The Weaving

by Gerald Costlow

This book is a work of fiction. The characters, incidents, and dialogue are drawn from the author's imagination and are not to be construed as real. Any resemblance to actual events or persons, living or dead, is entirely coincidental.

The Weaving. Copyright © by Gerald Costlow, 2010. All rights reserved. Printed in the United States of America. No part of this book may be used or reproduced in any manner whatsoever without written permission except in the case of brief quotations embodied in critical articles and reviews. For information address: Pill Hill Press, 343 W 4th St., Chadron, NE 69337.

FIRST SOFTCOVER EDITION

ISBN: 978-1-61706-007-6
ISBN-10: 1-61706-007-0

Cover art by Philip R. Rogers
Cover design by Alva J. Roberts
First printing: February 2010

Visit us online at www.pillhillpress.com

To My Wife

The Weaving

by Gerald Costlow

Chadron, Nebraska

One

The three Ladies stood around the scrying pool, searching the web of life, as images formed on the water. Men and women and other, stranger creatures appeared, were studied, rejected and discarded for the next. Using the pool was like walking through an endlessly branching labyrinth of corridors, peeking into keyholes in search of one particular room. It was an almost impossible task, but that didn't matter. The Ladies would continue searching for as long as it took.

The people who appeared were scrutinized in whatever endeavor occupied their time, caught in moments of heroism or compromise or passion. Neither bedroom nor toilet was inviolate. The dark of night provided no cover. Prince and prisoner were given the same careful consideration. The strongest of magical wards against such intrusion were brushed aside, the contents of the life rummaged through, heedless of the outrage. Even time was no barrier; the past and future both were laid open and examined. Still, the search went on.

"There! Go back!" the first Lady said.
"This must be it," the second Lady continued.
"But we have to make sure," the third Lady finished.

The three Ladies leaned in, studying the image. A small clearing in a woods was shown. It contained a cottage, a typical little homestead with a garden and several outbuildings. It seemed a common and mundane setting, the very picture of innocence. They saw a rather plain looking woman walking down a path toward the trees, carrying a basket and followed by her cat. She was recognized instantly.

The Ladies watched the thread of life unwind, more certain

than ever that here, finally, they had found the person responsible for turning a monster loose upon the world.

***

Rose stood before the two ancient ley stones and disrobed. Each garment was carefully folded and placed in the basket until she stood naked to the world, wearing only the crystal necklace. It was the sign of her office and never removed. The tomcat watched with disapproval.

"This is a decidedly unwise decision," the cat said, continuing an argument began days before.

"We've been over this enough, Tom. Leave it alone. I'm hardly going to change my mind now." She placed a lid over the basket, just in case it rained before she returned. Her weather sense told her today would remain sunny, but she didn't know how long she'd be gone.

"Well, what's the use of even having a familiar if you're not going to listen to it?" he asked, giving it one last try. "Have I ever steered you wrong? When the Elf King gave you a choice of gifts for rescuing his son, wasn't I the one who told you to pick the old, cracked hand mirror? Did you know it was the Mirror of True Seeing? Of course not." He sat down and sighed, shaking his head. "I blame those books you've been reading. *Love's Lost Labor*? *Passion's Embrace*? It's done something to your thinking. Not proper reading at all for a witch."

Rose looked back at her cottage. Inside the little house was a small table cleared of the breakfast dishes, a small cot made up from the night's sleeping, a small fireplace swept clean of ashes. Clean, neat, everything in place. *But empty, oh so empty.*

She knelt and scratched her familiar on his favorite spot, an old scar behind his ear, a souvenir from some long forgotten battle. He purred, never tiring of this sign of affection.

"Tom," she patiently explained, "I agree with everything you say, except the part about the books. And you enjoy them just as

The Weaving

much as I do, or you wouldn't be asking me to read out loud each night. What you can't understand is that it makes no difference. Even if you're right, I still have to do this. Now, I charge thee to guard what is mine until my return."

"*If* you return, is how you should be saying it. I've got a bad feeling about this one." He laid back his ears. "I bet other cats don't have this much trouble training their humans. I spend half my life tracking down a witch worthy of my talents and what do I get for my effort? Two years of trying to keep you out of trouble."

Rose smiled and straightened, looking toward the portal. "There's always an *if*, no matter how short the journey, isn't there?" she answered. "I'm asking you to understand and to do this for me out of our friendship."

He finally gave in and rubbed his fur against her leg, his twitching tail the only sign of his agitation. "Very well," he said. "I swear by our bond that I will stand vigil until your return. Now go do this thing, and get back here as quick as you can."

She turned back to the portal, the door into Otherwhere she'd built. Rose brushed her fingers over the weaving between the two upright stones, performing one final check.

"What do you see, Tom?" she asked. "Are there any knots or broken strings in the magic weaving I've missed?"

The familiar gave it a close look and pronounced it ready to go. To her, the magic was an invisible thing created out of pure imagination until activated by her power. Tom served as her eyes and could see the spell as glowing lines. He'd told her most cats have the Sight, but only a few are crazy enough to want anything to do with magic or the strange humans who dealt in it. His eyes had been a great help to her work ever since he'd arrived soaking wet in the middle of a winter storm, demanding to be dried and fed.

Yes, Tom was a good friend, but she needed more.

It was time.

Rose outstretched her arms, made contact with the portal, and began bringing it to life. Her hands danced along the pattern while her mind began the reconstruction of reality. With talent and training, she had learned to weave intricate magic out of the air and use it to change form for a brief time or force a permanent change upon someone else. Like all witches, she had a special gift from the Mother of All and could trade gossip with the animals of the forest. It was her birthright, her special talent.

Rose, the great Witch of the Woods, could do all this with little effort. What she was attempting now took effort, for the portal was the most difficult of the many spells in her books and one she'd never tried.

The sun was hot on her bare shoulders. Being sky-clad made the next step easier, and she needed to save her strength for the end. Expanding her senses beyond the limits of her physical body, Rose made contact with the life around her. Her eyes became those of the falcon overhead, searching for its prey. Her ears became that of the wood mouse, listening for the flapping of death's wings from the sky. She could feel the wind as it rustled across the leaves of the trees, could taste the rich earth as the worms ate their way through the humus beneath.

Drawing upon the spirit of her woods, her place of power, she reached beyond the world of form and substance to the realm of the Mother of All—or perhaps she simply reached deeper within herself. Such distinctions have little meaning in magic. Rose opened her mouth and began singing her song of power. Using her will and her song and her true name, she called for a doorway into the home of the Goddess.

Rose stepped through the portal and fell flat on her face.

***

"Are you all right, my dear?"

Rose lay face down on a thick rug covering the floor. As she rolled over, her first thought was how soft it felt against her bare skin, followed by some surprise the spell had actually worked. She hadn't realized how much she had doubted her success, until now.

"Take your time, child. You've just performed a great feat, so

The Weaving

it's natural to be a little shook up."

Rose was finally able to focus on her surroundings. She was in a great hall, looking at a ceiling high above, where openings let the light shine through. She sat up and looked for the source of the voice, eager to finally meet the Goddess.

Rose had always pictured the Mother of All as resembling her childhood memories of her own mother, or some other ideal of what all mothers should look like—slightly graying hair, a little overweight and careworn, pregnant, solid and competent. The woman standing over her looked competent, but showed no signs of being with child, and had all the regal bearing and classic beauty of the Goddess she was. At least the deity was wearing a green robe cinched around her waist, the same traditional outfit worn by her worshipers. The Goddess was looking down at Rose with an amused smile.

Remembering where she was and who was addressing her, Rose scrambled to her knees and bowed deeply, pressing her forehead against the floor. "Oh Mother of All, forgive this trespass by your subject..." she began, only to be interrupted by laughter. She fell silent in confusion.

The Goddess finally stopped giggling. "I wish you could see how silly you look, with your naked butt sticking up in the air. Oh, child, do stand up. I'd rather see your face when I'm talking to you."

Rose got to her feet and the Goddess handed her a robe. "Here, put this on before you catch a chill," she was told. "Let's go to my office where we can be more comfortable." Without waiting for a reply, the Goddess turned and walked off. Rose followed, struggling with the robe.

They left the hall through an arched doorway and Rose stumbled to a halt. She had thought of the first chamber as huge, but this one defied belief. The ceiling was the same height, with the same kind of windows illuminating the inside as bright as day, but the walls disappeared into the distance. Filling the space was what looked like row upon row of shelves. It was all too strange to believe and Rose stood in shock.

A hand passed in front of her eyes and she blinked, focusing back on her immediate surroundings. "Relax, dear," the Goddess said. "We're not going to get anywhere if you keep fading out like that. You're a child of nature, used to trees and fields and open sky. Shall I cloak my house to better suit your experience?"

The thought of having to be coddled in any way brought Rose's pride to bear and she gathered her courage around her. She was the great Witch of the Woods, after all, and hardly a child—no matter what the Goddess might say.

"No, Mother of All, I'm alright," she replied. "I'd rather see the true appearance and not understand than see an illusion and pretend I do. Besides, I'd kick myself for the rest of my life for missing this chance."

The Goddess smiled, seeming to like this answer, and they continued, passing between two of the racks. Rose saw what appeared to be books on the shelves, filling every space. Rose owned a small collection of books herself, most of them romantic fantasies and fables that helped while away the long nights in her lonely little cottage. There were also several books containing lists of herbal remedies and various spells, which were passed down to Rose by the old woman who had schooled her in the secrets of magic. She had added several new discoveries to the pages, something she was proud of.

These bound volumes were of every size and color and seemed uncountable, and she marveled there could be so many. *Like stars in the sky or leaves in the forest*, she decided, and found thinking of it this way made it something she could deal with.

They came at last to another door and entered a small room no bigger than her cottage. There was a desk with common writing utensils and a stack of parchment, chairs on either side. A large cabinet occupied one wall, with numerous little drawers bearing labels. The only other furnishing was a smaller table in the corner holding a pot and cups. The walls were decorated with several framed paintings showing scenes of outdoor life such as a field of flowers with mountains in the distance. Rose considered it a most peculiar setting for the Great Mother.

The Weaving

The Goddess motioned toward the chair. "Sit down, dear." She picked up the pot and poured steaming liquid into the cups, handing one to Rose and putting the other on the desk, then walked over to the cabinet of little drawers. "Now, let's start by finding out who you are. Name and occupation, please."

Rose sipped what turned out to be an herbal tea and, for the first time since arriving, began to relax. "I go by the name Rose," she replied, "unless you need my true name, and I'm the Witch of the Woods. But Mother of All, don't you know that already? You're supposed to see everything that happens."

"Seeing everything going on and being able to keep track of it all are two different things. You'd be in Adventure, then of course Witchcraft, and being out in the woods usually means Questing, and here you are." The Goddess had been going through one of the drawers and pulled out a little card from the middle of the file. She finally sat down across the table, studying what was written.

"Oh, yes. A beautiful world, and you've done a magnificent job helping to keep it that way. The previous Witch of the Woods and I had a long conversation. We both agreed she'd made the right decision in choosing you." The Goddess picked up her cup and took a sip. "Right now you have a lot of questions, so let's get them out of the way first. Ask and I'll give you what answers I can."

"Um..." Rose looked around at all the strangeness, the movement in one of the paintings catching her eye. She watched a brushstroke bird fly across a framed sky and realized she didn't know enough to even ask questions about it. She could swear those were paintings, not windows. One was even hung slightly crooked. "I guess I'd like to know what all of this is. Nothing makes any sense."

"You mean I'm not the mother figure you expected? I knew that would be the first thing we'd need to clear up. Well, I'm not the Mother of All, but then again I am. Even mortals have different roles they assume, depending on the need. A woman can be mother, wife and warrior in the space of a day. You might say it's the same thing with me, only taken to extremes. Life involves more than just birth, you know. In this case, we're opposite faces of the same coin. Since she's dumped you in my lap, your problem must involve my function, not hers."

Rose was even more confused. "You're another aspect of the Goddess? I've never heard of that. What do I call you? You wear the green robe, so you must be a witch. Are you the Mother of all Witches? Are you supposed to teach me a magic spell from your books?"

The Goddess snorted, seeming to find additional amusement in Rose's speculations. "Those are not really books out there made of parchment and leather," she explained. "Basically, those are lives that have reached their ending. It has been said that everyone has a story to tell, but in my realm, it is more accurate to say that a life being lived is a story being told. I sort and catalog each life, then place them into their reserved spot on the shelf. As for how to address me, calling me Goddess is rather formal, so why don't you keep calling me Mother? I like that. A part of me gave you life, and the part talking to you now holds that life in her hands. Literally."

She set the card she was holding onto the desktop and pushed it over for Rose to examine. "This is you, Rose. A life in the process of being lived—a tale being written as we speak. Your problem must lie here, in the story of your life. That is my realm, the function I control."

Rose was beginning to catch on, and what the woman sitting across from the desk was saying scared her. Her growing fears were confirmed when the Goddess continued.

"I have few titles and fewer worshipers," she said. "One world that prides itself on its scholarship calls me the Librarian. A few enlightened races that appreciate my work call me the Keeper of Stories, and that's probably the most accurate. Most people, including those in your own particular reality, have a less flattering title for me."

The Goddess leaned back in the chair, taking another sip from the cup. She did not seem amused anymore. "Now," she said. "It's time you tell me why you are here. What pressing need has brought you to disturb Death in her own abode?"

Two

"I'm waiting," Death said, impatient. "My uninvited guests usually can't wait to tell me about how their loved ones were taken unjustly, and then demand they be returned."

Rose sat in shocked silence. She had somehow broken the one rule she never should have broken, traveled to the one place from which there can be no return. *Once dead, forever dead*, was the way her old Mentor had put it. Magic can perform miracles, but once Death gets her hands on someone, all the powers in the world couldn't pry her fingers away.

Death sighed and shook her head. Rose felt something enter her mind, a force soothing all fears, projecting a compassion that could only come from the Mother of All. Rose had felt it before, as a quiet presence in moments of prayer and meditation, but that was a half-heard whisper compared to what she was experiencing now.

"It's all right, daughter," the voice said. *"Tell her what you want. Trust me."*

Rose knew then, in spite of her lack of understanding, the Mother of All had sent her to meet Death and would not abandon her in this realm. Rose also knew the prepared speech she'd started to give when first arriving would not do. She looked down at the cup in her hands and spoke her heart.

"I'm lonely, Mother," she said.

"Look at me, child. Talk to me, tell me the story."

She looked at the Goddess and took a deep breath. "Recently, a Prince named Valant came to my door," Rose began. "He was strong and handsome and well mannered. Instead of asking me for help, he told me I was the culmination of his quest, that he'd had a vision of me as his true love. He swore as soon as he'd laid eyes on me, desire had blossomed in his heart and he would pine and die should I refuse his love."

Once she started, the rest spilled out. "My heart sang, for never had those words been spoken to me. I invited him into my house and was courted with sweet words and affection. Soon I was ready to give him everything, to surrender my body and spirit to our joining—but my familiar, Tom, had his doubts. He cautioned me to look in the Mirror of True Seeing. I laughed at his fears, but gazed at the reflection of my newfound love, even if only to appease the cat."

The memory made Rose choke up with emotion, but she pushed on. "What I saw turned my delight into anger," she continued. "I saw an evil, lying, hateful man, one who used his looks and sweet voice to deceive women, who planned on doing the same with me. He would capture my heart, then use our bond to have me do his bidding. He wanted me only for my witchcraft, to use my powers for his selfish purposes."

The Goddess shook her head. "There are many people like that. What happened next?"

"Oh, nothing too drastic. I turned him into a snake with a spell that won't break until he sheds a tear over someone else. I doubt that will ever happen, and it's no loss to the world. But after that, I did much thinking and came to a realization. My anger was mostly at myself, for being so eager to believe his lies. Mine is a small world, and my people occupy only a tiny part of it. The men I meet either see me as a power to be feared or treat me as a prize to be mastered. Every King has his Queen, but there are none my equal in the arts. I used all my skill to search the land, even persuaded the three Ladies to check the web of the future. I asked them if I would ever find my true love. Their answer was plain—the man who loves me does not exist and never will."

The Goddess reached across the table and took hold of Rose's hands. "Do you regret the path of power you have chosen, then?"

"Of course not, Mother," Rose replied. "It is my pleasure and my duty, as much a part of what I am as my womanhood. But must I choose one over the other? If you write the stories, can you not find

The Weaving

it in your heart to let me be both witch and wife? I have served the Mother of All unselfishly. Surely you have the power to grant me this small favor?"

Rose fell silent. She had done her best. Now she could only wait for the reply.

The Keeper of Stories got to her feet and poured more tea, then walked over and looked at one of the paintings, seeming to consider her request. Rose watched the Goddess straighten the hanging picture frame, then saw it change to what looked like her own little hut and familiar forest glen. Maybe a sign of hope?

The Goddess spoke as she continued to examine the framed scene. "Rose, I do not write the stories. The Creator has reserved that privilege for each mortal alone. It is done with every decision you make, every action you take in your life. And, while each life is unique, no story stands isolated and complete in itself. All that has ever been, every tale being told or yet to be, is part of a greater whole. If I change what has been written in one life, I would have to change countless others. There are limits to what I can do, even for the most devoted and deserving of my children."

Rose's dream died, but she had always known, for one reason or another, the request might be denied. Yet, a part of her refused to give up. She looked down at the card on the table, still amazed her whole life up until now could be squeezed into a few words. Rose looked closer at the card while considering her next move. She reached over and fingered the pen, glanced back at the Goddess, then acted on impulse and picked it up. It was an idea born of desperation, probably the most foolish mistake she would ever make—maybe even her last.

She was going to do it, anyway.

Change made, she placed the pen back in the holder, her heart thumping. Now she had to worry about getting home as only the Goddess could send her back. "Very well, Mother," she said. "I will perform my tasks and do your bidding. Thank you for considering my petition. If even you cannot change what is to be, then I will accept my lot in life. My story will be that of a witch who lives alone in the woods, one who spends her days with only a cat to keep her company."

The Goddess turned and held up her hand. "Don't jump to conclusions. I said there were limits, not that I couldn't or wouldn't try. Whatever I can manage to do for you, there will be a price— what you have learned here will not be remembered. I've found it isn't healthy for even those who deal with magic to know too much. You'll start second-guessing your decisions and spend your nights wondering when your own tale will be finished."

She came over and pulled Rose to her feet. "Oh, and you'll find that portal spell won't bring you here again. You must work out your own life, child, and accept the consequences of your actions. The next time we meet here, it will be the final time."

So it wasn't a definite no, after all, but a maybe? "That is a price I willing accept. I don't know how I can express my thanks to you, Mother."

The Keeper of Stories gave the young witch a hug, and Rose felt the body against her change. When the Goddess stepped back, Rose saw a middle-aged woman, a touch overweight and with slightly gray hair. The woman was obviously pregnant. "I'm proud of you, daughter," the Mother of All said. "All my children are special, but between you and me, some are more special than others." And with those parting words, the Goddess sent Rose back to her own world.

***

The Keeper of Stories put the cups back where they belonged, then picked up the card from the table and looked at the writing scrawled between the lines, the ink still wet. Rose had managed to scribble the one word, 'Romance,' during the brief moment the Goddess had turned away.

"Crafty little witch," she murmured as she put the card back in the file. "The Creator knows I gave her enough opportunity. If she only knew the trouble she's getting herself into." The Goddess sighed as she considered all the work she'd have to do to correct for this one

The Weaving

small change. But there would be some satisfaction in the task, for the Mother of All was also a woman—was in some way all women—and knew very well what it was like to be alone and yearn for someone to share her life with.

***

Rose appeared back in front of the portal and stood blinking in the bright sun.

"That didn't take long. Hey, you've brought back a new robe, at least. What was it like?" Her Tom was waiting, as he had promised, as she had never doubted he would.

She looked down at the robe and frowned. "I...had some tea. The Goddess gave me this robe, told me my butt looked funny, I think. I'm not sure. It's hard to recall."

Tom laughed. "Well, if that's all you got out of it, at least you came back safe and sound. And I think you have a fine butt. Come here, great Witch of the Woods. Give me a hug."

Rose hugged Tom, her husband and love. As his arms held her close, she found herself crying without knowing why. Finding this man had been a miracle. He had stumbled into her life several years ago, lost and confused and half-dead from exposure in a snowstorm. He knew his name, but had no memories of his past. She'd nursed him back to health and romance had bloomed with the arrival of Spring. He loved Rose the woman, while accepting that as the Witch of the Woods, she had a duty to perform—and sometimes duty came first. Even though Tom was a little on the lazy side, not very handsome, and snored something terrible, he was her love and she was his, bonded by the strongest magic of all.

She ran her fingers through his black, curly hair, scratching behind his ear where there was an old scar, a souvenir of some now forgotten fight. He made a low rumbling noise deep in his throat. It was a familiar sound. Over time, a husband and wife developed these little rituals.

"Thank you, Mother of All," she whispered, although she still couldn't quite remember why.

***

    The Ladies stood around the scrying pool and watched as Rose hugged her husband.
    "Here is the start," the first Lady said.
    "The cause of the unraveling," the second Lady continued.
    "As we had feared," the third Lady finished.
    They broke the circle and began preparations for their journey. One started gathering supplies while another left to get the horses. The third went to tell their son he would be staying with the Dragon Queen for a while, and then convinced the dragon to child-sit again after what the boy had pulled the last time.
    All was done in silence, for the three women were joined to their Sisterselfs within the mind, and were capable of carrying on conversations through their shared thoughts. The Ladies did not even need individual names. To speak to one was to speak to all. The people who did have cause to address them used the term Lady and treated them with great respect.
    Right now, the Ladies were engaged in a fierce argument over whether or not Rose would have to be destroyed in order to set things right.

Three

The three Ladies had always known it was possible for the monster to escape, but their ability to check the web of the future had assured them the prison would not be disturbed for at least another mortal lifetime—anything beyond stretched the limit of their ability to predict with certainty. Free will ensured the future was not set for eternity. The Ladies had even placed a reminder on their calendar to recheck the future every fifty years.

Thus it was, when they felt the magic wards fail, it caught them by surprise. Something, some *force*, had changed the web of the near future, and that could only be done by changing the past.

Impossible!

They used the scrying pool to verify the unfeasible was indeed happening, then began their desperate search for the cause. Who was this man they could now see at the cave and when had the thread of his life been altered?

***

The Wizard Maynard stood next to his employer outside the cave, watching the rope unwind. His boss, Prince Valant, had the bulk of it coiled at his feet, with one end tied to a large stone and the other end tied around the arm of the servant. At least Maynard assumed it was attached to the servant, since more of the rope was still being pulled into the cavern where the man had been sent, torch in hand. The farthest point the previous servant had reached was marked with a bit of tied cloth, and the scrap of fabric was fast approaching the cave, sliding over the tumbled stones once blocking the entrance.

Suddenly, a scream came from the darkness and the rope

whipped through the air as several more yards were jerked within the cave. Then it went slack and all movement ceased, the same as the last time.

"Drat," the Prince remarked. "I should have brought more servants." He looked at his wizard. "About a hundred paces, same as the last man. Well, it looks like it's your turn, Maynard. Time to earn your pay."

The wizard watched his employer pull back the rope, the bloody stump of an arm still attached. Maynard was noisily sick while the Prince examined the remains.

"Sliced as clean as a sword cut, by the Gods! No, wait," the Prince peered at the rope."See here? It's kind of scalloped on the edges. Looks like it was bitten off. Say, Maynard old boy, you wouldn't have led us to a dragon's den now, would you?" The Prince waved the dismembered arm at the wizard.

The wizard fumbled in his robe and found a bottle of pills. He popped several into his mouth, chewing for immediate effect. He grabbed a canteen to rinse his mouth before replying.

"If it was a d-d-dragon, it would have came out to see what idiots were p-playing games with it, and we'd all be r-roasted by now. No, the magic wards we found at the entrance are p-proof enough. It's in there. It just doesn't want to be disturbed." Maynard struggled to calm down. Being upset always brought about his stuttering.

"Or maybe it just woke up cah-cranky," the Prince replied, tossing the arm in the direction of the other dead servant's leg. "After all, according to what you've told me, it's been trapped in there for a thousand years. And, by the way, it doesn't look like that magic charm you gave this guy was very effective. Any comments?"

Maynard shrugged. "I lied. It was the only way to get him in there. That was just a p-piece of j-junk j-jewelry. They're s-spelled to look g-genuine. I trade them to girls in the t-taverns for—"

"So you kept the real magic charm for yourself?" the Prince cut in, not interested in Maynard's love life."Don't ever disobey me again. That man's death was a waste—good servants are hard to find." Valant wiped the end of the rope against some dry grass to remove

The Weaving

most of the gore and held it out to the wizard. "Then, if you have the real protective amulet, you don't have anything to worry about. Grab another torch and off you go."

The wizard felt his stomach flip again and reached for more pills with a shaking hand. "I c-can't! I just won't be able to! It's not that I doubt the charm will work." He looked at the black hole in the ground and shuddered. "I just can't stand being in tight spaces. I know it's stupid, but something like that cave...I won't get two steps and I'll feel like I'm suffocating. I won't be able to b-breathe. I'll pass out."

The Prince considered the excuse. "You wouldn't be trying to duck out on me, would you? Or maybe hoping to get rid of the guy who threatened to squeal on you for stealing forbidden spells? Let's get one thing straight—I've set it up so if anything happens to me, a certain incriminating package is going to be sent to the Wizard's Council."

"But I'm telling the truth! Look, here's the real key." The wizard pulled on a cord he wore around his neck and held up a small disk hanging there by the hole in its center. "You can see the engravings match the runes that were sealing the cave. Hold this out so the thing inside can see it and you'll be safe. Even with the entrance unblocked, whatever is in there can't leave until you place this key in the matching depression inside, and it can't attack you while you have this in your p-possession. Once free, though, there's no controlling the monster. You'll need to make a deal first."

***

Those who knew him had rightly called the Prince many things. Cold-hearted, traitorous, scheming and vicious were all on the list, but stupid or cowardly were not. Standing at the entrance of the cave, he turned and addressed Maynard one last time.

"You're sure this little charm you stole is the real thing?" he asked. "Nothing you forgot to tell me? It's going to be unfortunate if I don't make it back out alive, you know."

Gerald Costlow

Maynard shook his head. The Prince believed his wizard was telling the truth this time. Valant had trussed the wizard up with the rope once used to haul body parts out of the cave and had gagged him to prevent any spell casting. Considering the remote wasteland surrounding them, Maynard had to know there was no chance anyone but his employer would cut him free.

Prince Valant crept into the cave, torch in one hand and magic disk in the other, wishing he had a third hand to hold his sword. The entrance to the cavern started large enough for him to walk upright, but soon narrowed into a smaller passage, forcing him to stoop. Valant experimented and found holding the torch low to the ground was the best way to advance. It still caused shadows to dance on the rock walls in a disturbing rhythm, looking as if something was moving just out of the light's reach. He was more worried about the uneven floor—he didn't want to trip and drop either the torch or the disk.

Valant came to a section where the rock was chiseled flat and covered with the strange writing Maynard called runes—the wards inside the cave imprisoning the creature. The Prince made note of the spot carved to match the key, but was careful not to touch the walls.

He'd been counting paces as he went along and was approaching the point where the servants had met their fates. The tunnel began to change, widening and emptying into a large cavity. The Prince was able to straighten and stretched to get the kinks out of his back. He could hear the constant dripping of water from somewhere close and jumped when an additional sound echoed against the rock. It sounded like something was slurping soup out of a bowl. Visions of the horror lying ahead filled his mind.

Well, time to go for broke. He held out the key and marched the final paces. *Ninety-six, ninety-seven, ninety-eight, ninety-ni—.* He froze, one leg still in the air, as the torch light revealed the monster. Its skin was pasty white, the hair on its head tangled and matted with blood. The creature watched him approach, perched on the stacked, mutilated bodies of Valant's servants, waiting in the dark for another

The Weaving

victim to arrive. One leap and it could add another corpse to the pile.

"About time you got here," the naked woman said, picking at something stuck between her teeth. She glanced at the disk Valant clenched with white knuckles, then raised a bowl, slurping the liquid it contained. She smacked her lips. "So you've got the keystone?" she asked. "I can finally get out of this dump." She waved a hand in his direction and watched, like she was waiting for him to fall down dead or something. Valant didn't feel any different. After a moment, the creature leaned forward and took another long look at the amulet.

"Those sneaky wizards," she said, reaching down and tearing a finger off one of the bodies. She used its nail as a toothpick while she studied the man in front of her. "Thanks for the meal, by the way. I haven't eaten since those damned Ladies sealed me in here. Even demigods enjoy a snack once in a while. Call me Lilith. What's your name, handsome?"

"P-Prince Valant," he stuttered, then winced, wondering if Maynard's affliction was contagious. He put both feet back on the ground, ignoring the puddle of blood rippling around his feet.

"Valiant? Your parents actually named you Prince Valiant?"

The Prince sighed at the familiar response to hearing his name. The magic disk appeared to be working, or maybe the monster was full. He didn't relax too much—Lilith might enjoy playing with her food. Now, if only he could determine what sort of creature he was dealing with. She'd called herself a demigod, but that told him nothing useful.

"Everyone always asks that," the Prince said. "It's Val*ant*, not Val*i*ant. That other guy must really get around. Um...I take it you're some kind of witch?"

"Oh, Valiant had a good press agent, but it was all brag. And no, I'm not a witch, although the body I'm wearing used to be one." She dropped the finger into the bowl, leaned back on her hands and thrust out her chest while she studied him.

"There's something else I haven't done in a long time," she added with a toothy grin. She was staring at his tight pants.

The Prince smiled back and hung the disk around his neck.

Gerald Ghostlow

He had no experience in dealing with monsters or demigods, but there was a well-rehearsed script for this situation that practically guaranteed success. It had only failed once, when the Witch of the Woods had laughed and sent him on his way, saying she was already happily married. That wasn't his fault. Who ever heard of a happily married witch? This expedition was his fallback plan, a wild shot—and it looked like it was paying off.

Valant stepped forward and fell to one knee. "At last I have found you!" he exclaimed, placing a hand on his chest. "I am indeed a Prince, youngest son of King Morgan of Morania. I am heir to a castle and fortune, but was sent into exile because of treacherous lies. In the dark of my despair, I was given a vision of you in my dreams. I knew my destiny was to search the world for your radiant beauty. The moment I laid eyes on you, love blossomed in my heart. I will pine and die if you refuse me."

He watched the flattery have its intended effect as he wedged the torch between a couple of rocks. The stone floor would be uncomfortable, but maybe they could arrange the bodies as a cushion. She wasn't a bad looking dame, despite her filthy locks, so he wouldn't have to keep his eyes closed. He just hoped she wasn't into the kinky stuff—that had a tendency to turn him off. After all, he did have his principles.

***

The Prince and Lilith eventually emerged from the cave. She had cleaned up a bit and put on a dress. She'd even rinsed and combed her hair, and the Prince had to admit she was a striking woman, even if a little on the pale and skinny side. She swore when the bright sunlight hit her eyes, stepping back into the shadows long enough to pull something from the chest Valant dragged behind him. When she straightened, she wore some kind of covering over her eyes against the glare. It looked like pieces of dark-colored glass on a metal framework, designed to fit across the bridge of her nose. The sun was painful to his eyes after being in the gloom of the cave, and

The Weaving

he became determined to have eye protectors made for himself.

"My world is a much darker place," she said, as if that should mean something to the Prince. There was only one world as far as he knew, and they were standing on it. "Even then, we live mostly underground. I'm pretty much a night person, you know. In fact, I'd prefer to travel after dark. I don't tan and I hate walking around with my skin peeling."

The Prince sat on the chest, catching his breath. There were several more back in the cave she'd pointed out as necessary to take along. Besides a good amount of bracelets and other bangles made of gold and precious jewels, they contained clothes and personal items. This Lilith creature did not believe in traveling light. At least they had a couple of spare horses, their servant-riders dead in the cave, and the rented pack mules didn't have to be returned.

"Beloved," he said, "It's best we travel at night anyway, with this heat. It will give us time to discuss our future plans together."

Lilith stood and looked around the bare landscape, enjoying the sight of...well, sight, for a change, he supposed. "At night, this looks like my old homeland," she said. "It's why I picked this cave. I should have known better than to assume I could keep it hidden from the Ladies. I won't make that mistake again." She spotted something at the bottom of the hill. "What's this? Do you have another gift for me? How sweet! I'm really not hungry right now, but I suppose he'll keep for a day or two."

Valant remembered his wizard, left tied during his journey into the monster's lair. The man was probably half-dead by now, suffering heat stroke.

"That's Maynard, a wizard who works for me," Valant explained while starting down the hill. "I sort of promised him he could be my Royal Wizard when I'm on the throne. I'll find you someone else to snack on, my darling." The Prince might still have a need for the wizard.

Lilith knelt and picked up a stone block as big as her head. She examined the rune carved on one side—it once crawled with magic and trapped her in the hole. With a heave, she threw it. The Prince

Gerald Ghostlow

watched, open-mouthed, as it whistled through the air, landing far away and rolling until it was out of sight.

"You don't have to bother, my darling," she said. "I prefer harvesting my own food. Now, tell me again about this little kingdom you want. Morania, was it? And perhaps you can find out if this wizard will tell me where the Ladies might be found, since you haven't heard of them."

Four

The Lady threw another stick on the campfire, listening to the sounds of the forest. It was unnaturally quiet, as if even the insects had been scared into silence. Something or someone was out there watching her, and it wasn't the man she had come all this way to find. Even the combined experience of the three Ladies drew a blank on what sort of creatures lurked in this particular forest. The vast wilderness was claimed by the elves but, in reality, belonged to nobody. It was one of the wild places of the world, unexplored and populated only by creatures preferring their privacy. The elves had a name for this forest that translated as "Only Fools Go There." Unfortunately, this was exactly where the Lady had to be, fool or not.

This...*whatever*...had been following her for the past few days, ever since she'd stumbled upon the ruins of an old temple overgrown by massive tree roots. The carvings on the blocks told her it was built by the Old Ones, the strange race of beings who lived on this world before even the elves appeared. It remained to be seen whether or not this mysterious stalker was dangerous or curious. It had grown bold enough today for her to catch a glimpse of a long, rat-like tail as it slithered among the trees. She conferred with her Sisterselfs through her mindlink—they all agreed if it didn't show itself tonight, tomorrow she must abandon her search long enough to hunt it down and force a confrontation. She resigned herself to another sleepless night.

At least this little clearing she'd found next to a small lake was a good spot to make a stand, if it came to that. The Lady wished she could use her scrying to find out when the creature would attack, but the Sisterselfs didn't bother to remind her of the impossibility. Each Lady was allowed to look at her own future only once, and then would be required to give up her powers and return to normal life. The thought of being without the other two Ladies made her shudder.

The sun had barely set and she was quieting her restless horse when one of the twigs she'd carefully scattered around the edge of the clearing snapped, telling her the wait was over. She whirled and crouched, hands outstretched and balancing on the balls of her feet, a fighting stance taught to her as a young child and perfected by centuries of practice.

There was a brief glimpse of a toothy nightmare bounding into the light cast by the fire, then a howl as it was jerked back into the trees by its long tail, followed by further screams as it battled something in the dark. The Lady pulled a small knife from her belt, took a brand from the fire, and ran to the spot where the struggle was taking place. The commotion ended before she arrived and all she found was a torn-up piece of ground. Dark, wet patches that might be blood reflected the torch light. Whatever this thing was, it had either met its match or had fled to consume a hard-won meal. She saw some tracks in the dirt and bent to examine them. They looked familiar.

"You shouldn't travel alone in this wilderness, my Lady," said a voice from behind her. "There are things here even you can't handle."

The Lady turned and saw Keyotie sitting next to the campfire, acting as if he'd been there all along. With his brown leather outfit, dark skin and long black hair braided down his back, he looked as much a part of the forest as the leaves. Only the Trickster could make such a dramatic entrance.

"I doubt that," she replied, walking over to the lake. "However, I do thank you for your help." She knelt and picked up a makeshift fishing pole, then pulled the dancing line out of the water. The fish had a bright yellow and black banding, suggesting it was poisonous. Her stomach rumbled, willing to take the gamble, but the Lady sighed and tossed the fish back into the water.

Her Sisterselfs were getting impatient and accused her of stalling. She turned to face Keyotie. At least he'd finally come out of hiding—Keyotie must have known she was in the area long before

The Weaving

this. As for the price he might demand for his help, if it came to that... well, she'd find out before the night was through. *I'll do this my way or not at all,* she told her Sisterselfs.

Her stomach grumbled again, refusing to be ignored. "If you'd like to be of more help," she said, "could you round up something to eat? I've been traveling through nothing but forest for weeks and ran out of supplies some days ago. My snares have been coming up empty and I don't think I can bring myself to eat another bowl of toad stew."

***

Keyotie returned a few moments later with their dinner, finding the Lady hadn't moved from her spot next to the lake. She stood, looking out over the water, while he prepared their meal. The woman was taking her sweet time letting him know why she was here. It was unlike the Ladies not to come to the point, but he could wait. If anything, he preferred she take her time. It would allow him the pleasure of her company for a while—before the inevitable request, the refusal, followed by the argument and parting. Whatever the Lady had come for, his plans took precedence and did not include returning.

"This place reminds me of a story," she finally said. "In fact, it's about you. A Coyote legend. Would you like to hear it?"

Keyotie licked the blood off his fingers and set the rabbit on the fire. "Coyote, my Lady?" he asked. "You're sure it's not one I've told you in the past that you're just repeating back to me?" The People had carried stories of the Trickster along in their migrations. Since this particular land had never seen a coyote, his character in the traditional legends had been replaced by a talking fox named Cotie. That sort of thing galled him to no end.

"No, this one predates our arrival on this world and has the ring of authenticity. You might not have heard it before."

Keyotie settled down next to the fire, always ready for a good story. There was only one better way to pass the night with a beautiful woman, and the Lady didn't appear to be in that kind of mood. "Then by all means, you have my full attention."

"Very well. I suppose you could title this *Coyote and the Moon Maiden*. Is something wrong? You look startled."

Keyotie coughed into his hand, then looked back at her with a forced smile. "No, nothing wrong. I really would like to hear the story."

"Well, here's how it goes..."

***

Coyote crouched in the cattails next to the lake, watching with interest as Moon Maiden prepared for her bath. He had stumbled across this remote spot by pure accident. It was well off the usual trails, surrounded by tall pines, and there was only one reason he could think of for Moon Maiden to be here. Many times he had returned to see if he could catch her during one of her visits, and now his curiosity was finally being satisfied.

***

"I can see why you think it sounds authentic."

The Lady came over and sat down next to the fire. "The rabbit smells delicious. I'll have mine rare. I have said this is an old legend, perhaps the most ancient of the Coyote stories I know. Do you want to hear it or not?"

"Sorry, my Lady. Please go on."

***

Moon Maiden hummed as she removed her clothes and placed them on a handy rock. Coyote caught his breath as he saw the beauty before him. She quickly dove into the water, leaving him an all too brief look at her charms.

The Weaving

"I must have her," Coyote thought. He watched her swimming out into the lake. Being Coyote, he looked at the discarded clothes, then at Moon Maiden cooling herself in the water, and came up with a plan to trick her into his arms. He quietly removed the clothes from where she had left them and carried them into the forest, where he hid them in a hollow tree. Then he trotted back to the lake and sat down openly on the shore.

"Moon Maiden!" he called. "I am overwhelmed by your beauty! Your hair is like a cascading waterfall, your skin as soft as clouds. Your breasts are like rolling hills and your legs are like.... well, I've never seen better. Your clothes seem to have been stolen by a wandering thief. If you come lie with me for a while, I may be persuaded to track them down for you."

***

Keyotie couldn't contain his laughter. "Ha! Breasts like rolling hills? The fine art of flattery has certainly improved over the years."

She glared at him. "Keyotie, if you interrupt me one more time, I'm not finishing the story. Do I interrupt your stories?"

"Sorry, it was rude of me. Please continue. You were saying?"

"Where was I? Oh, yes."

***

While Moon Maiden was understandably shocked at having Coyote show up at her private bath, she had listened to his praise with approval. She was starting to swim back to shore to continue the conversation when his final ultimatum made her stop—for it is the nature of all women, that what may be freely given upon asking will be denied upon demand.

"You place the price of my love at a single set of clothes?" she asked. "Keep what you have stolen, for that is all you will steal today." Then she swam in the opposite direction, to exit the water on the other side of the lake.

Gerald Gastlow

  Coyote had thought of this, however, and simply ran around the shoreline. When she arrived at the edge, there he was again. She retreated back into deep water and thought of waiting him out. But, it soon became apparent that Coyote was determined and didn't mind spending the day watching her swim in the clear lake.

  This stand-off continued for some time, with Moon Maiden occasionally making a break for it and Coyote circling around to meet her. When it finally started getting dark, she decided this had gone on long enough. She smiled and swam directly to where he waited.

  "All right, you old trickster," she said, "I guess you win. Here, help me out of the water."

  Coyote was eager to claim his prize. After looking around briefly and failing to find a stick to reach out to her, he turned around and told her to grab hold of his tail and pull herself to the shore. No sooner had she gotten a firm grip, then with a huge tug, she pulled him into the water instead!

  Now, Moon Maiden was at home with water, but Coyote was an indifferent swimmer at best. It was no problem for her to hold him under, despite all his splashing and struggles. In the end, it was she who pulled Coyote from the lake. He lay there, soaked and exhausted and coughing, while she stood over him in triumph.

  "Coyote, for all your tricks, you are a fool," she said. "Like most men, you see a woman's body and forget she also has a mind. Since you enjoy looking at me so much, then know that all you will ever be able to do is watch me from a distance and long for what you can't have."

  Coyote spit out some water and whined. "It's not my fault you're so beautiful! I wouldn't have forced myself upon you. I just couldn't bear the thought you might refuse. I hoped once I had you in my arms, my skill would arouse your passion. I think…I think I'm in love!"

  This softened Moon Maiden's heart just a little bit, and she bent down and kissed him on his wet nose. "I did like that stuff you told me about the clouds and hills and waterfalls. Tell you what,

The Weaving

if you say nice things to me when you see me, and keep singing to me of my charms, then maybe...maybe someday I might forgive you. You do know how to flatter a girl." Then Moon Maiden, pulling a piece of the night sky about her shoulders to replace the stolen clothes, ascended back to her place among the stars.

And that is why, to this day, Coyote and all his clan cry out in longing and sing praises to the Moon when the robe of sky slips from her shoulders and she appears overhead in all her naked beauty.

As for Coyote, soon after this happened, he disappeared from the land of the true people. Perhaps he did feel love and not simple lust for the beautiful Moon Maiden, and took the path of many men with broken hearts, to wander and seek distraction from the pain in far-off lands. Yet, the land would have to be distant and strange, indeed, for Coyote to escape from Moon Maiden's scorn, for she holds sway over the night in all the known worlds, even when she is called upon by a foreign name given to her by foreign people.

One day Coyote will grow tired of waiting, for no man will wait forever, no matter how desirable the woman. Or perhaps one night Moon Maiden will relent and give old Coyote another chance. Great is the ability of a woman to hold a grudge, though. She hasn't shown any sign of forgiving him yet.

***

"There, that's the whole story," the Lady concluded. "What do you think?"

Keyotie sat cross-legged in front of the campfire, chin resting in one hand. He remained lost in thought after she finished and the Lady seemed content to allow him his silence.

Finally, he reached forward and gave the rabbit roasting over the fire another turn, then picked up a stick, poking around in the embers. He looked up at the Lady. "That's really the way they tell it now?" he asked. "It makes the Coyote in this story sound like a misbehaving child who got spanked."

"No one's told this story in quite a while," she replied. She rose to her feet from the opposite side of the fire, walking over to a saddlebag draped across a log, continuing the conversation. "The people who once passed it down to their children are long gone and lived in a world far removed from here. We Ladies are the only ones who remember it now. Besides the Keeper of Stories, of course."

"Then perhaps it's best you let it die and take its place in her realm, along with the countless other legends that have come and gone. Is this why you left your two Sisterselfs and tracked me down? To tell me another musty old story about the infamous Trickster?"

The Lady pulled some blankets from the pack and began clearing sticks and pinecones away from a piece of ground next to the fire. "My Sisterselfs are on their own missions. It's not like we are joined at the hip. When our duty requires it, we can get more done by splitting up. Even now, we are all present within each mind. They say to give you their regards, by the way. They...no, *we* regret what was said before you left."

"Before I was sent packing, you mean?" Keyotie watched her movements from across the flames. The Ladies might share a common will, but he had lived with them and knew they were as different in their thinking as any three women could be. Nor did they look at all alike. Coyote had been attracted to this one from the beginning. He admired her long black hair, slim build and short stature, barely taller than his own small frame. He'd often wondered if she had the blood of his people running through her veins.

"Surely you didn't make this trip just to apologize?" he asked. "Everything you Ladies said was true. I had no business trying to come between you three, and I've long since stopped blaming others for my faults. I'd like to think we're still friends, at least." He grinned at her and rubbed his cheek. "If you're worried about that parting slap you gave me, I deserved it for the way I acted. It's not the first time a friend—or lover—has tried to knock some sense into me. You are the first to make my ears ring, though."

She had the grace to look embarrassed. "That was wrong of me. I'd like to think we're more than friends. That's not the only reason I tracked you down, although it did need to be said."

The Weaving

"Lady," he prompted, "we have known each other too long and too well for these word games. Let's agree that apologies have been made all around and move on. What have you come for?"

"What I have come for," she replied, "is to ask a question, and then perhaps make a request. I ask only that you answer truthfully for a change."

"Don't I always?" He gave his best innocent look.

She laughed. "Keyotie, I believe you have refined lying to the point where even you can't tell the difference. But my question is this—is what the story suggests true?"

He snorted. "What, that I tried to make out with the moon? You can't be serious."

She spread one blanket on the ground, then came back around the fire and sat down next to him, using the other blanket as a cushion. "I wouldn't put it past you. But no, I'm talking about the speculation at the end. Did Coyote feel love, not simple lust for the Moon Maiden? Is that why he took to wandering in strange lands? The rabbit looks done, by the way."

Keyotie removed the rabbit and tore off a leg to hand to the Lady, then took a bite of his own while he thought about his answer. He watched the sparks from the fire, following them as they floated up to the leafy canopy almost hiding the night sky. *Moon Maiden.* Even though he'd shared a bed with the Ladies, he'd never spoken about that part of his life. Not to them, not to anyone.

"There's nothing simple about lust," he answered, "and no reason why it has to be one or the other. It's only that lust comes naturally, with your first breath out of the womb, while love is something that happens over time."

He suddenly became very conscious of her closeness to him and found it harder to talk because of it. His sensitive nose caught a faint scent of lilac on her clothes from the bushes growing in her mountain valley.

"The Coyote in the story was young and full of lust," he explained, "lust for life and everything life had to offer. He acted out of ignorance, making the mistakes of the young. All he felt at first was the natural desire of a man for a woman. The love came later, when he saw the beauty and strength of spirit within the woman, but by then it was too late. Perhaps it was too late even before he saw her charms."

He grew uncomfortable enough to stand and walk a few paces away from the fire, looking at the darkness of the trees. "My truthful answer, Lady, is that Coyote felt both lust and love for the beautiful Moon Maiden. Both lust and love also fuel his wandering. Lust for adventure caused him to seek new worlds, where he would always grow to love the people around him. Then, as time passed, he would find himself surrounded by generations of ghosts and reminders of old friends and lovers. He would wander again, in part to escape the memories."

The moist air of the woods filled his nostrils, beckoning with a promise of moonlit trails and new horizons. He had spent the past year or so living in the wild forest, growing farther from human contact with each passing day. He could fade into the brush and she wouldn't be able to follow this time. He was glad to see her, but he wished she hadn't come. He hated goodbyes.

Then it dawned on him why this particular Lady had been sent, and how desperate they must be. She was not just the messenger— she was also the payment, if *that* was the price of his help. Keyotie turned his back on the forest and walked over to the Lady's side, looking down.

"I asked you once to be my wife," he said. "You refused. Time has not diminished my desire for you. But I am not the cub that so long ago tried to bargain for a woman's love. That Coyote no longer exists. It is Keyotie who stands before you tonight, and I will accept no love that is not freely given."

He shifted to true form, a transformation so quick, an eyeblink would have missed it. The man standing next to the Lady was replaced by a large, dog-like animal. He placed a paw on her knee.

"Why are you here, Lady?" he asked again. "You are the Three Who Are One. You can order the skies to rain and see the future in a drop of water. You are a power not confined to this world and your

The Weaving

stories go back at least as far as mine. Yet, you are troubled, and that troubles me."

***

She looked at the famous Trickster of a thousand myths and legends. When he first appeared in this world, the Ladies had met him at the door, so to speak, with the intention of telling this troublemaker to keep on traveling. It was she who had looked into his eyes and let him stay. Now those eyes were staring back into hers once more, and she was surprised to find herself feeling disappointed Keyotie had not insisted on taking her as payment.

Damn it, Keyotie, how do you keep doing that to me? "I came to find out why you're leaving this world," she said, "and ask you to stay, for my sake, if nothing else. We need you to track someone down for us. If you leave now, this land and all the people in it will die."

Five

The Ladies had considered the witch's request for a reading to be routine, although Rose had never shown any interest in their services before. She brought along the required gifts, along with an invitation to a conference of powers to be held at the Palace later in the year. Mail service to dragon country was spotty to say the least.

One of the gifts was a book, and they gave it to their son, who ran into his room and began reading. He later told them it was all about adults kissing and fighting and then kissing some more, but if he skipped over the kissing part it was a nice enough adventure. He also asked what a bosom was, and why it was always heaving. The Ladies confiscated the book and spent a pleasant few nights reading it themselves.

Rose had asked the Ladies if she would ever find true love and was told the disappointing truth of her future. Then she had asked, why not? They said only the Goddess could answer her question. Rose didn't even bother with her last allowed question. Instead, she rode away with a thoughtful look on her face.

If they could reconsider the incident, they would realize Rose was going to take their last response literally. She specialized in quests such as this and, to her mind, even destiny was just another obstacle to be overcome with magic and ingenuity.

Of course, when the past was changed, this incident became just another of the many possibilities that never happened. There was no need for Rose to ask the Ladies her question—she'd already found true love.

***

The Weaving

"But I just took a bath last week!"

"Tom, I swear. I've never seen a grown man who hates getting wet as much as you do!"

It was an old argument, a script played so often enough neither Tom nor Rose had any doubt of the outcome. She emptied another bucket of water into the big wooden washtub behind their cottage. She tested the temperature with a finger, allowing enough magic to flow down her arm to heat the water until it was steaming.

"Here, one more trip ought to do it," she said, handing him the pails. "You've been working in the garden and need more than your usual quick wipe down. I've just changed the sheets, so you're not getting in bed tonight unless you're clean. It's your choice. And as an additional treat, I'll climb into the tub with you."

Tom strode toward the spring with a bucket in each hand, whistling. She'd always suspected some of his reluctance to bathe came from not wishing to perform the chore of fetching water for the tub. "And don't spend all day at the stream!" she called before he could disappear into the woods. He waved a pail in her direction in response.

Rose bent down and picked through a basket of clothes, pulling out a pair of pants. She held them up and shook her head. Another rip in the knee. She squinted in concentration, muttering a general purpose mending spell. The torn edges started to rejoin, the fiber stitching back together. She followed with a cleaning spell and the dust and grime became detached from the cloth. A good shaking and the pants were ready to be folded and placed on the finished stack. He'd need a new pair before winter. Every repair left the fabric weaker and it would probably tear again.

She quickly worked her way through the rest of the pile. Rose had never been shy about using her power to get out of the hard work constituting the daily lives of most wives. She was less willing to coddle her husband in his chores, figuring he needed the exercise. He'd even asked her one time why she didn't just use one of those laundry spells on him if she thought he was in such need of cleaning. After some thought, she'd decided doing so would probably result in the removal of his hair along with the dirt. She didn't tell him how tempting it had been to try it anyway and feign surprise at the results.

She was folding the last shirt when she saw Tom coming back up the path from the spring. He was singing and swinging the buckets along to the tune, losing half the water in the process.

"*...Oh, the Dragon tried his valiant best, but in the end cried stop! When dragonhood met maidenhead, the Maid came out on top!*" He was belting out the end of the song as he set the buckets down. He grabbed Rose, planting a big kiss on her lips and his hand on her butt.

"Ah, my fair maiden," he growled. "Shall we try for two out of three?"

She laughed and put her arms around his neck. "I never think of it as a contest, you randy old tomcat. Wherever did you learn that song? It's enough to make a midwife blush."

"I heard the Minstrel sing it during our trip to the Palace. It's called *The Maiden and the Dragon*. Catchy tune, isn't it? Want to hear the one about the farmer's daughter and the traveling wizard? It's even better."

Rose shook her head and began unlacing his shirt. "I'm not sure my maiden ears are up to it. Here, get in the tub while I clean—" She was interrupted by a sparrow landing on her shoulder and chirping for attention. She stopped what she was doing and extended her awareness into the woods, briefly looking through the eyes of one tiny bird after another until she spied the intruder. Then she relaxed her talent, bringing her consciousness back to her own body and sighed, retying his shirt.

"We have company coming, so the bath will have to wait. Could you bring in the clothes for me? I need to change into the green robe and do something with my hair."

Tom looked toward the wide path cutting through the woods. "Must be someone special for you to go through all that," he said. "Anyone I know?"

"It's the Ladies," she replied, already heading back inside. Tom followed with the basket of laundry. "They're the ones who ran into the trouble with their boy at the Conference. They almost never go anywhere, so no one really expected them to show up. The Ladies pretty much stayed in their room and left early, so I didn't get a chance to introduce you."

Tom had spent most of his time during the meeting of the powers hanging out in town—at the town tavern, to be exact. Not being a power himself, there hadn't been any reason to attend the meetings with her. Rose had asked her old friend, Keyotie, to make sure her husband wasn't bored. She should have known better. Whatever went on, both men refused to talk about it, and considering Keyotie's reputation, she didn't want to know.

Tom sat at the table where he'd be out of her way, watching as Rose pulled a folded green robe out of a trunk and changed clothes. "I think I saw them," he said. "A tall blonde, a freckled redhead about your size, and a skinny little thing with black hair? So witches come in threes now?"

"The Ladies aren't witches," she answered. "They're...unique. The Ladies are the only power in the land that can actually see the future. People go to them and get their fortunes told." She tied the cord around her waist to complete the outfit, looked at her reflection in the mirror and tisked. "Where's my brush?"

"They actually know the future?" Tom shook his head. "That's sad. I feel sorry for them."

Rose stopped brushing her hair and stared at her husband. His unusual way of looking at the world because of his missing past sometimes surprised her. "Feel sorry for them? Why, I'd love to have that power. There are lots of times being able to see what's going to happen next would save me a lot of trouble."

Tom shrugged, leaning the chair back against the wall and grinning. "Or not. You're excited about meeting the three Ladies. If you knew something bad was going to happen tomorrow, you still couldn't stop it, but it would ruin the good time you're having today. So why would you want to know?" He waved his hands in the air. "It's better to, I don't know, live for today and let tomorrow take care of itself."

Gerald Ghostlow

Rose laughed. "You know, I think you're trying to turn laziness into a virtue. Live for today? Sounds like something you thought up last time you spent the day fishing instead of doing chores." Rose gave herself one final check in the mirror, a large ornate thing on a gilded stand. She'd chosen it as her reward for rescuing the Elf King's son and Tom had complained ever since about how much room it took in the little cottage. "It's not the three Ladies showing up, though. There's only one of them, *a* Lady. I've never heard of one traveling alone. It must be a real emergency."

She set down the brush and stood, ready to take on the world. "How do I look?" Tom got up and took her in his arms. She scratched behind his ear, a sort of good luck ritual she'd developed. "Tom," she said, "I believe it's time for the Witch of the Woods to walk the land."

They went to meet the Lady. Once more she would pack and leave Tom behind to wait and worry. He claimed it was something he'd grown accustomed to, filling his time doing chores around the cottage.

As Rose stepped out the door, she realized Tom had managed to skip out on taking a bath, after all.

***

Rose and Tom were standing in front of the cottage as the Lady came riding out of the woods. Tom recognized the woman from his brief glimpse at the palace. It was one of the three he'd seen in the hall—the tall, busty blonde. The woman rode without a saddle, only a thick blanket between her rump and the horse. He was impressed—even with Rose's lessons, it didn't take much to send him flying off one of the beasts.

The Lady was staring back at him, and he began to feel uneasy as she continued to stare. When the horse was a few paces away, the Lady placed a hand on its neck and it stopped. Only then did she turn to address Rose.

"We greet the Witch of the Woods in her place of power," the Lady said. "We have come a long way to see you and would ask for a few moments of your time."

"The Witch of the Woods greets the Ladies in return," Rose answered. "I offer you the sanctuary of my place of power and the shelter of my home. All that I have is yours, for as long as you are my guest." She leaned closer to Tom. "There," she whispered, "if she wants to be formal, let's see her top that."

The Lady slid down from her horse without showing so much as a glimpse of the long legs under her skirt. "Your hospitality is appreciated," the Lady replied in turn, "but we cannot stay as long as we would like. We are on our way to see the King about a pressing emergency. We came here to ask you to accompany us and cannot stop to indulge ourselves in pleasantries." She looked at Tom. "May we speak privately?"

"This is Tom, my husband," Rose explained. "He would never betray a confidence, so you may speak freely in front him. If you insist, we can go inside while he takes care of your horse."

The Lady looked back at Rose. "You misunderstand us," she said. "You again have our apologies. Even now the Sisterselfs are reminding me that my way of speaking is confusing in this language." She pointed to Tom. "I was asking this man if he and I could speak in private. I need to talk to him alone."

"Um...what? You mean me?" Tom was caught off guard by this turn in the conversation.

"May I speak to you alone?" the Lady repeated.

Rose spoke. "Please excuse us for a moment. Why don't you take care of your horse while I talk to my husband. There's a small stall stocked with grain behind the cottage. You can fill the water bucket from the tub." The Lady nodded and led the horse away, leaving Tom and Rose some privacy.

"What's going on?" Tom asked. "What does she want with me?"

Rose shook her head. "I have no idea, but the Ladies have always been a mystery. I'm interested in learning what this is all about, as well. No harm in finding out, I guess. Just don't accept any gifts or make any promises without checking with me first. Of course, these women do have the habit of turning the people who cross them into enchanted frogs. I can't imagine her trying that on you in my place of power."

He grinned. "Well, if I don't come back from the stream, look for a frog that doesn't like getting wet."

"If you end up as a frog, I swear by our bond I will be known throughout the land as the Witch Who Kisses Frogs. But it won't come to that. We'll just have to go along for now. You were bound to get involved in one of my adventures sooner or later. You can't marry the Witch of the Woods and spend your life tilling a garden."

Tom remembered his encounter with the Ice Queen during the conference. Rose hadn't been told about the adventure—it was too embarrassing. He was still trying to figure out how Keyotie had ever talked him into it. "Being married to you is never boring, honey. Here she comes. I'll go see what she wants, then help you pack. It can't be too important. After all, I'm just your ordinary, everyday man. What could I possibly be able to do that would make a difference in the world?"

Six

Tom escorted the Lady down the wide, cool path. The woman was silent, looking at the surrounding woods. It was nature left to itself, teaming with life. A hawk watched from its perch upon an old dead spruce and a fox trotted from around the base of the tree to stare at them.

"I haven't been here before," the Lady remarked, "but it's beautiful. You can feel the Mother of All's presence. Did you know ten generations of witches have lived here?"

"Rose has told me a little of the history." Tom reached down and picked up an acorn, chucking it at a nosy fox following them. "I realize Rose is someone special."

"Did she tell you none of the previous office holders ever married? That any witch being married is unusual? In fact, you might be the only man in this generation to take the chance. There's a widespread belief that the bond of wedlock allows a witch to read the husband's thoughts. That scares most men spitless."

They had reached a little wooden bridge spanning the stream. Tom leaned against the rail while the Lady sat down on a log beside the path.

"No, the subject never came up," he replied. "Even if Rose could read my mind, there's nothing in there I'm trying to hide. Is being single supposed to be part of her tradition? I don't get in the way of her work. In fact, Rose discovered I have something she calls 'the Sight,' so I even help her a little when she's trying new spells" Tom became troubled by the turn of conversation. "I knew who and what she was before I married her and accepted that part of her life. If you're worried I'm one of those men who try to keep their wife at home and pregnant...well, don't be."

Gerald Ghostlow

"What can you recall of your life before meeting Rose?" she asked.

Tom looked at the woman, wondering how she knew of his missing memory. "Not a thing. Rose found me right about here, half-frozen in a snowstorm. I spent the rest of the winter sick with fever. I've never been able to remember anything about my life from before that. Rose says it's not unheard of, that the fever erased the memories somehow."

Tom remembered the Lady's unique powers and he whipped around, excited. "You can see through time! If you can tell the future, can you also see the past? Can you tell me where I came from?"

"We don't—"

"No!" came a cry from the surrounding woods. A fox popped its head up from the brush and the form shimmered, transforming into Rose. She struggled against the clinging brambles, then jerked them loose, heedless of the damage to her robe. She stomped to the bridge. "Lady, you will not do this. I am a power equal to you and demand you keep your nose out of my personal life!"

"You demand?" The Lady jumped to her feet. "I don't recall inviting you to this discussion. This is none of your affair, witch."

Rose stood arms akimbo, glaring at the taller woman. "This is *my* place of power and you're discussing *my* husband. You are no longer welcome. You would sneak behind my back after accepting hospitality? You break the rules, Lady."

"You speak of rules? You spied on a private conversation, asked for and granted with your full knowledge!"

Tom watched, forgotten in the argument, growing frustrated as the two women yelled at each other. Watching the two powers go head-to-head, he suspected it might be a good idea to step away from an incipient magical duel. The wind picked up and storm clouds formed overhead in response to the Lady's anger. The life in the woods responded to Rose's state of mind, birds filling the surrounding trees and looking ready to attack in mass. He decided to try restoring some order before it got any worse.

"Will you two women stop bickering!" he yelled at the top of his

The Weaving

lungs. "You're both acting like spoiled brats!" The arguing and chaos ended abruptly as both women turned to glare at him. He wondered if being turned into a frog hurt. He hoped flies tasted better than they looked.

***

Rose was at the point of deciding whether to turn the Lady into a snake or go for something more creative when Tom's words slapped her like a wet cloth in the face. She became aware of the agitation of the life in her woods and forced herself to calm down. That didn't mean she was going to back down from a duel. If this woman hurled one more insult her way, there was going to be a groundhog where a Lady used to stand.

"But she started it!" was all the Lady said, probably in response to a scolding from her Sisterselfs.

Tom looked scared, but was determined to have his say. Rose admired his courage—it was one of the many reasons she loved the man. At times she doubted his wisdom, but no one was perfect.

"I don't understand what's going on," he said, "but you two fighting doesn't provide me with any answers."

Tom first addressed Rose. "Darling, if you think I shouldn't ask the Lady for help, I'll take your advice. But first let me find out if all this is even necessary."

He turned to the Lady. "Could you help if I asked for it?"

The Lady looked at Rose, folding her arms across her chest and looking away. "As I was about to say," the Lady replied, "we don't answer questions about the past. We look into the future, then tell you what you need to do now in order to get where you want to go, if it's possible at all. We will tell you how to find your memories, but you have to ask the right questions and have the wit to understand the answers."

"And the price?" Tom asked. Rose was proud he thought to ask. Most people didn't stop to consider the cost when it came to magic.

Gerald Ghostlow

"There are rules involved," the Lady explained. "You get three answers to three questions, no more. What we say is for your ears only." Rose glanced up to see the Lady looking at her again, but decided to let the implied criticism slide.

"Normally, you'd present us with a gift first," the Lady continued, "something dear to your heart. Then we decide if it's worth a reading. But in your case, we'll state our price later. You'll just have to trust us."

"You traveled all this way to offer me this service?" Tom asked. "What makes me so important?"

"Is that your first question? I'll have to whisper the answer in your ear with Rose here."

"No!" Tom caught on fast to how tricky the Ladies could be. "Excuse us, please." He came over to Rose and pulled her a little way down the path. "Rose...darling. Tell me what I should do."

She searched for the right words to say. "Is it really so important that you remember? Aren't you happy the way we are now?"

He took her hands in his. "Very happy. I awaken every morning in amazement at my luck in finding you. But I lie awake at night sometimes, wondering who I am—who I *was*, before you rescued me and gave me this wonderful life. I don't feel complete. I'd like to know, Rose. I think I need to know."

She felt a tear starting and resolved not to cry. This was the moment Rose had been avoiding for the past two years, but she'd always known it couldn't be put off forever. "What if...what if you already have a wife, maybe children?" she asked. "What if there's a family out there, and they want you back?"

"Is that what you're afraid of? It never occurred to me" He paused, then shook his head. "It's disturbing to think there might be a family out there I left behind. I suppose if that were true, they'd consider me dead by now. Maybe I could keep it that way. It could get complicated, but I'd never leave you."

He gently wiped the tear from her cheek. "I'm more afraid it would turn out I'd been an outlaw, some bandit who escaped the King's justice. What if I'm a murderer or rapist? How could you still

44

love me, then?"

Rose laughed, needing the relief. "Oh, Tom, people don't change what they are by losing a few memories. You're an honest, caring man. You didn't get that way overnight." She could see the pleading in his eyes, but he'd promised to take her advice. He'd walk away from the Lady if she told him to. Maybe one day he would walk away from her as well, in search of his past.

She did what she had to do. "Tom, ask the Lady your questions. Then together, we'll go find out who you were. I won't even eavesdrop this time." She sniffed and managed a smile. "I can say I've never been happier in my whole life. Maybe when this is through, you'll be able to say the same."

She walked back up the path, leaving Tom and the Lady alone to conduct their business. For the first time, she wasn't at all excited or happy about going to battle as the Witch of the Woods. She wished she was just an ordinary woman whose biggest challenge was getting her husband to take a bath more often.

***

Tom watched Rose depart, then turned to the Lady standing patiently in the same spot by the bridge. He figured the woman had known the outcome all along.

"How do we do this? Do you read my future in the palm of my hand or what?" Tom asked.

"I'm not a hedge witch, trading false hopes for coin," she replied. She reached into a hidden pocket of her skirt and pulled out a small bowl. "Could you fill this for me from the stream?"

He did as requested and she sat back down on the log, holding up the bowl and looking into the water. "I will tell you the price. You must accompany Rose on this trip, in spite of her objections. Also, what answers you receive here, you must not share with Rose. You will understand why after we're through. If you agree to this, then I'm ready when you are."

He stood in front of the Lady, crossing his arms. "If you knew

Gerald Ghostlow

Rose, you'd know what a high price I will pay. Let's get this over with. I get three questions, and it's up to me to figure out what to ask? Here's the obvious one. What do I need to do in order to get my memories back?"

The Lady studied the water in the bowl for a moment. "Follow Rose into the maze." She looked up at him. "You have two more questions."

"What kind of answer is that? Wait!" He held up a hand, stopping her from replying. "I know, you'll tell me something like 'it's a true answer' and I've just wasted my second question." He thought for a while, and then tried again. "When will I find out about my past?"

She took a little longer to answer, but eventually said, "When you encounter the beast within. You have one more question."

He grunted and stood in silence, trying to decide what to ask next. He hadn't realized the Ladies were so stingy with their answers. *What did that leave? Of course.* "Will knowing the truth about my past hurt Rose?" If the answer was yes, he would stay at home and resign himself to living with the mystery.

The Lady didn't even look into the bowl this time. "Knowing the truth will hurt her," she replied. "Not learning the truth will mean her death." The Lady poured the water onto the ground and put the bowl away while he stood, shocked . "That is your final answer. You can see why it would be better for Rose if you didn't burden her with this. The quest for your missing past must be your task alone to solve." She got to her feet and placed a hand on Tom's arm.

"Please understand," she said, "I do not know everything that's going to happen in the world. That is more than three minds together can encompass. If destiny was fixed and unyielding, there would be no reason to do anything but sit and wait for the inevitable. The future is..." She looked around and pointed to where a large spider was building a web in the bushes next to her. "...like that. What has already been built determines the shape of what is to be. The anchor lines reaching out from the center support the web and cannot be moved once placed in position. To do so might bring the

The Weaving

whole structure to ruin. But, the spider has the freedom to connect those lines into a web of her own design, within limits. Now, imagine a whole world of spiders, all working on the same great web."

Tom watched the spider pause in its spinning and rush to where a luckless furry moth had stumbled into the web. The result was predictable. The web was torn, but the anchor lines still held, and the spider stopped her building long enough to dispose of the moth and repair the damage.

"I don't understand," he finally said. "And it doesn't matter, anyway. You tell me my wife will die if I don't enter some maze and meet some beast, and then expect me to care about destiny and spiderwebs?" He started walking back up the path, wondering how Rose was going to react when he refused to discuss what he'd learned here. It was going to be a long trip. "If Rose's life depends on my completing this quest, then I'll find my missing past or die trying."

The Lady nodded. "I know you'll do your best, Tom. I can tell you're a good man. Now, the three of us have some spinning of our own to do."

***

The blacksmith in the small village stopped his work when he heard an insistent knocking. He limped over and opened the door. A woodpecker flew in. It landed on the center beam and began rapping, adding another round of dents to the hard wood.

"All right, I get the message," he told the bird. "Go back to your mistress and tell her I'll send Yarnie right over with her horse." The bird seemed unsatisfied, adding two more sharp raps, then looked at the man. He frowned. "Both horses? You'll need Yarnie to stay and look after the place, then. I'll tell him to take a few supplies."

The blacksmith yelled for his son. The boy shuffled in, expecting to be ordered to pump the bellows. The lad brightened when he was told about the bird, and soon had the horses saddled and the wagon hitched for his ride to her cottage. The man watched his son leave and knew the boy would never be happy as a blacksmith. On the other hand, tending the witch's garden while she and her husband were gone had taught the lad quite a bit about the plants she used in her healing and there was a ready market for those. The boy could support himself when it was time to take a wife and make his own way.

The blacksmith laid down his hammer and walked to a workbench, pulling a ledger from its hiding place. He sharpened the quill, kept handy to figure the accounts, then opened the book, marked the date and noted a woman had stopped in earlier, asking directions to the woods where Rose lived. He described the woman as best he could, then added Rose and Tom were now travelling to an unknown destination.

The blacksmith slid the ledger back in its hole. Every once in a while, a stranger would arrive and let the blacksmith know it was *that* time again. His list of events would be traded for a blank book and a few coins and the watching would continue. The blacksmith didn't do it for the money—he made a good enough living from his forge. He was doing it because his old Captain, the Duke, had asked him to.

The Duke had saved his life several times during the war, so he figured he owed the man this favor.

Seven

Prince Valant looked down at his father, King Morgan the Sixth. He wasn't surprised to find the old man slept alone. The King had not taken a woman to bed since his wife died giving birth to Valant. The castle's servants admired their King for his fidelity, talking about his undying love for his wife and other such nonsense.

The Prince knew better.

He'd once bribed a serving girl into seducing the King, just to satisfy his princely curiosity. His father couldn't rise to the occasion—he was as impotent as his tiny little kingdom, as useless as his limp army would be against the neighboring might of a true ruler, such as King Justin.

The Prince sat on the side of the bed and shook the man's arm. "Wake up, father," he said softly. "Your not-so-beloved son has returned and wants to have a word with you."

The King awoke slowly, squinting into the darkness. "What—who is it?" He tried to sit up, but Valant pushed him back down. "Valant? Is it really you? What are you doing in my bedchamber?"

"You might as well ask what I'm doing back in the castle at all, father. You did threaten to have me publicly flogged and locked in the dungeon if I returned to this dismal place. It's been years now—aren't you even a little bit glad to see me?"

"How dare you come back! Guards!" The King struggled to sit up again but Valant easily held him down. "Let me up! Guards! Attend me!"

The Prince patted his father's arm. "There's no reason to shout. The guards aren't going to come to your rescue. Save your strength, old man, you'll need it."

"What have you done? You and your henchmen have murdered

my guards? Do you plan on killing me now, like you did your brother? The people will not stand for it!"

Valant sighed. "The guards aren't dead and I didn't murder my brother, either. Well, not on purpose. If you'd cared about me at all, you would have listened. You always did love him more."

Prince Valant leaned over, took a match from the holder and lit the lamp on the night stand. "It's true," the Prince continued, "Sometimes I wished something would happen to you and my older brother would assume the throne. He'd listened to me when I told him our destiny was to rule the Empire. But now you've convinced everyone I'm a common murderer. It's a problem I've been working on. I'd like to introduce you to my solution. Dad, say hello to Lilith. Lilith, darling, this is the King I was telling you about."

Lilith stepped into the light, revealing herself for the first time to the old King. "Who's this?" Morgan asked with a quavering voice. "Did you bring a witch to do your dirty work? Going to turn me into something, are you? My advisors will find out and you'll both hang!"

Lilith chuckled. "A witch? Oh, I'm much better than a witch, old man. I'm here to make sure you do whatever my handsome Prince orders."

"Never!" The King propped himself up on one elbow, pointing a shaking finger at his son. "You haven't changed one bit. You only want the throne so you can march on the Empire. Our poor land would be destroyed by your vanity. You have no regard for the people of this kingdom. Torture me all you like, but I will not accept your authority!"

The Prince was insulted his father thought so little of him. "I have a high regard for the people. Without their taxes, I'd have to work for a living. A King without his people is like...a shepherd without his flock of sheep!"

"Beloved," Lilith said impatiently, "you're wasting time arguing." She waved a hand at the King. He gasped, flopping onto his back. His eyes bulged, staring vacantly at the ceiling. He lay there, quivering and moaning.

The Prince leaned over and checked the man's pulse. "Amazing

The Weaving

how that works. Are you sure his old heart can take it? I did say he wasn't to be killed."

"I won't let that happen, my darling. I have a lot of experience in this. After a short while—that will seem like an eternity to him—I'll release him from his nightmare. Oh, he might stay stubborn at first, but a few more sessions and he'll be too afraid to do anything but obey." She placed a hand on the Prince's shoulder. "But let's talk about what you said just now. Is that all I am to you, a solution to your problem?"

The Prince stood and pulled her into his arms. "It breaks my heart that you might think such a thing! Once I am truly the King, I will order my subjects to worship you the same as I!"

"You say the sweetest things, beloved," she purred in response. "Now can you remove that silly amulet? Haven't I proved my love for you tonight? It's so cold against my skin when we...*you* know." She batted her eyes, looking innocent and oh-so-love struck.

Valant wasn't the least bit fooled. She'd tried every trick in the book to entice him into removing the protective charm. Lilith was good at seduction, but she was up against another pro at the game. Now that he'd gotten to know her, Valant was not about to trust this demon. He'd been having nightmares lately of being forced to lick her feet while she sat on his throne and cackled.

"Please be patient, darling," he replied. "I do love you, but a part of me is still afraid you're only using me to get what you want. It's my failing, not yours. I've been hurt too often in the past. Just give me a little more time and I'm sure I can bring myself to trust you completely." Valant hugged the demon, anticipating the day the charade would be over.

The King lay moaning and twitching on the bed, ignored. He was living out his worst nightmares in his mind and not anticipating much of anything.

***

Valant could tell the day had finally begun by the voices

outside the door. One voice complained the night guards wouldn't get out of the way of the breakfast cart; another man asked what was wrong. He'd ordered the night guards not to speak to anyone or allow anyone to enter, and after Lilith's touch, they would have killed their best friends for trying.

Valant opened the door before someone was hurt. When the new guards saw him in the King's chamber, they attempted to rush in, only to be blocked by crossed spears.

"Father," he called back into the room, "I believe you forgot to tell your staff about my *expected* return. If you could straighten this out, please?"

The King was sitting on the bed, struggling to put on his boots, looking tired but unharmed. The old man cleared his throat and looked at Lilith standing beside him.

"There's...no reason to be alarmed," he said. "I forgot to tell the Captain of the Guard, that's all. I sent for my son. I decided to end the exile. Please..." Lilith waved her hand at him—he flinched and continued. "Please gather the staff in the throne room for an announcement." The Prince cleared his throat and the King continued. "Have the Captain of the Guard report here first, for a... private conference."

"And send down to the kitchen for more food," the Prince added. "I'm starved."

When they arrived at the throne room, it was packed with the many people who made a living off the Royal treasury. Valant imagined word of his arrival with the mysterious woman had been passed around, speculation running wild. The Prince and Lilith walked directly behind the King and stood on either side of the ornate throne.

"My subjects," the King began, "you all know Valant, my... beloved son. It was obvious to me from the beginning that he had nothing to do with his brother's murder. It had to be a...conspiracy against the Royal family, by members of our own court. The only way to flush out the enemy was by...pretending to go along with the lies. Valant has spent the past few years searching...I mean seeking...I

The Weaving

sent him on a secret mission..."

So far, King Morgan was sticking to the script Valant had made him memorize, but the old man seemed to have forgotten the rest, or simply got lost in his lines. King sat in silence while the crowd's murmurs grew louder. Valant looked at Lilith, and she just shrugged.

All right, here we go. Valant stepped forth and raised his hands. "Fellow countrymen!" the Prince cried. "I bring you grave news! For too long you have been kept in the dark, but now the terrible truth can be revealed. There is a plot against your King, against the ruling family, against the whole of our small kingdom. My brother was murdered by an agent of this most despicable of enemies. The foe is planning on invading our country, to take our land as his own."

The murmuring became shouts of disbelief and alarm. Finally, the Duchess, Advisor to the King, stepped forth and addressed the crowd.

"This is nonsense!" She turned and pointed to Valant. "I've known this scoundrel since he was a boy, have watched him lie and scheme his way through life. He's done something to our King!"

The Prince had anticipated the Duchess' actions and nodded to the two nearby guards. She was grabbed and dragged away under protest. The rest of the audience became silent as more guards filed in and surrounded them. Lilith had made sure the Captain of the Guard was now on their side.

"Countrymen, please!" Prince Valant had a captive audience. "The Duchess has been an agent of our enemy all along, a fact only discovered recently in my search. And who is this enemy, you ask? It is none other than that despot, King Justin!"

"That's a lie!" A young woman wearing a green robe stepped forward. "There's no plot! My King is an honorable man! I tell you—get your hands off me, or—" She was silenced by a blow to the back of her head. The guards dragged away the unconscious witch to join the Duchess in the dungeons.

"And there, my fellow countrymen, is the proof!" The Prince lowered his voice. "This witch was sent to us under guise as an ambassador, but was actually a spy, using her witchcraft to pass secret messages back and forth. She would have turned the King into a toad at the moment of attack."

One last, courageous man stepped forward, addressing the silent King. "Your highness," he began, casting nervous glances at the remaining guards, "If what our...um, *innocent* Prince says is true, what are your orders? What do we do about it?"

The King leaned forward, his head in his hands. "My son is in charge. I am too old and feeble to protect you. Forgive me. Do whatever he says, and may the Gods have mercy on us all."

The Prince smiled at Lilith over his father's back. He had a Kingdom, finally, but knew there was a greater destiny in store for him. Now it was time to acquire an Empire.

***

Valant's first order of business was to provide for his father's comfort and health. The old King was locked in his comfortable quarters under guard, away from pesky advisors and staff. No need to upset the old man with questions that should remain unanswered.

Then Prince Valant got down to the business of turning Morania into an instrument of his will. His secret mission cover story was written into broadsides and messengers were sent to read the tale in every town and hamlet. The small group of companions he'd brought with him moved into the castle to become his trusted, loyal inner circle.

Word about Lilith's brutal talents spread. Soon, the threat of her attitude adjustments were enough to bring the people in line. She started skipping the endless meetings with his generals and other staff and retreated to the castle library, where she made the librarian read to her from the history books. She was especially interested in tales mentioning the Ladies.

In the meantime, Valant kept busy. Running a kingdom turned out to be harder than acquiring one.

***

The Weaving

The delegation of merchants stormed the castle, demanding to know why their goods were being held up at the river crossings. They were joined by the delegation of miners, complaining of their workers being conscripted for the army.

"But, Prince Valant, you simply can't close the border!" they pleaded.

"Why not?" he asked. "It seems to me you could just sell your merchandise to our people. We'll do without anything we can't make or grow on our own. This is war—people have to make sacrifices!" Had the protestors' tax revenue not funded the kingdom, he would have thrown them in the dungeon.

Further protests, where terms like balance of trade and profit margins, were thrown about. Finally, one of Valant's new council members stepped forward, a cunning riverman named Ambrosius recently promoted to Councilor. "Prince Valant," he said, "I can take care of this. Why don't I take these men into the back room and see what we can work out?"

Valant was all too happy to turn the problem over to someone else. He was surprised to see the merchants and businessmen leaving soon after their meeting with Ambrosius, shaking each other's hands and smiling. The Councilor came back into the throne room, whistling. The Prince dismissed the rest of the staff so they could speak in private.

"Care to tell me how you got rid of them?" he asked.

"Oh, they just got a piece of the action. It's what they wanted all along. Your army needs food, clothes, boots, weapons and such. Those guys now have exclusive contracts. I've also told them that what they need smuggled across the river, I can handle for my usual rates."

"And who's going to pay for all this?" Valant didn't like the new councilman assuming the authority to make deals.

"Have you looked at your treasury?" Ambrosius asked. "You're loaded. Besides, you win either way. If you come out on top in this war, you can tax the money back out of them. You lose the war, you'll

Gerald Ghostlow

be hiding or dead."

"How much are you getting out of this deal?" he asked.

Ambrosius shrugged. "Ten percent off the top."

"Make it five for you and five for me. We'll work something out to stash the money safely. I've already endured one exile with no source of income."

The Prince felt much better. He was beginning to get a handle on how to run a kingdom. A King didn't have to be noble, or wise, or loved by the people. He could get the job done by making his subjects afraid. Ambrosius might become a useful agent, since it appeared the man knew how to get things done. He'd keep an eye on the Councilor and determine if he could be trusted with the royal treasury. If not, there was always Lilith or the dungeon. He smiled at the man.

"Ambrosius," he said, "I believe this is the start of a wonderful friendship. Now, I'm trying to figure out how to keep King Justin's army from crossing a river. Any ideas?"

Eight

King Justin took the crown off his head and held it high. "In keeping with the laws of succession under the watchful eye of whatever Gods have nothing better to do this morning, I hereby crown thee Queen Cindy, ruler of the one and only Empire. Long live Queen Cindy!"

He set the band of gold on her head. It slipped past her ears and nose, finally resting on her shoulders like a heavy gold necklace.

"You're silly, daddy!" his daughter giggled. "Mommy's a Queen, I'm a Princess." She tugged at the crown. "It's heavy."

"You have no idea, Princess." King Justin motioned to the servant for more scrambled eggs. "So, your Mom told me what you want for your birthday. A horse and riding lessons?"

The real Queen stopped feeding the baby and waited to hear the decision. His wife insisted it was too dangerous and her little girl should ride the pony for another year. Whatever his decision, his Princess or his Queen would throw a fit.

There was a cough from the doorway, and for once, Justin was relieved to have his chamberlain interrupt their private breakfast. He motioned for the man to enter the room. "What emergency can't wait this time, Fredrich? Palace on fire? Dragon landing in our courtyard?"

The chamberlain coughed into his hand again. "I regret to announce, sire, that a power has arrived and requests an immediate audience. It's one of those...*Ladies*. We've escorted her to the side conference room."

King Justin wiped his mouth and tossed the napkin on the table, getting to his feet. "I'm afraid we'll have to continue this discussion later, my darlings." He turned to his daughter. "Princess, your daddy needs his crown back. It's time for me to go to work."

Gerald Costlow

***

"His chin was a little more pronounced...put in more of a cleft. And he goes around with the right eyebrow arched half the time, not the left."

The Lady was bent over the artist in the corner, her critiques guiding the artist in his drawing. King Justin took the opportunity to go through some reports at the conference table in the center of the room.

A guard knocked and stuck his head inside the room. "The Duke is here, my Lord," he announced. When the King nodded, the guard swung the door wide as the King's Advisor, the Duke, filled the doorway with his immense girth. He came strolling into the room, his large, powerful frame carrying his great weight gracefully.

The Duke sat in his special chair at the table and laced his fingers across his ample stomach. "You sent for me, sire?" he asked.

The King put down the report he'd been trying to decipher. The writer was in need of a new quill pen and lessons in spelling. "Budrich," he said, "the Lady claims we have a problem." He jerked his head in the direction of the woman holding the sketch pad and shaking her head. The artist frowned.

"Then we have a problem, sire. It was only a matter of time before one of the border kingdoms gave us trouble." The Duke had done no more than glance at the Lady before reaching forward to tap the paper in front of the King. "By the way, since that's Captain Stewart's unique penmanship, I can save you the trouble of figuring out what it says. He wants more men, better food, and a replacement so he can visit his betrothed.

"It wouldn't have made it to your desk, but the General denied his request and the Captain is persistent. I happen to know his betrothed is currently enjoying the company of his brother, the Captain of your fifth guard unit. Might I suggest a simple exchange of duties? The betrothed seems to enjoy the variety and it will keep the two brothers from each other's throats. The additional men are not

The Weaving

available and the food will improve when the crops come to market."

The King picked up his quill and made a note on the report before placing it in the small pile of finished business. He looked at the large stack of unread reports and threw down his pen.

"I swear this endless pecking away at my time will be the death of me!" he complained. He sat back and looked at his trusted friend and Advisor. "All right, tell me how you know this trouble involves a border kingdom."

The Duke shrugged. "The Lady brought this problem to you, so it involves the Empire in some way. Having a sketch made shows she wants you to identify someone. Since we can hardly be expected to know on sight everyone in the land, it would be someone of noble family. Since her description so far has not jogged your memory, we're dealing with minor nobility from a small border kingdom you don't often visit. Going through my list of suspects and considering scattered reports of my own, I'd say it would be the southern kingdom of Morania, and the person in the drawing a young man named Prince Valant. That last is only a guess, though."

The Lady brought over the sketch and set it on the table. The artist left, muttering something about lack of creative expression. The King studied the likeness. "I'd say you amaze me, but I've repeated it so often it goes without saying. I'd never have guessed Morania. King Morgan has a large dungeon reserved for troublemakers and isn't afraid to use it." He thought for a moment. "Prince Valant, the youngest son? The last time I saw him, he was still in diapers. I thought both of Morgan's sons were killed several years ago and he didn't have any daughters. A distant cousin was going to inherit the throne."

The Lady sat down at the table. "This man is very much alive, I assure you," she said. She pushed the drawing over to the Duke. "We could see through our scrying pool that he dressed like nobility and grew up in a castle, but couldn't tell which one. The father actually named the boy Prince Valiant? He must have high hopes for his son."

The Duke shook his head. "Val*ant*. The drawing matches the description I have. He was exiled after he put an arrow through his brother's heart during a hunting trip. He was accused of doing it on purpose to become the heir. It probably was an accident. Valant man is deceitful and cares only for himself, but he's no fool. His brother—Morgan the Seventh—was kindhearted, stupid, and loved his younger brother. Prince Valant would have ran the kingdom in everything but name, so had no reason to take such a gamble. My agents lost track of him a few years ago. What's Valant gotten himself involved in?"

They were interrupted by another knock on the door and the King's chamberlain entered, bearing refreshments. He set the tray on the table as far from the Lady as possible and practically ran from the room, neglecting to perform the courtesy of pouring the wine. The Duke performed this task for them.

"The poor man hasn't been the same since the conference of powers," the King explained. "Turning him into a frog once was justified, Lady, but *twice* might have been excessive. Not that I blame you, but he does a fine job of supervising the Palace staff and I might have to replace him."

She picked through the bowl of fruit on the tray, finding a choice nectarine. "My Sisterselfs and I were not in a good mood at the time. We could sense a break in the web of destiny, but we didn't know it would release the monster until it was too late. The chamberlain provoked us, but we apologize for it, nonetheless. As your guest, we should have left his chastisement in your hands." She did not look the least bit regretful.

The Duke leaned forward. "A monster? You bring us notice of a problem involving the kingdom of Morania, seek information about a known scoundrel, and tell us a monster has been set loose? It does not take great powers of reasoning to know Prince Valant has done a terrible thing and now resides in that little kingdom, hatching some plot. Could you tell us what you know about this monster and what is happening in our neighbor's land? You have my full attention, and I'm sure our King's, as well."

***

The Weaving

After meeting with the King and Duke, the Lady was escorted to the guest quarters to recover from her long trip. She'd informed them her Sisterself was due to arrive in several more days, along with the Witch of the Woods, and asked to postpone further conversations until their arrival.

The staff took the opportunity to light the lanterns and bring dinner from the kitchen. The Duke shoveled food onto a plate. "Well, sire," he remarked once they had privacy, "Looks like we have work to do. What's your take on the Lady's story so far?"

The King put down the reports and walked to a cabinet. He grabbed a rolled map and spread it out on the table, studying the tiny border kingdom. "A power like Rose or our Royal Wizard can best deal with the monster while we handle Prince Valant. If that man becomes the ruler of Morania, he can cause all sorts of trouble."

The King traced a line around the small kingdom. "The Elves would come down hard on the Moranians if they expanded into the forest on their eastern and southern borders, and since that would break the treaty between nations, we couldn't come to their aid without sucking the whole land into another war with the Elves."

The Duke looked at the minute symbols clustered around the tiny area. "They've overcut their trees. Without the lumber trade, people could only find work in the mines. That little kingdom doesn't have enough farmland to feed their own population, so they import wheat from us. People have been going hungry because of the high prices. On top of that, those mountains contain huge deposits of iron ore. They make most of the weapons that supply our army.

"For all our size, our forces are scattered and we cannot afford to leave our other borders unguarded. Valant could field a smaller army in a span of weeks and then use the river on his border to hold us off until winter. The other vassal kingdoms might decide to join in the rebellion to grab their share of the loot, and that would be the end of the Empire."

The King pinned the map to the wall. It was going to get a lot of use in the coming days. "All from one minor Prince with ambitions above his station. The Lady says this monster will allow Valant to assume the throne. Is she right?"

"She's certainly telling the truth," the Duke replied, helping himself to another hunk of beef. "I don't think she's capable of lying. But she's not telling us everything. Soon two of the Ladies will be here, but where's the third? Telling us she's on a secret mission is evading the answer. Then there's the real mystery, and that's why they've approached us in the first place."

"Isn't it obvious? There's a danger to our Empire, so she's warning us."

The Duke shook his head. "I've made it a point to learn all I can about the various powers and keep track of their movements. The Empire has been threatened in the past, and I'm not just talking about our eternal conflict with the Elves. The Ladies have played a remarkable role in our struggles."

The King settled back, knowing his friend would eventually get to the point. "And what remarkable role would that be?" he asked.

"No role at all, or at least, none directly traced to their doorstep. The Ladies stay in their little mountain village and mind their own business, except for providing cryptic answers to useless questions for the right price. The elves say the Ladies arrived here with our people, that they're either immortal or have a life span equal to a dragon. The description of at least one of the women has changed over time. I'm assuming as one gets killed, another woman is recruited to take her place, but that's only conjecture. The important point is this—they never get involved in our conflicts."

"That's interesting to note. What about this monster, this 'Lilith' she's worried about?"

"Never heard of it. We'll have to ask our young Wizard, Bertram—that's his specialty. I've already taken the liberty of sending for him. But you just mentioned the key to the puzzle. The Ladies are worried about this creature, so there's some personal history between them, something they're not telling us about. I believe we are being maneuvered like pieces on a chess board, and the real fight is between those two. Or four, or whatever. The Ladies are more worried about the monster than what happens to us."

The Weaving

The King considered the Duke's words. "Budrich, you have a devious mind. So, we'll play along, but gather our own information and follow our own wisdom. What she's describing is certainly a danger to us, so our goals should be the same for now. If we're pieces on a board, I'm glad you're standing by my side. I've never seen you lose a game of chess—you're the best in the land."

The Duke wiped his mouth, having finished his entire dinner, including most of the King's portion. He knew the King would have little appetite until it was time for action—the planning stage of a campaign always made him edgy.

"Sire," he remarked, "I'm flattered at your confidence and won't pretend to false modesty, but I've never played chess with someone who could see my every move before I decided to make it. It will be a real challenge. I might even ask the Lady if she'd like to play a game or two. Just be aware—unlike the Ladies, I'm only human. It's possible I've met my match."

The King watched his friend leave. He knew the Duke would enjoy exercising his remarkable intelligence against a worthy opponent. He shoved the reports into a pile, glad for some excuse to put off reading any more. He decided to make a surprise inspection of the barracks and get in some sword practice, then he would spend time with the Queen and their children. The Ladies might consider him a pawn, but he would not sacrifice all his ancestors had built to win a game.

Nine

Keyotie sat panting, his tongue hanging out in the heat, his paws scorched and sore from the hot ground. The sun was already baking the land of cracked mud, even though it was still morning. It reminded him of another land he'd seen in his early days. Then, as now, he wondered what use Old Man Creator could possibly have for such an inhospitable place.

A slight movement caught his eye and a tiny lizard skittered from a crack, pausing long enough to stick out a forked tongue at him and bob its head, making a chuckling sound. Then it scampered back into the shade, leaving Keyotie nodding his head in agreement. He was reminded of something else from way back then, something he overheard a shaman say. *Old Man Creator made the worlds, because he needed beauty to exist. He made the people, because he needed to see this beauty through the eyes of his creation. He made the Trickster because he needed a good laugh.*

Keyotie shifted into human form while returning to their camp. The Lady sat under the canopy, sharing the shade with their mules. She wore a loose white robe, thin enough to allow air to circulate, with a hood to cover her head. She held out a chunk of bread and a canteen. He refused the food but took a swallow of the warm, stale water and poured a little into a pan for the thirsty mules.

"Your sense of direction was exact," he told the Lady. "One night's travel has brought us to the cave—it's just on the other side of the hill. If you're not too tired, we can check it out now and get in a nap before returning tonight."

She uncrossed her legs, getting to her feet, and picked up the pack she'd been sitting on. "That's better than enduring an extra moment of this heat. I'm tempted to draw in some rain, but then

The Weaving

we'd be wading through mud the whole way back." She held out the pack. "I have an extra robe you could use. You've got to be boiling inside that heavy outfit."

Keyotie looked down at his fringed leather pants and shirt, then wiggled his toes inside the matching boots. They fit him like his own skin. "Better not. This is my fur when I'm in true form. If I changed clothes and had to shift out there, I'd be a bald coyote wrapped in a big robe." He fingered the fringe running up one arm. "I suppose I could change its appearance, but the first people I ever lived among wore their clothes this way. I continue doing it to honor them."

He started walking back to the cave. "Besides," he added, "women really go for a man wearing leathers."

***

The Lady pulled her hood over her head and stepped into the sun. She followed Keyotie around the hill and climbed the short distance to the cave.

Keyotie examined the surrounding hillside. He called when he found human remains. The dry heat had mummified the arm and leg, so he couldn't tell her if they were weeks or years old.

She knew exactly how long they'd been there.

She stood looking at the jumbled blocks that once sealed the entrance. They had been brought here with great effort, in heavy wagons dragged through mud after a seasonal rainstorm. She remembered the desperate race to complete the trap while the monster was asleep inside, recovering from her wounds. She knelt, running her hand over one of the stones. A thousand years of weathering had turned the deeply carved runes into shallow grooves.

A shadow fell across her hands. Keyotie stood next to her, holding a coiled rope and a couple of spent torches.

"Not much to find," he said. "There were four horses and several pack mules. One or two people came to a bad end. They were here for several days at least. They rode in from the north, same as

Gerald Ghostlow

us, and probably from the same border town, but used a less direct route so our tracks never crossed until now. They left in a slightly different direction. There were four men and one woman walking around. The woman came out of the cave with no tracks leading in." He shielded his eyes from the sun and looked to where the horizon disappeared in the shimmering hot air. "I have their scent now," he continued. "I can track them down for you, like I promised. That's guaranteed. With the lead they have, though, it's going to be a long hunt."

The Lady was confident the man would deliver. Once Keyotie was on your trail, there was no place on this or any other world you could hide. She stood, looking at the hidden entrance to the cave. Finding the monster had been no accident. This wizard had done his research. He knew Lilith was in there, knew what the demon had done, and released her anyway. For all their learning, wizards could be incredibly stupid.

"Well, Keyotie," she said, "We know who the woman is. The rest matches what we saw in the scrying pool. We also knew one of the men was a wizard." She picked up a small empty bottle and read the label. "A wizard with a weak stomach."

Keyotie looked at the dark hole. "I can make a torch from what's left here if we need to go inside."

"I don't want to, but I need to. Scrying can tell us many things, but there's no substitute for being there." She walked over to the opening. "It's a short way in and you won't need the torch." She reached up, touching previously unnoticed carvings running along the roof of the cave. The ceiling began to glow dimly, lighting up the interior well enough to see.

"Lilith set this up, but made a big mistake," she explained. "In her weakened state, the only way she could turn the light on or off is out here. We turned the light off when we sealed her inside. Being in the dark was a small enough punishment for her crimes."

"A thousand years of sitting in complete darkness with nothing to do but scheme?" Keyotie shook his head. "Why didn't you just kill her when you had the chance?"

The Weaving

"Kill her and her spirit will wander the world until she finds another body to possess. It must be a risky process for the demon, because Lilith tries desperately to keep whatever body she's using. This was her secret retreat, reserved for the time she might need to repair damage to her current host. That's when she's unconscious and vulnerable."

They were barely into the cave when Keyotie sniffed and put out his arm, stopping her from following. "It reeks of decay in there. We'll find the rest of one dead intruder, at least. The smell will grow stronger the farther in we go, maybe becoming too foul to breath." He looked at his leather outfit, then at her long robe. "If you could find me a bit of thin cloth to tie around my nose and mouth, I'll go in alone. Just tell me if there's anything special you're looking for. There's no need for you to endure this, my Lady."

***

She didn't have to wait long for Keyotie to pop back out of the hole. He welcomed the fresh air, taking large gulps to clear his nose, then held up the undergarment she'd somehow been talked into giving him to use as a mask. "I'd planned on saving this as a reminder of our time together," he said, "but the only scent on it now is the stink of the cave. Might as well throw it away."

She snatched it from his hand, her face red as she heard her Sisterselfs laughing in her thoughts. "I'll wash it later, thank you. I didn't pack much in the way of clothes. What did you find in there?"

"There's two bodies, swollen and fly-bloated," he informed the Lady. "Dried blood everywhere and it looks like she ate part of the bodies. There aren't any animal tracks, so it has to be her work. Several opened chests, with clothes thrown about. She seems to prefer wearing black all the way down to her underclothes. Other than all that, it would be a nice enough place to use as a shelter. There's even a little pool in the back, fed by dripping water. I certainly don't want to drink it, now. I checked the carvings on the tunnel wall like you asked. The disk you described isn't in the slot, so they took it with them."

The Ladies' good humor was gone by the end of the description. She wrinkled her nose at the odor left on Keyotie's clothes when he came closer. With no water for washing, he'd have to air out. Until then, she would remain upwind as much as possible.

"Lilith has the nasty habit of treating humans like cattle," she said. "A demon doesn't really need to eat or drink once it's fully taken over a body. I think she enjoys the effect it has on people. Lilith feeds on terror. She stores this fear inside her somehow and can give someone an overwhelming dose of it. On top of that, she has a limited ability to work magic. Nowhere near the level of someone like Rose, fortunately."

They started walking back to their own camp. "You defeated her once," Keyotie said, "so it's always possible to do it again. What do you see in the future, Lady? What do we need to do in order to ensure victory?"

"We don't know, Keyotie," she replied. "We can't tell how this is going to end." He turned at this admission, staring at her in shock. "We are forbidden to look at our own future—that is the price of our power," she explained. "By being part of this campaign, we have eliminated our scrying as a weapon against her. We have rendered ourselves helpless." She looked back at the cave. "We are not used to being blind."

He came over and put his hands on her shoulders. "My Lady," he said, "you are never helpless—and I'm speaking to all your Sisterselfs when I say this. Do you think your little pictures in the water are your only skill? You have the ability to weave events together into a desired outcome that impresses even the great Trickster. On top of that, you now have Keyotie's pledge that he will never rest until this Lilith creature is somehow shoved back in her box."

The other Ladies paused in what they were doing and merged their minds long enough so all could share equally in hugging Keyotie. The kiss he stole in return left the two absent Ladies with unexplained blushes on their cheeks.

"Keyotie, you always did have a way of flattering a girl," the

The Weaving

Lady eventually said. "Now, it looks like you won't have to track our quarry the hard way, after all. My Sisterself at the Palace has just found out where Lilith and her Prince are hiding. Do you know of a place called Morania?"

***

The next day they arrived back at the nearest town, where Keyotie dropped off the mules at the livery and picked up their horse, taking the time to entertain the rather closed-mouthed owner of the establishment with some of his wit. The man was eventually coaxed into talking about the Prince and his wizard. The two men had also stopped at the livery, using the only available resource for supplies. The stableman spoke mostly about how the fella had neglected to return the mules. The stableboy earned a small coin for remembering the wizard had been called Maynard.

Keyotie received his substantial refund upon returning his pack animals and handed back a large part of it to buy a second horse and more supplies. Later, a smaller amount was spent at the tavern, paying for his drinks while waiting for the Lady. She finally appeared, coming down the stairs, followed by a tavern serving wench. The girl was gushing over the honor of having her future told in exchange for letting the Lady freshen up in her room and wash out some clothes. He handed over the rest of the money along with the little bit of information gleaned.

The tavern girl started to make her usual offer to Keyotie, then thought better of it when she saw the Lady's expression. She looked around the room, deciding no one was in need of her services, and retired back upstairs to rest before the night's work began.

The two left to begin the next stage of their journey, Keyotie helping the Lady onto her horse before vaulting up behind her. It was starting to rain, a natural event the Lady had nothing to do with. She could have told the clouds to go away, but the farmers needed it for their crops. Keyotie didn't mind being in the rain and his Lady had the amazing ability of letting the raindrops bead up and slide off of her without so much as wetting her hair.

He gathered the reins of the second horse, acquired on the Lady's orders. This one wore no saddle and would be used only to carry their packs, since Keyotie preferred to range ahead on the trail in four-footed form. He'd wait until they were out of sight before shifting.

"Let me guess," he said. "The girl wanted to know how to catch some rich man and live a life of luxury?"

"Keyotie, you're too cynical," the Lady replied. "The questions and answers are private, but let's just say a local farm boy will finally get his wish the next time he asks, and the local customers of the establishment will have to go elsewhere for their entertainment."

He looked back at the town. "Oh, I imagine soon enough there will be another young girl fresh off the farm providing this service—and learning that slopping hogs is not the worst of fates. It's not like there's much else a poor young waif can do to support herself, unless she's lucky enough to be born with the talent. Some things are common in all the worlds."

They stopped when they came to the dirt road connecting them to the Empire. Keyotie let his hands wander a little from where he was holding onto the Lady's waist and whispered in her ear. "My Lady, I saw your reaction to that girl's attempt to move in on your territory. All you have to do is ask, you know." He slid off the horse and shifted to coyote form. He strutted up the road with tail held high, giving the flustered Ladies a view that caused them to blush for the second time in as many days.

The rain didn't stop their travel, but the dirt road soon turned into clinging mud and neither they nor the horses would enjoy a wet camp. They stopped at a farm while it was still daylight and traded the family an evening's conversation for staying in a dry barn.

Keyotie was bedded down for the night and listening to the rain beating on the roof when he heard the Lady softly call his name. He went over and knelt next to her in the sweet-smelling hay. She took his hand and placed it on her breast.

"As long as you know nothing has changed," she said. "My

The Weaving

Sisterselfs are as eager for this as I am, and will share equally in the pleasure. Should they take a lover, the reverse would hold true. I can never give you my private love."

He slid his other hand under the blanket and down her body, making her gasp. "My Lady," he replied, "your Sisterselfs may toss and moan in their lonely beds tonight as long as *they* know I'm doing this for your benefit, not theirs." He undressed and slid under the blanket.

Much later, when his Lady was snuggled against him, spent and sweating, Keyotie whispered in her ear. "And what do your Sisterselfs have to say about that?"

She sighed and wrapped her arms around him. "I believe the consensus is, 'Wow!' We have missed that, you know. Flattering is not all you know how to do."

Ten

The Lady and Keyotie travelled southwest from Lilith's old prison, skirting the dense forest where the elves lived. Keyotie had learned the ways and means around this world in his wandering and had spent some time in Morania, although he'd never heard of Valant. King Justin had been a young Prince, barely old enough to shave, when Keyotie was last there—and the Trickster had lived up to his reputation. He'd avoided the place since, just in case there were still people living who might recognize him.

They replenished their supplies by stopping at prosperous looking homesteads. After her near starvation in the forest, the Lady insisted the packhorse stayed burdened with enough food to feed an army garrison. She had brought enough funds for an extended trip, although the ancient coins caused comment. They used the silver for now, saving the gold for a real emergency.

***

They arrived at the ferry station in Rivercrossing to catch passage across the wide river serving as the border between Moriania and the Empire. There was no ferry in sight and the pier overflowed with stacks of goods, waiting to be loaded onto the barge when it returned to this side of the river. That seemed normal to Keyotie, who remembered buying passage for a small fee the last time he was through here.

There was a large and noisy crowd of people around the ticket station. The Lady stayed on the outskirts while Keyotie pushed his way in to see about buying tickets. The office was closed and a harassed-looking man in the King's uniform stood in front along

The Weaving

with several other guardsmen keeping the mob back.

"People, please!" the man said. "There has been no change since yesterday or the day before that. We have received no messages from the officials on the other side of the river since they closed the border. Until this is cleared up, I've issued orders that no one be allowed to cross, even if you find another boat. I am drafting a notice to our King requesting instructions, but that will take some time."

Several men in the crowd shouted back, all talking at the same time. "No," the official said, "We don't know what's going on...No, we don't know how long this is going to last...No, we don't know where our subjects are going to stay in the meantime...No, we don't know who's going to pay for what this is costing you...No, it's not our job to storm across the river and force them to reopen the border...No, we don't know what we're going to do with the subjects of Morania stuck on this side...Yes, your taxes are paying our salary, and yes, it is our duty to assist the subjects of our King with their problems. You will be the first to know when we find out how to do so. In the meantime, you'll just have to be patient."

A well-dressed merchant in front wasn't satisfied and waved his hands, saying something Keyotie couldn't hear. The official got red in the face. "I *am* the ranking officer here," he replied. "You can file all the complaints you'd like back at the Palace. Until I get further orders, you'll do what I say." The man stomped away, leaving the guards to keep the crowd from taking their frustration out of the ferry office. Keyotie went back to the Lady and passed along the information.

***

The Lady considered this new development. "So, we find another way across? How long will that take?"

"Well, if the river crossing is closed, it's probably also guarded over there," Keyotie concluded. "If we follow the river for another day or so, I'll liberate a large enough boat for the horses, or maybe the river will become narrow enough to let them swim across." He looked at the setting sun. "We'll get far enough away tonight for privacy, then head upstream."

"You know I'll have to pay for any boat you *liberate*," she replied, "but we should probably keep a low profile. Lilith couldn't know we're already on her trail, but the Prince might be on the lookout for spies. At least my Sisterself can let the King know what's happening. She tells me this is the first she's heard of it." She looked around at the chaos. "There has been peace in the land for so long, these people cannot recognize what this means. I need no scrying pool to know two Kings settle their differences using armies."

Keyotie was about to answer when a voice interrupted from the shadows. "Not all of us are babes, yer Ladyship," it said. "I know the signs of war. If ye can pay, there's another way ta get across the border." A man stepped into the light. He was a big, scruffy looking fellow, badly in need of a shave and haircut. The Lady noted the large knife sticking out of one boot. The man's accent marked him as one of the river clan, families who lived along the river for generations and supported themselves by supplying fish to both kingdoms. This had possibilities, but might also mean trouble.

The man continued to walk toward her. Keyotie dropped the reins to the horses and stepped between her and the stranger. He reached behind his back, as if he had a weapon hidden there. Keyotie carried no knife, preferring to use his sharp teeth in true form when faced with a fight. Right now, they couldn't afford the attention shifting would bring.

"Ah, now, there's no need a'that," the stranger said. "Call off the servant, yer Ladyship. All I want is ta make a business proposition." He looked around at the people close by. "Ye've not much experience in sneaking around, I'd wager. Too many ears ta hear. What say we find a place more private, like your guide said, and see if ye don't find it worth your while ta hear me out."

The Lady considered the offer from her vantage point in the saddle. She needed to know how much this ruffian had overheard and decided to play along.

"I hired this man as a guide because I don't have experience in such matters," she replied. "Since he seems to have failed me, I will hear your offer. I assume you have a private place in mind? Then by all means, let us retire there to continue our discussion."

She nudged Keyotie in the back with her stirrup as a signal to play along and he put on a sullen expression. "Is that wise, my Lady... Ladyship?" he asked. "I am more than capable—"

"Silence!" she hissed. "Your big mouth has gotten us into this trouble. If you talk again before I give you leave, I will terminate your employment without pay."

Her servant looked properly chastised as they allowed the stranger to lead them to a lonely spot on the riverbank some ways away from the ferry landing. By then it was full dark and the man lit a prepared campfire in a spot screened by the surrounding trees before speaking. The Lady remained on her horse and Keyotie stayed close by her side, watching the night around them.

"Now, yer Ladyship," the stranger began, "Ye need ta get across the river real quiet-like. My gang and I are able ta provide this service."

The Lady looked across the river. Faint in the distance, she could see an answering signal from a fire on the opposite shore. She decided her role called for caution. "Who are you?" she asked. "Why should I put my life in your hands? We need more than a boat. I have no desire to explain myself to the guards on the other side of the river."

He looked cagey. "No names. I don't ask yours and ye have no need of mine. Ye are not the only ones with a need ta escape the notice of guards, even before the border closing. We'll get ya across and make sure the patrols look the other way. My friends on the other side share in the profits."

She heard Keyotie cough and remembered she'd given him orders not to talk. "Well, man," she told him. "I'm paying you for your advice in these matters, not just to lead the horses. Earn your pay."

Keyotie looked up and said, "They're smugglers, my Ladyship. They would have the guards over there bribed, probably on our side as well. There would always be illegal goods that need this service. In particular, there's an addictive flower unique to Morania that causes pleasant dreams. The Empire has been trying to stamp out this trade for generations, with little success. This won't be cheap. Best let me handle negotiating the fee."

She waved her hand in dismissal. "Money is no problem," she said, watching the stranger's eyes light up. She heard quiet splashing from a boat drawing near in the night—the riverman had called in the rest of his gang without waiting for her reply. She doubted they would be allowed to ride off if she declined. "How much do you charge, my good man?"

He scratched the stubble on his cheek, looking at their horses. "Two mounts and two people? Make it one gold coin for each and ye'll soon be on your way."

Keyotie made a strangling sound upon hearing the outrageous demand, but was again silenced by a gesture from the Lady. "Done!" she said. "I am weary to death of this hiding in bushes." She untied a pouch from her saddle, then paused, trying to look cagey. "Only two coins for now, the other two when we cross safely," she said. She allowed the coins in the pouch to jingle invitingly while she sorted out two small gold ones by feel. She could swear the smuggler was drooling as he stared at the fortune in her hands.

***

Keyotie found it hard to keep a straight face. *Yer Ladyship, indeed.* The smuggler probably thought he'd stumbled across a Princess fleeing an arranged marriage—as if anyone with sense could confuse this woman for one of the pampered nobility. He knew what the Lady was doing. Her rules forced her to keep a deal once made and carried out in good faith, so she was inviting the man to attempt a robbery. Only then could she use her powers to eliminate one smuggler from the land and silence someone who would certainly sell the information he'd overheard to willing ears.

The boat arrived while she was handing over the partial

The Weaving

payment. Their transportation turned out to be a small barge pulled by six men in a rowboat. The barge carried two men with poles to help guide the vessel. The rivermen were practiced, moving with silence and speed to bring it to shore. The Lady dismounted as the horses were coaxed onto the vessel. The men strained at their oars, heading for the light on the other side. The smuggler stayed close to the Lady and her pouch of coin, so Keyotie had no opportunity to discuss their next step.

The trip across seemed to take forever, but the signal light gradually grew larger until they reached land and the men began the routine of turning around the barge. He figured the attack would come when everyone was on shore and they'd be surrounded and outnumbered. Keyotie caught his Lady's eye and motioned to the big leader. She nodded, giving him the privilege of handling him. Keyotie lived by his own set of rules and didn't need to wait for anyone to attack first. Many men had mistaken his small size for weakness and were taught a lesson about the deceptive qualities of appearances.

He had no worries about his Lady taking down the rest of the gang. The other two Ladies preferred settling conflicts by using their magic to increase the local frog population, but this one enjoyed a good fight. Once, Keyotie had taken her up on an invitation to wrestle, just to find out what she could do. He was repeatedly thrown to the ground.

The robbers were going to be surprised.

Keyotie watched in surprise, instead, as the men in the boats pulled away and left, leaving only their original riverman behind. The man walked over to stand on the other side of the signal fire. He cleared his throat and when he spoke, his thick accent was gone.

"I have a confession to make, Lady," he said. "I'm not one of the local smugglers. Those were the men who just left. My name is Ambrosius and I work for Prince Valant. If I could bother you to look over to your right, there's something you should see."

Torches flared to life and a dozen guardsmen appeared, standing motionless in the night with crossbows pointed in their direction. The man cleared his throat again. "I beg you to hear me

Gerald Gostlow

out, Lady, before making any move at all, and I'd advise your guide to do the same. These men have orders to shoot if you so much as raise a hand. I have been given careful instructions and their arrows will blanket this area. Some will shoot in front, some behind, and some where you're standing now. I was told you can dodge a shaft or two, but no doubt one will find a mark. We will only use them if you refuse the deal I'm about to offer."

The Lady had watched the soldiers only long enough to check on the truth of the man's description of the situation, then turned back to their betrayer. She showed no sign of alarm but Keyotie could smell her fear. He was concentrating on watching her and measuring the distance between them. The instant she moved, he would throw himself between the arrows and his Lady. As a shapeshifter, he could survive wounds that would kill her instantly.

She sized up the situation. "What kind of deal do you have in mind?" she asked. "One way or another, my life is now forfeit. At least this will be a quick death. Why should I put it off?"

"I have been sent here by Prince Valant to capture the women known as the Ladies. What I overheard assures me you're one of them. If you agree to be his prisoner and not try to escape or harm any of his men, then you have his word that you will be locked in the dungeon as a hostage and not harmed in any way, by himself or the people who follow his orders.

Keyotie could see his Lady shifting her weight. He focused on the reins she still held in her hand. *When she lets go...*

"So he can hand me over to Lilith at a later date?" She began to open her hand. "I still don't—"

"No, Lady!" The agent took a step back. "He also says to tell you, Lilith will be kept unaware of your presence if he can manage it. That's why he picked the dungeon. He knows she has other people searching for you and figures that's the last place anyone would check. He wants you as a weapon against Lilith, not a gift for her!"

The Lady paused as she conferred with her Sisterselfs. "Yes, we think it might work," she said. "There would be enough misery in that place to mask my presence if she checks her web of terror. We might agree, on one condition—my servant is to be let go, unharmed. He was given my promise of protection and I cannot let him be taken without a fight."

"My orders only concern the women known as the Ladies. If I give my word that he will be left here to make his own way back, will that suffice? He looks capable of dodging the patrols on his own."

"Very well, the Ladies agree to the deal on those terms." She ignored Keyotie's stricken look.

The Captain made a signal to his men and they lowered their crossbows. "You may relax, Lady, and get back on your horse. Please don't do anything to make my men nervous, though."

She walked over and took the money pouch from the saddle, reaching inside to remove two more gold coins. She tossed them at the man's feet. "I said you would be fully paid once we were safely across, but neglected to add I not be taken prisoner after that. You have kept your part of the bargain." The man ignored more wealth at his feet than he'd probably earn in a month, instead taking the two coins she'd already given him from his pocket and throwing them down to join the others. He left to fetch his horse, looking not at all happy about being successful in his mission.

She turned to Keyotie, hesitated, then gave him a long, uncharacteristic hug. "Stay close for now," she whispered in his ear, "then find a way into Lilith's lair. Look for my Sisterselfs near the entrance at the next full moon. I'll be there if I can." She stepped back before the returning agent could get suspicious.

"Here," she said loudly, putting another piece of gold in his hand. "You have performed to my satisfaction, but I no longer require your services. I suggest you leave this land and forget we ever met. Soon, it will not be healthy for anyone to live here."

The Lady climbed back into her saddle and took the reins of the packhorse Keyotie handed to her. She addressed Ambrosius. "You may now escort me to your dungeon. I'm looking forward to meeting your Prince Valant. I believe we have much to discuss."

Keyotie stood helpless, watching the Lady ride off surrounded by her captors. He dropped his coin and shifted. It would be no trouble keeping up with them in his true form and they wouldn't suspect the occasional glimpse of a stray dog.

The Lady had been determined to find some way into the castle—this probably wasn't a disaster in her mind. She might even insist everything was going as planned, but Keyotie was more skeptical. So far, this plan of the Ladies seemed awfully like making it up as they went along.

Eleven

Tom stood against a wall, watching the activity in the room. The King stood before a map pinned to the opposite wall, pointing to various parts of his Empire and debating with several men in heavily decorated uniforms. A man who had been introduced as the treasurer sat at a desk, scribbling numbers in various ledgers. Tom looked at the fine summer day showing through the window, licked his lips, then looked once more at Rose arguing with the two Ladies in a corner. He walked over and sat down at the report-covered table in the center of the room, sighing. Apparently, until the wizard arrived back from his journey, all these great and powerful people could do was spend their time getting on each other's nerves.

All he could do was wait and get on his own nerves.

"Care for a game of chess?"

He looked at the Duke. The big man sat quietly, thick hands folded on his large stomach. Tom had thought the man asleep, since he had been sitting in the same position for the past hour with his eyes closed—now they were open and looking directly at him.

"I don't know. Not anymore, I guess," Tom replied.

"An interesting way of putting it. Would you like to have your mind read, then?"

"Pardon me?" Tom still hadn't figured out the Duke. The official had been introduced as the King's Advisor and the job title seemed simple enough. But as Tom had observed in the last few days, even Rose listened respectfully to the Duke's occasional comment.

Mostly though, the man just sat and listened.

Or slept.

It was hard to tell.

"Read your mind," the Duke repeated. "You were just

Gerald Gostlow

thinking that if you have to put up with another day of these endless discussions, you'd die of boredom. Then you looked out the window and thought about sneaking off to the local tavern for a tankard of ale. Then you thought better of it, deciding to stick close to your wife. Then you observed that this waiting was getting on your nerves and sat down."

Tom pondered for a moment, trying to relive his recent past and smiled. "That's good. You made one mistake—I was thinking of something stronger than ale. Ale was several hours ago. Now I'd love a good shot of brandy. That's a peculiar skill you have. Are you a power?"

The Duke snorted. "Hardly. I am the Advisor to the King, nothing more. Somewhere in my rooms I have a medallion I'm supposed to wear, so everyone will show proper respect to my position of authority. In truth, I've never considered myself anything more than a reasonably intelligent man with some talent for observation."

The King came over to rummage through the reports strewn all over the table. "The Duke is being modest," he said. "I consider him irreplaceable. If my Advisor looked at the sky and told me the world would end in a flood tomorrow, I'd start building a boat." He found the needed report and returned to his general, waving it in front of the man's nose.

"So you figure things out by observing?" Tom asked. "Let me try it." He looked around the room again, then back to the Duke. "All I see are people engaged in debating each other, like they've been doing all along. There's no mystery to solve here."

"I beg to disagree. There are many mysteries in this room. You have neglected the first step of solving a puzzle—you must begin by asking the right question. Let me start you off. Why, do you suppose, have I been studying you since you showed up at the Palace?"

"You have?" Tom sat back and studied this man in return. "What makes me so important?"

"Yes."

"Yes? Yes, what?" Tom was getting lost in this verbal exchange.

"Yes," the Duke said, "that is the mystery I am trying to solve.

The Weaving

I'm wondering why you are here and it amounts to the same thing as asking what makes you so important. There's no role for you in our plans and that's why you're bored. Of course, Rose is your wife, and that is unusual enough to note, but she does not strike me as the kind of woman who would drag her husband around because she doesn't trust you out of her sight. I must confess, so far the solution escapes me. I don't have enough information to go on."

Tom leaned forward, struck with a possibility. The Lady had said to follow Rose into the maze and the Palace was certainly a maze of hallways. He didn't see how this Duke could be the beast within, but maybe Tom had misheard the Lady. At any rate, there would be no harm in seeing if this solver of mysteries could provide a clue to his missing past.

"If you have the time, I'd like to tell you why I'm here," Tom said. "I'll have to warn you—it's a personal quest, not involving your problems."

The Duke got to his feet, waving at the King to indicate his intention to leave. The King nodded and continued giving instructions to his field generals. He put a hand on Tom's shoulder. "I was hoping you'd decide to ask. Why don't you let your wife know the Duke has requested the pleasure of your company for a while? Follow me to my office and I promise you that brandy you wanted."

***

The Duke's office was a welcome relief from the sparse accommodations of the conference room. Rather, it was designed for comfort, from the overstuffed chairs facing each other to the well-stocked sideboard. The Duke waved Tom into one of the chairs, then eased his great bulk into the other. The butler, who met them at the door, was given a request for brandy. Tom could see into another room containing a sturdy bed with a deeply carved, elaborate headboard. The Duke's offices served as his living quarters.

Tom looked around at the expensive furnishings, comparing the luxury to the little cottage Rose and he called home. He became conscious of his plain, homespun outfit and worn boots, and began to wonder all over again why this important man was taking the time to listen to his problems.

"My father shoveled horse manure for a living," the Duke remarked. Tom didn't know how to respond to such a statement and accepted the brandy from the butler and waited for the Duke to speak.

"It was the Royal stable," the Duke continued, "but I assure you, all manure smells the same, even if the horse belongs to a King." The man took a sip of his brandy. "I started a career in my father's boots—literally, I couldn't afford to buy a new pair—but joined the cavalry as soon as I could reach the stirrups. I found I preferred riding a horse to cleaning up after one. I was a much slimmer figure back then.

"When the last war with the elves broke out, I was a member of the company assigned to guard the young King. Our losses were such that I quickly rose through the ranks to become Captain of our unit. The King and I became friends during the campaign. By the time the war was over, he had asked me to be his personal Advisor and conferred the title of Duke."

He set down his now empty glass, shaking his head when the servant offered a refill. "The King knows, as do I, that the measure of a man or woman lies not in their station, but in their character and intelligence. So please take that 'I'm-not-worthy' expression off your face. If it will make you more comfortable, we can go down to the stables and shovel out a stall or two while we talk. I haven't forgotten how."

An image of the Duke slinging manure made Tom laugh and he decided he liked the man. "I'm tempted to take you up on your offer," he said, "just to see the expression on the faces of the regular staff."

The Duke laughed along with him, throwing back his head. "Probably not as bad as the expression on the face of your wife when you tell her how you picked up the smell." He turned his gaze back on Tom. "If I can help you, I will. Why don't you start from the

The Weaving

beginning?"

Tom told him everything, from the confused panic of waking up in his sickbed and not knowing who he was or how he got there, to his hesitant courtship of and marriage to his beloved Rose, ending with the arrival of the Lady and their conversation. Through it all, the Duke sat in his favorite position, hands clasped across his stomach and eyes closed. When he was finished, the Duke opened his eyes and took a deep breath, letting it out slowly.

"A remarkable tale," he said. "It clears up one mystery and leaves one unsolved, while creating one more. When I first received reports that Rose had a man around the house, I made my own inquiries in that direction and came up empty. All I can say is, there are no missing persons or wanted outlaws matching your description, and no one in that area even saw you arrive. If it was possible, I'd conclude you didn't exist before that day."

"Well, what mystery does this clear up, then?" Tom had not really expected the man to suddenly begin spouting names and details, but any help was better than nothing.

"It explains why you are here, of course. You are wrong in thinking your problem has nothing to do with this monster. My last report of Valant placed him in the area of your home shortly after you two married, where apparently Rose held a brief interview and sent him on his way. That kind of thing must happen often enough and she still doesn't realize she's met our Prince. The meeting might be coincidence, but now the Ladies are determined to drag you into this mess. Their answers are designed to make sure you become part of our band of champions. That in itself tells me you're going to play an important role."

"Yes, Rose gets requests for her help all the time—and turns down half of them. But what role could I play in this? Am I supposed to remember I'm a great warrior and slay the monster?" Tom didn't think he'd been a swordsman. The old rusty sword he'd found in the shed always slipped from his grasp after a few swings. Rose had caught him playing with it one time, pretending he was slaying a dragon, and laughed until she got the hiccups.

The Duke dismissed the thought with a wave of his hand. "The Ladies are involved, which means the most obvious conclusions are the wrong ones. You'll just have to wait and see. Be prepared for anything."

Tom sighed. "It's worrying me to no end, thinking Rose might end up counting on me to save her life. So now I have to save the Empire, as well? What's the new mystery you've dug up?" *Like I don't have enough on my mind.*

"Why don't you remember your past? I've seen minds damaged by blows or sickness before, and the people either recover over time or show an obvious confusion in their thinking. You fit neither category. I suspect some part of you doesn't want to remember." The Duke held up his hand to block the immediate protest. "You were excited when the Lady told you she could help. But think for a moment, Tom. You are married to the Witch of the Woods, a power who specializes in quests such as yours. She's never been known to refuse a worthy cause. That doesn't mean she had to step in and volunteer, I suppose. You must have known all this. Why didn't you ask your wife for help in finding out about your past?"

Tom sat stunned. Sure, the missing memories bothered him at times, but he'd always pushed it out of his mind as something he had to live with. Only when the Lady arrived did remembering become something he needed to do.

A messenger knocked on the door, interrupting their conversation to announce Rose and the Ladies were retiring for the day. The Royal Wizard had returned and the King needed his Advisor.

The Duke pushed himself out of the chair, grunting with the effort. "Tom," he said, "I'll keep your problem in mind and provide what help I can. Rose is a great asset to the Empire, so if her life depends on your success, it concerns us all. At least now we can start working on our problems instead of talking them to death. You are not alone in being sick of meetings."

***

The Weaving

Rose watched the bathtub fill, delighting at the luxuries of modern life. *Water on demand, indoors, with no need to pump or fetch!* This world was already full of marvels, and here was one more. She'd heard about the Palace bathrooms, but the room she'd stayed in during the Conference hadn't included one. The wizard had outdone himself, including a spell to heat the water. Bertram was doing more than turning out luxuries for the pampered nobility, though. His method of duplicating books was already being praised by the common people, who could now get their hands on cheap copies. Teachers of reading skills were in demand. Booksellers were eager to supply the public's thirst for entertaining stories. Many of the books in her library were gifts from the Queen, who was becoming famous as a writer of romantic tales women, in particular, enjoyed.

Rose was reminded of her appointment to have a private dinner with the Queen, to get an expert's opinion on her own attempt to write a story. She'd better hurry.

"Tom!" she called. "Get your clothes off and get in here!" When the expected complaint wasn't heard in response, she emerged from the little bathroom to see if he'd snuck out of the room. Tom was still sprawled on the couch, staring moodily at a painting on the opposite wall, a picture of an old woman with a baby on her lap.

He'd been doing this since returning from his visit with the Duke and she decided it was long enough. Rose went over to stand directly in front of him. "Alright, I can see whatever the Duke said upset you, even worse than the Lady. If you'd let me know what's wrong, I could help."

Tom stared at her with an expression she hadn't seen on his face before. He was angry—at her! "How old do you think I am?" he asked. "How long do people usually live, anyway? I've realized I don't even know that much."

His response was unexpected and she had to think for a moment. "Well, if people don't die of accident or illness or childbirth, and don't work themselves to death, they might live to be eighty years old, maybe a little more. You look to be in the prime of your life, probably a little younger than me. That could place you in your late twenties to early thirties. It's hard to tell."

"That's one way of looking at it," he replied. "Another way is to say I'll be three years old this winter." Tom was finally opening up. "The Duke pointed out there is no good reason why I can't remember before that. Did you do something to my mind, to make me forget? Is it your fault? Did you put a spell on me? Is there something in my past you don't want me to know about?"

Rose stood with mouth open, astonished he would ask such a question. "Tom! How could you think that of me? To root around in a person's mind and change what they are? That's forbidden! Witches have been persecuted in the past for doing just that. We won't traffic in love spells anymore, either. Believe me, we've learned our lesson. One of my duties as High Priestess is to track down and punish any witch caught doing something like that!"

Tom's anger melted into misery. He stood and took her in his arms. "I'm sorry, darling. It's just…why didn't you help me? If a stranger came to you with a missing past, I bet you'd find a way to fix it."

Rose clung to him. "Yes, I could have tried," she admitted. "Instead, I did my best to convince you there was nothing I could do so you wouldn't ask. Tom, the men in this land are raised to believe a marriage with a witch is doomed to failure. They won't even take the chance. You'd forgotten all that nonsense along with your past. When I fell in love with you, and you came to love me…I was afraid of losing you. I should have done my best to fix your problem, but instead, took advantage of it. Can you forgive me?"

Tom answered, caressing her hair. "You should have trusted me. I'm still angry at you, but of course I forgive you. Darling, you told me that losing a few memories didn't change what I am. Well, doesn't that mean gaining a few memories won't change what I am, either? I know you are the only woman I've ever wanted. Don't ask me how, I just know."

Tom held her in his arms, her ear pressed against his chest, listening to the deep rumbling sound he made sometimes. She thought about their brief time together, how he'd held her in his arms

The Weaving

like this after she returned from seeing the Goddess.

Then something else nagging at her mind became clear.

Prince Valant.

She'd met a man with that name, briefly, a short time before building her portal. Could it be related? With the Ladies involved, coincidence was always suspect.

But for now, she'd concentrate on being a wife. Rose grabbed her husband by the ears, planting a long kiss. "If only I was as certain of that as you are. I'll trust you more, darling. But right now, you're getting in that tub, even if I have to use my magic to force you in there."

Tom looked over her shoulder at the bath. "Why bother? It looks like the water's coming to me."

Rose turned and saw the tub was overflowing and ran to turn off the tap. "Maybe indoor running water isn't such a good idea," she said. "This sort of thing must happen all the time. I don't think this particular marvel will ever catch on."

Twelve

The Duke arrived back at the conference room to find it cleared of everyone but the King and Bertram, who had stopped at his quarters long enough to wash and put on his official uniform—a long-sleeved, loose-fitting white robe covered in gaudy gold symbols.

The Duke bit back a chuckle. Their Royal Wizard might have looked impressive wearing it had he been an old man with a long white beard and bushy eyebrows. Instead, Bertram was tall and skinny, with ears that stuck straight out, and the wizard looked ridiculous in the robe.

King Justin sat in his chair at the head of the table, but had not invited the wizard to sit. Bertram stood at the other end of the conference table, sweating under the steady gaze of his King. The Duke didn't bother asking for permission and sat down in his usual chair.

"Bertram," the King said, "The Empire pays you to assist us in all things magical. I have not had cause to complain in the past. All I wanted were some answers, but now you've dragged the Wizard Council in on this and kept us waiting when action is called for. I trust you are not going to disappoint me again?"

The King was a fair man, but like all absolute rulers, did not get many refusals—especially from his staff. Bertram was in danger of becoming the first Royal Wizard fired from the job.

"Your Highness," the wizard replied, "I would never keep you waiting if there was any alternative. I simply had to make sure of my facts. The Council has now placed the entire resources of the College at your disposal and given me authority to handle this as I see fit."

The King sat back, looking at the Duke. "The translation of that little speech is 'the old farts at the Wizard Council are putting

The Weaving

this problem in his hands and getting ready to blame him if anything goes wrong.'"

"Our Royal Wizard really didn't have any other choice, sire," the Duke replied. "Wizards cherish their secrets like a miser hoards his gold. I believe Bertram is ready to join us in our campaign. If I may, I'd like to invite the young man to come over here and sit down. He looks worn out from his trip."

The King waved toward a chair and Bertram slid into it, breathing a sigh of relief. "Now," the King said, "let's start with some history. The Ladies say this monster is named Lilith and has the form of a human woman. They say you wizards were involved in sealing the cave, probably have records of what happened, and only a wizard with access to these records could have let the thing escape. The Ladies won't say anything more about how the monster ended up in that hole, telling me they don't answer questions about the past. What can you tell me?"

Bertram pulled a small leather case from a hidden pocket and carefully extracted an ancient scroll. "This involves events that happened at least a thousand years ago," he explained. "Much of our past was lost to us over the years and here is the only record of that time. If I may read from it, you'll have your answer." The King nodded. The wizard cleared his throat and read from the scroll.

"There are many worlds that make up creation, and each has their own nature and rules and deities. Why the worlds are designed this way, only the Creator of All knows, but the fact that it is true cannot be doubted. There are cracks and passages between the worlds, some natural and some forced. People and other creature sometimes use these portals to travel from one world to another. Their reasons for doing so are varied, but these travelers between worlds are responsible for much mischief.

"The People came to this world through just such a portal, led by the mighty wizards of the time, although the exact reason for doing so—whether because of some calamity that engulfed our old world, or simply an accident of wandering—has been lost to us. For generations our people lived here in peace, building their homes

and thriving..."

The King cut in. "All of this is fascinating to wizards and historians, I'm sure, but please get to the part about the monster."

"Um..." Bertram unrolled the scroll some more.

"*...The wizards of that time were mighty and uncontrolled in the use of their power. They created their own portals to explore the worlds and ignored the consequences. They competed in discovering ever stranger, more distant lands populated by creatures difficult to comprehend.*

"*Eventually, something noticed one of these portals to our world and used it to invade our land. Its name was Lilith and it was evil such as this world had never known. The demon enslaved the people with a web of terror and lived on the fear. The mightiest wizards were defeated and forced to flee from her power. Her touch could overcome the most courageous of heroes...*"

Bertram paused. "It goes on for some length at the suffering in the land and the evil nature of the monster. I can skip forward again, if you'd like."

The King looked over at the Duke, who nodded. "If it will bring us to when the Ladies get involved in this, then by all means."

The wizard unrolled the scroll to the last of the writing.

"*When it seemed all was lost, there came to our rescue the Three Ladies, who brought with them a champion, a woman of two natures. The Ladies were captured by the monster, but Lilith was unable to defeat the champion of two natures with her touch and was sorely wounded in the battle that followed.*

"*The monster fled to a secret retreat, but the Ladies had prepared for this, knowing the location of the hiding place through their divination. The wizards who had escaped Lilith's yoke of terror came out of hiding and joined with the Ladies in sealing the monster inside, where she will remain for all time.*"

The wizard looked up from his reading. "The rest is a map showing the location of the cave and some discussion of the spells used. Oh, and then there's this." The wizard pulled a small carved and polished stone disk out of the case and set it on the table. "That's supposed to be the keystone that goes with the scroll."

The King leaned forward, careful not to touch the disk. "What does it do?"

"It's how they turned the spells on and off back then. Probably one of the few left in existence and a priceless relic, but the one that should be with this scroll is even more special. It contained a tiny bit of Lilith's spirit, stolen while she was in her deep sleep, and used for protection. Only the real keystone could free the demon and keep her from tearing you into bite-size chunks as a reward. The scroll is specific about her taste for human flesh."

The Duke began his interrogation. "So you're telling us this amulet is a fake, that Maynard switched it for the genuine article, and then used the knowledge in the scroll to free the monster. Who is this most stupid of wizards?"

"No one of importance, until now. He graduated from our College about the same time I did, but received barely passing grades in his exams. Stuttering is a severe handicap to spell casting." Bertram picked up the disk and compared it to the drawing in the scroll. "It's actually a very good forgery, but totally useless. If we get back the real keystone, the cave will still hold her."

The Duke dismissed the suggestion. "The prison failed once, so only a fool would repeat the mistake. Besides, this Lilith will never allow herself to be taken that way again. I'll see if I can work out some way to acquire the real keystone, though. So far, it's the only thing you've mentioned that has any power over her at all, besides this mysterious woman of two natures. What exactly does the scroll mean by that?"

"We have no idea. The writer could have either assumed we'd know, or more likely, had no idea himself and was just repeating what he'd heard. This scroll was written long after the events."

The Duke leaned forward. "You are the Royal Wizard, tasked to advise the King in these matters. Advise him."

The wizard looked pained. "I suggest we let the Ladies handle Lilith. If they fail, then it will be my duty to battle the monster." Bertram rolled the priceless scroll back up and slid it into its protective leather tube, dropping the worthless amulet in with it. "I thought I could lead a team of wizards whose combined might would leave the world in ruins, but this Lilith might be left standing in the rubble, laughing. Her spirit is supposed to be immortal."

The Duke turned to his King. "The translation of that is 'the wizards have no more idea of how to defeat this monster now than they did back then, and hope the Ladies will once again come to their rescue.'"

The King stood. "This audience is at an end. Tomorrow we march for Morania and I would have the Royal Wizard by my side, for whatever good it will do. We will deal with Prince Valant and leave what happens next to fate." He left the room, leaving the Duke and Bertram standing at the table.

"That is not a happy King," the wizard remarked. "Magic seems so powerful; it's hard for people to understand it has some real limitations."

The Duke got to his feet. "It's not the limitations our King is worried about." He walked over to the map and placed a finger on a spot marked in red. "Wizard's Folly, and rightly named. Enough farmland around that abandoned tower to feed a small town, but for a hundred years now, not a weed will grow there. That's what magic can do in the wrong hands. We're going to be working closely together on this. You can start by loaning me the scroll so I can study it more carefully."

"I'm not blind to the faults of my fellow wizards, you know," Bertram said as they left the room. "I've been working hard to change our reputation. I'm well aware that, for all our power and knowledge, some wizards can be incredibly stupid."

Thirteen

With all the work going on, Prince Valant had little time to spend with Lilith. She accepted the excuses for his occasional lack of enthusiasm for the physical demands of their relationship and sought her own entertainment. The morning reports on his desk did begin to describe how men were being found bitten to death in back alleys, but it was confined to the part of town where the men more often preyed on the women. He let it pass for now.

When Lilith announced her intention to move into nearby iron mines and borrow a few guards, he signed the authorization, gave her an allowance from the treasury and figured the honeymoon was over. He also assigned Maynard to keep track of her and report if she started anything that would interfere with his own plans. Promises or not, if Maynard wanted to be his Royal Wizard, the man had to prove he could follow orders and get the job done.

***

The great wizard stood before the assembled nobility of the land, resplendent in his flowing gold and white robe. The King knelt before him in the Palace throne room.

"Oh, Great and Powerful Maynard," the King said, "We are here to honor you for saving our Empire from the monster. In our greatest hour of need, when all the other champions of the land lay vanquished, only you had the power to slay this Lilith."

"It was nothing," Maynard replied. "I happened to be in the neighborhood and had some time on my hands."

"You are being too modest, but that is only one of your

countless virtues," the King said. "You must be rewarded for your great service. I have already made you our Royal Wizard and the minstrels sing your praises throughout the land. The treasury is at your disposal. The other powers acknowledge you as the master of all magic and many have announced their retirement. Please accept this further token of our gratitude."

The King waved his hand and a dozen fair maidens were brought into the room, every one of them dressed in scant outfits to display their beauty.

"Each of these women begged for the honor of being your consort. Each is a virgin and wants only to wait on you hand and foot, providing for your every need. Pick one. If you'd like, take them all. You deserve it!"

"And how do the fair maidens feel about sharing my bed?" Maynard asked, turning to the women. The most beautiful one in the bunch stepped forward, licking her painted lips. She opened her mouth to speak.

"Get your lazy butt out of bed," she said. "I've got work to do!"

***

Maynard groaned and rolled over. An old woman wearing an apron was standing at the foot of the bed, holding a stack of clean sheets and scowling. She tried to jerk the blankets off him and he sat up, clutching at them.

"If you d-don't mind," he stuttered, "I'm naked under here. Please remove yourself from my chambers immediately. You will show the proper respect for a wizard."

"Look, young man," she replied, "I have three more rooms to clean before I get a break and I wouldn't care if you were the Prince himself—although you wouldn't catch Valant lazing around half the day. For all his faults, that boy has always put in a hard day's work."

She headed for the door, dumping the sheets on a chair. "Here, change them yourself, they'll probably need it. Like I don't know what you're hiding under there, anyway. Seen it all before, I have.

The Weaving

You need to get yourself to the tavern, boy. There's women there that could use the money. They'll show you the *respect* you deserve."

Maynard flopped back on the bed, groaning. This moment was only the latest in a list of things gone wrong, starting back at the cave. Up until the first servant was killed, Maynard had assumed what they'd find inside was a pile of dry bones and the dead monster's treasure. No one prepares a secret retreat without having it well stocked in advance. When he pictured the monster still alive, it was of some nasty, tentacled beast out of a horror story, something Valant would require a wizard's talents to control.

The woman coming out of the cave with the Prince was more than a surprise—she was a *disaster*. He'd seen what the monster could do during their trip back to the Prince's homeland. He'd followed Lilith one time, when she left their camp to visit a nearby farmhouse. What she had done to that family made him sick to his stomach for the rest of the night and he'd used up his supply of pills before they left the wasteland. Worse, she'd let him know the next day that she'd been aware of his spying and asked if the wizard was 'one of those people who like to watch', whatever that meant. Maynard had avoided her ever since.

Now the Prince was demanding he do something about the creature. Oh, it had been couched in language to suggest Maynard should just keep an eye on the monster, but he knew better. Lilith had served her purpose and could be disposed of. If something went wrong, his employer would deny any involvement, insisting the wizard had acted on his own.

He couldn't put it off any longer. Time to go see Lilith. He got out of bed and dressed in a clean robe. He caressed the single gold stripe on the sleeve, the badge of a graduate of the wizard's college. Receiving the robe had been his proudest moment, the day he proved his father wrong and amounted to something.

Maynard straightened his shoulders, drawing on the power he felt all around him, his special gift enabling him to become a wizard. He placed several protective spells on himself first, wishing his boss had given him back the keystone instead of laughing at his request.

Gerald Gastlow

Then he picked up a bottle of wine from the table to take along. It had been doctored with enough sleeping potion to knock out a horse and his plan was to get her to drink some. He supposed chopping her up with an ax and throwing her remains in a deep pit would do, after that. It was the best he could think of. He sallied forth to do battle with a monster.

Maynard the Great would earn his name this day!

***

Lilith slipped out of the dress and stepped on the pedestal. She held out her arms, cupping her hands as if she held something between them.

"Like this," she said. "There will be a bowl made of solid gold, designed to fit here. It will hold the bloody heart when my Priest or Priestess performs the sacrifice at the altar below. Make the statue about twice life size."

The sculptor walked around the nude woman, twirling his mustache while he studied her figure on display. "Magnificent!" he exclaimed. "A classical statue come to life!" He sat down on a stone and reached for his sketch pad. "I can use one of my paid models for the rough work. You'll need to pose some more before it's finished. And I'll need to buy the finest marble from the best quarry. We haven't discussed payment."

She stepped down and snapped her fingers. A guard she'd brought from the castle came running. "Fetch me the small locked box in the bottom trunk," she ordered, "and don't touch anything else."

The artist picked up his charcoal and started sketching. "It's been a long time since people went around sacrificing animals to the Gods," he remarked, "and I've never heard of a witch spilling blood in the name of the Goddess. Well, that's your business. How, um, detailed do you want it? If it's going to be on public display, there are laws against full nudity. Some of my best work is in private establishments where men seek, um, *entertainment*. If you know

The Weaving

what I mean."

"I know, that's why I sent for you," she replied. "One sculpture in particular caught my attention, the one titled 'Submission'. I love the way you captured the expression of agony and how realistic you made the whip marks. You have a talent that shouldn't be hidden. Yes, of course the statue must be detailed and accurate." Lilith ran her hands down her body. "I'm an artist, too, you know. I work in living flesh and this body is some of my best work. You should have seen the condition it was in when I started. I'm particularly proud of how I was able to increase the strength while keeping the figure slim and supple.

"The black hair against the pale skin makes a statement about opposing values, don't you think? It's taken me longer than you can imagine getting it this way. The previous host body was almost as good, but then some idiot hero ruined it with an axe. He was tortured for an entire year before I sacrificed him. I hate it when I lose one of my host bodies and have to start over. Imagine someone taking a hammer to one of your sculptures. Don't worry about the law. Worry about doing something that will please me."

The artist had stopped his sketching to stare at her while she talked. He wiped a bead of sweat off his forehead and gulped. "Ah, well...maybe you can show me again the exact pose you want?" he said. "I don't think I quite caught it the first time. I certainly want you to be satisfied with my work."

Lilith climbed back on the pedestal, freezing in the desired pose. She could picture the scene when it was done—the altar with the struggling sacrifice, the crowds of worshippers, the wave of fear mixed with lust she would soak in as the red blood ran down the polished white steps. Every detail would be perfect and beautiful, her artistic vision brought to life.

This sculptor would be paid for his work and, as his patron, she would commission other statues to fill her temple. Of all the humans she'd collected over the ages, the artists were her favorites. She left their minds untouched without chains of terror to bind them to her will—that destroyed the spark of creative genius of her kindred

Gerald Ghostlow

spirits.

She had a good view of the surrounding countryside from atop her pedestal and noticed a horse and rider coming their way from the direction of the castle. Lilith tensed when she saw the rider was wearing a wizard's robe, but relaxed when she recognized the man wearing it. While she had no doubt a mighty wizard would pop up eventually and learn what it meant to be her slave, this one was just that useless Maynard.

What did this idiot want? He was waving a...bottle of wine around? Why would he bring—*oh, come on! Even Maynard couldn't be that stupid, could he?*

***

The little boy was crouching and hugging his knees in the darkness, whimpering softly. He had to crouch—the tiny box would not allow him to stand or lie down. The air was stale and hot and smelled of sweat and urine. There weren't enough air holes. He didn't know how long he'd been in the punishment box, but finally the pain of his cramped muscles overcame the fear of his father's anger.

"*D-d-daddy!" he screamed, "I'm s-sorry! Let me out. I won't wet my b-bed again!" There was no answer. He continued to cry and plead, believing Daddy had left him in the box for good this time, like he always threatened to do.*

***

Maynard awoke lying in the dirt, his body still feeling the ache of the cramped box that haunted his childhood. His head was thumped and he was shaking. A familiar nausea caused bile to rise into his throat. He knew he was beaten, since his one attempt at casting a spell had been brushed off as a minor nuisance.

Lilith stood over him, breathing in his fear. He waited helplessly for her teeth to begin tearing chunks from his throat. "And

The Weaving

people call me a monster," she remarked. "At least I don't pretend I'm doing this for your own good. Now, I'll ask you only once more. *How does the keystone work?* It talks to me in my own voice, telling me not to take it by force or harm its owner. I find I have to obey. What's the secret to its magic? Can I turn it off?"

"I tell you, I d-don't know! I couldn't understand that part. All I could make out was the directions to your cave and how to get p-past the wards." Maynard was close to tears.

She nudged him with her foot. "Get up, Maynard. You're not much of a wizard, but I suppose you can still be useful. Come with me."

Maynard scrambled to his feet. He was still alive and now it seemed he had a new employer. He held no loyalty to the Prince, after all. If this demon wanted a wizard, he was the man for the job. Maynard, the High Priest of Lilith, would not be a bad title. It would certainly get him the respect he deserved. A new fantasy formed in his mind, of virgin slaves desperate to avoid the sacrificial altar.

***

Lilith strolled into her sanctuary, pulling her dress back on as she went. She didn't bother looking back to see if Maynard followed as ordered. She knew the wizard was telling the truth about the keystone, his fear of being given another punishment controlling his actions.

The guards on either side of the entrance stood in rigid attention as she passed by and the stone carvers putting the finishing touches on the entrance worked even faster as she paused to check their work. The stone was being carved to resemble the fluted columns of her old temple.

She strolled down a wide corridor lit by torches set into the walls. In another day or so, she'd have the strength to weave the spells to give the tunnels her preferred dim lighting. A few weeks ago, this had been an abandoned mine. It was amazing how much could get done with constant work and some motivation. Lilith reached the end of the torch-lit section and continued walking. She snapped her fingers and a glowing ball of light appeared before her, leading the way. A new, more powerful Lilith was beginning to emerge as she continued to feed. She could feel the wizard's fear of close places fight his fear of her touch— and lose. The globe became brighter as she fed on the result.

She began to take side corridors, turning left and right in a random manner designed to confuse. They eventually came to a huge chamber deep in the earth, already illuminated by her magic with no way to turn it off. Large oil lamps on cast iron stands provided additional lighting. Tunnels from all directions entered the room, some of them leading to secret outlets. Lilith was not going to get trapped again in a dark underground prison. She walked over to inspect a mural being painted on the freshly plastered walls.

"This will have to be improved," she told the artist doing the work, "but I'll wait until you can paint from life. Right now, there's only a passing resemblance." She traced a circle around a group of three women, pictured in chains and bowing before her. The Ladies were never far from her thoughts.

Lilith went to a massive stone throne draped in furs, sat down and crossed her legs, letting the slit up the sides of the dress fall open. She could see the gold bracelets on her ankles reflected in the wizard's eyes as he stood before her, awaiting her next command. Greed was already showing in Maynard's face. Domesticating humans was almost too easy.

"Now," she said, "I'll give you another chance to be of service. What do you know about portals?"

Fourteen

The Lady was forced to ride through the night despite having traveled all day. When they made camp, it was past dawn and both she and her horse were stumbling from exhaustion. Ambrosius took advantage of all their horses' speed and she wondered if Keyotie was able to keep pace. She hadn't seen a dog since leaving the river.

Back on the road at sunset the next day, Keyotie still hadn't made his presence known. She grew convinced he'd run into some trouble. Though her options were severely limited, she eventually had an idea—the men allowed her some privacy in nearby bushes during a call of nature. She started drinking lots of water and asking for frequent breaks, hoping to provide a scent for Keyotie to track. It was still possible these men were part of some trap Lilith had planned.

He appeared out of the bushes on one of the breaks, then sat and watched her squat, ignoring her hand motions to turn away. When she was finished he came over and sniffed where she'd been, then cocked his leg, adding his own bit of moisture to hers. He faded back into the night as she rejoined her guards.

"Lady, you wouldn't need to visit the bushes so much if you hadn't drunk a full canteen of water." Ambrosius was losing patience. "Do you think you can put a stopper in it long enough for us to actually get somewhere? We need to reach the castle before dawn to make sure the wrong eyes don't see you, and at this rate, we'll never make it. I'm beginning to suspect you're trying to delay us on purpose."

She took the reins from his hand and got back on her horse. "I understand the need for haste," she replied. "I will 'put a stopper in it', for now." Ambrosius seemed satisfied.

They reached the castle just before dawn, where she was led

Gerald Ghostlow

around to a hidden, guarded door set deep in the massive stone wall. Scaffolds stood outside the entrance, although thankfully, there were no bodies left swinging by their necks.

The other guards were sent on their way, leaving only the leader and a handful of men. Ambrosius waved them back a few paces and, at his signal, they raised their crossbows. "You're a brave one, m'Lady," he said, "but nobody walks willingly into a dungeon if they have any sense, promises or not. If you need a moment to gather your courage, we'll wait."

She was grateful for the moment and decided she'd misjudged this man. She *had* grown frightened. While her Sisterselfs were present in her mind and providing some comfort, she was unused to being without their physical company. She took a deep breath and dismounted from her horse.

"I gave my word and I will keep it," she told the man. "It remains to be seen if Prince Valant will do the same. I believe you, at least, are a man of honor. Will you care for my horses and keep my possessions safe? I might need them again. You may take whatever fee you want out of the coins in the pouch."

Ambrosius got down from his horse and walked toward her, taking the reins from her hand and then bowing deeply at the waist in the best courtly manner. At first she thought he was mocking her, but when he straightened, his face was very serious.

"Lady," he said, "I have done many things in my life I am not proud of, but putting you in this dungeon will always be my greatest shame. If I did not know the Prince to be a man of his word, I would never have brought you here. Perhaps one day I will be able to make it up to you."

He got back on his horse and turned to his men, who looked amused at his posturing. "I will keep her horses, supplies, and purse, until her release—no matter how long that takes. If any of you think to challenge me over this, do so now."

His men looked disappointed, but only glanced back and forth among each other, none of them willing to look their leader in the eye. She believed her possessions would remain safe and wondered how

The Weaving

someone like Ambrosius could end up working for Prince Valant.

She was escorted into the dungeon as her captors rode off. The clang of the heavy door locking behind her echoed Keyotie's warning, whispered when he'd handed over the reins to the packhorse back at the river.

"*Oh, Lady, getting into a dungeon is easy. It's getting back out again that's the problem.*"

***

Keyotie kept pace with the horses, loping along the road out of sight and taking an occasional shortcut through the fields. He never let the group get far ahead. If something unexpected happened on the way to the castle—like Lilith showing up—he'd hear and come running. When he saw they were going to bed down for the day, he took the opportunity to grab a meal from a nearby chicken coop, then found a hiding spot near the horses.

The next night, Keyotie became puzzled by the Lady's constant need to urinate. When it dawned on him that she was marking her trail for his benefit, he let her know in his own way it wasn't needed. *Honestly, sometimes she treats me like a pup!*

After she was escorted into the castle, he continued on to the nearby town. There was nothing else he could do for his Lady from outside the walls.

Keyotie had other work to do.

First, he needed to find out what was going on in the local area. The best way was to stay in true form as one more stray dog hanging out, begging for scraps. It was a perfect disguise he often used when entering a new town, but he needed to address one problem first.

***

"Trespasser!" the alpha growled. "Not welcome! Leave!"
"Up yours!" Keyotie growled back. "Staying!"
"Leave or die!" the alpha snarled in warning.

Gerald Ghostlow

"Lick me!" Keyotie barked in reply.

The two fighters circled in the middle of the dirt street. The argument had been going on for only a few moments but was already drawing a crowd. Both people and dogs shouted encouragement, with the people laying bets on the winner. Keyotie was expecting this encounter with the local pack alpha, and while he had no personal desire to take over the position, the nature of the pack demanded Keyotie either submit or fight the top dog. A member of the noble coyote clan, he was not about to sniff this mongrel's tail.

With the preliminary insults out of the way, the alpha rushed his opponent. Keyotie danced to one side and bit down hard on a back leg, letting go and getting out of range before the dog could retaliate. The alpha was limping and in trouble. Keyotie was bitten a few times but was eventually able to get past the dog's defenses and clamp down on the throat. The dog whined his surrender and there was a new alpha.

The loser limped off to lick his wounds and the rest of the pack came over to show their allegiance and engage in an orgy of sniffing. When the people saw it wasn't going to be a fight to the death, they settled up their bets and considered the entertainment over.

Now the pack followed Keyotie wherever he went and provided cover for his spying. Several days later, Keyotie stepped out of an alleyway in human form, holding a small purse of coin liberated from a passed-out drunk. By eavesdropping on town gossip, he'd discovered how to accomplish the next stage of his campaign.

He stopped and slapped behind an ear, scratching at a sudden itch. He captured the flea and crushed it between his nails in disgust. He could feel others crawling under his leathers, a parting gift from the pack. Keyotie hated the little biters and headed toward the bathhouse.

After he was clean, he would find the roughest tavern in the most dangerous part of town and spend every last stolen coin buying drinks.

***

The Weaving

While the Lady had observed plenty of dungeons with her scrying, she had never actually been inside of one before. This dungeon seemed typical. Massive stone walls and heavy locked doors were simple, effective and pretty much described the basement of most castles.

She was prepared for the sight, but not the smell.

As she was led past the first holding area, the odor from the barred doorway hit her and she retched, covering her mouth. Raw human waste mingled with vomit to produce a foul stench. She caught a glimpse of several men inside, lying or sitting in the filth. The cave, with its decomposing bodies, couldn't have been any worse.

One of the men behind her spoke. "Aww...did you forget your perfumed hanky? You're in *my* little kingdom, now. This cage here is where we keep people who are going to be with us for a short time. Some are waiting for the noose and some are waiting for their family to pay the fine for a minor transgression of the King's law. We don't get many repeat visits from either type. Haw!"

Turning to tell this man what she thought of his humor, she came face-to-face with a spear point.

"Nuh-uh, Princess," the man standing behind the guard said. "We'll tell you when to stop—and when to speak, for that matter. Now keep walking." He was a greasy looking character, mostly bald and with a belly and red nose that spoke of constant drinking. Judging from the large ring of keys hanging off his belt, he was the jailor in charge. He smiled, showing a row of decaying teeth, motioning for her to go on.

She continued walking, passing other cells, most with solid doors with a small opening barely big enough to fit a head through. The lamps set into the walls of the wide corridor didn't allow her to see the occupants, but she could hear moaning or crying.

"Those cells aren't for you, either," he continued. "These are the men waiting around for the King to decide their fate, if he ever remembers they're down here. You certainly don't want to share a bunk with some of these animals. We have special instructions, we do. Nothing but the best for our mystery Princess. Stop here and face the wall."

The Lady did as she was told and lost control when fingers probed her most private places. Her Sisterselfs had to take over briefly to stop her from attacking, keeping her body locked in place while telling her this was only a routine search. The hands continued feeling around, found the small wooden bowl used for their scrying and a small pouch of coins, and took both away from her.

"All right, turn around. There, now that wasn't so bad, was it?" the jailor asked with a leer. She didn't bother to reply. The man used his keys to open a door, motioning for her to enter. When she was halfway in, a shove on her back propelled her the rest of the way and the door slammed shut behind her. She could hear the men laughing as they left, talking about spending the money they'd confiscated.

"It's about time," a woman's voice said from the gloom inside the chamber. There was a small, barred window allowing a little of the morning sun to shine in, but most of the space was left in deep shadow. She squinted, seeing three women already in the room. The one who'd spoken was old and gray-haired, wearing a dress in the latest court fashion now wrinkled and worse for wear. There was a young woman in a maid's outfit sitting on a bit of straw in the corner, hugging her knees. The third woman was even younger, lying on more straw piled up to serve as a bed and covered with a threadbare blanket. She seemed to be asleep with her head on the old woman's lap.

"It's about time for what?" the Lady asked.

"For you to arrive, of course," the old woman replied. "Beatrice here kept talking about how another woman—a power—would show up, and how you'd straighten out this mess."

The Lady walked over and looked closer at the girl. She could see a bit of green sleeve sticking out from under the blanket. It was a young witch. "She's not saying much now," the Lady remarked.

"Oh, that was before, when the fever had her rambling," the woman continued. "Couldn't shut her up, then. Kept talking about three women and something called a portal and witches living in woods with their cats. There was a cave mentioned a time or two."

The Lady was truly amazed. This girl was too young to be more than an apprentice, and spirit walking through time and space went beyond the talent of any witch she'd heard of, even Rose. She knelt down and felt the wrist. The skin was dry but cool to the touch, the pulse slow and steady.

"How long has she been like this?" she asked the old woman.

"Since yesterday night, when we finally arranged a trade with the jailor for a potion. Poor Beatrice took a nasty hit on the head before being thrown in here, but the swelling is finally starting to go down now that the fever broke. I didn't know how much to give her and the witch wasn't any help by then. Hope I didn't do more harm than good. Here, this is what I forced down the girl's throat."

The Lady took the small bottle, reading the label. It was a remedy for fever and infection with half the content gone. One of her Sisterselfs interrupted a conversation with Rose to describe the emergency and was given an expert's opinion—an overdose, but not life threatening.

"She should be fine," the Lady told the woman. "The deep sleep is a result of taking too much, but she'll wake up feeling much better." The Lady looked around the bare cell. Except for a little straw, all she could see was a bucket in the corner covered with a bit of cloth and another bucket full of water. The sewage smell was gone, replaced by the musty odor of moldy straw. All the women were in need of a bath and could use a change of clothes, but at least they were trying to keep the place livable. She thought about how she'd been searched before being put in the cell.

"The jailor doesn't seem the kind of man to take pity on a sick prisoner. What could you have possibly traded him? This potion wasn't cheap."

The woman in the corner stirred and spoke. "There's only one thing we have left a man like that wants. He wasn't interested in the Duchess and the witch wasn't in any condition. That left me."

She looked up at the Lady. There was a large bruise under one eye. "Even with the Prince in charge, the jailor hasn't the guts for an obvious rape, not yet. Valant let everyone know the King's law would continue to be enforced and rape is a hanging offense. The jailor set his terms for the deal, including I do a little play-acting at enjoying what he did. Now, tell me you can get us out of here, like the witch said. Tell me I didn't go through that for nothing."

The Lady looked at the locked door to their cell and remembered her deal not to escape or harm any of the Prince's men. Her plan didn't include rescuing anyone from the dungeons. Her Sisterselfs agreed the plan would have to be changed.

They just had to figure out how to do it.

Fifteen

It was a parade, the event of the year, and everyone came out to watch. Most of these people had never traveled more than a few days' walk from their homes, so this would probably be their only chance to see King Justin in person. The crowd lined both sides of the dirt road leading through the avenue of shops, watching the company of soldiers go by in formation and cheering them on. Occasionally, a girl would dart out of the crowd and hand a bouquet of picked wildflowers to one of the soldiers. This generation would tell their grandchildren about the historic day when their King and his army came through their remote village.

Tom stared at the crowd of people staring back, wondering where they'd all come from. Surely this small town didn't contain this many people? And how did everyone find out the King was going to be riding through, anyway?

Tom was near the front of the long column of horses along with the select leaders of the expedition. He kicked his horse, spurring it to trot for a second. The painful bouncing of his rear on the saddle reminded him of something he'd forgotten to ask Rose. He caught up to her at the front of the line, where she rode next to the King. The ruler was relaxed, waving to his subjects.

"Are you sure I can't tempt you to work for me?" the King was asking Rose. "There are several witches with shops in town, but I can't always count on finding them if I need their services. Besides, I like to hire the best. You'd have a position and salary equal to my Royal Wizard. Bertram is also the best at what he does, although I'm letting him sweat a bit right now."

Rose shook her head. "I could never leave my place of power, but I know of several well qualified witches looking for a home. I can arrange for some interviews later, if you'd like."

His wife was occasionally visited by young witches new to the robe, asking to be her apprentice. Rose told him she had no plans of taking on the responsibility for several more years, but hated sending them away to wander the land. She'd developed a network of contacts among her peers in the magical arts, becoming a sort of unofficial job placement councilor somewhere along the way.

Fortunately, there never seemed to be enough witches to go around. Unfortunately, many of the places Rose identified as needing a witch's service were unglamorous postings in far flung settlements and vassal kingdoms, where payment was more likely to be in chickens than coin. Tom knew the Palace would be flooded with applicants once word spread about the opening.

The King leaned forward and peered at Tom riding on the other side of Rose. "I wish all the powers were like your wife," he said. "She doesn't cause more problems than she solves, unlike most of them." The blonde Lady riding close enough to overhear laughed and waved off the King's apology.

He turned back to Tom. "I see you don't wear a sword. The Duke tells me you've expressed interest in learning the art of sword fighting. That's wise. A man never knows when he'll be fighting for his life. I can have my Captain issue you one, if you'd like. There's no shortage of weapons."

This time Rose laughed and Tom cut in before she could tell him about the pretend dragon slaying. "I'd appreciate a sword, if your army can spare one. Could I also ask your Captain to give me a few lessons in how to use it? While we're on the subject, can I ask you a question about your army?"

"By all means. They're a fine bunch of men and have served me bravely in the past. I'm always ready to sing their praises."

Tom looked around. Several hundred men on horseback clopped along in disciplined columns. Freshly painted supply wagons rode in the middle, closely guarded. Each man carried a long spear sticking straight in the air, a sword at his side, and a crossbow slung across his back. Farther in the distance, a motley collection of wagons

The Weaving

occupied by civilians brought up the rear and endured a cloud of dust kicked up by the army.

It was an imposing sight, this many warriors in polished metal breastplate and helmets, but nothing compared to the descriptions in the adventure books. "I thought an army was...well, *bigger*. In the stories, there are men as far as the eye can see."

The King laughed. "Oh, these are just my personal guard. I have no desire to lay waste to my own fields, with thousands of marching feet trampling what they don't eat. That's what you try to do to your enemy. In fact, that's the real threat an invading army presents, not the possibility a village or two might be put to the torch."

"So where's the rest of your army? Or is that a secret?"

"Well, I wouldn't want maps passed around," the King remarked. The man seemed eager to talk about his area of expertise. "During the past week, my Generals have been busy issuing orders. My army will be there when I need them. If not, the officer responsible will find himself back with the foot soldiers, digging privy holes. You can never have too many privy holes. Disease can kill more people than crossbows."

"Privy holes? The stories skip over where the men take a dump. The warriors in those tales spend all their time marching, fighting or bragging about how many elves they've killed. Did you kill any?"

"A few," the King answered with less enthusiasm. "A few too many. I was barely old enough to shave when I first saw battle. Being heir to the throne meant having a unit dedicated to making sure I wasn't killed or captured. I had to be careful about putting myself in danger, for the sake of my men. Take one time, when we rode into an ambush. The elves had hidden themselves..." The King stopped, thought for a moment, then looked at Tom. "You've given me an idea. Your King thanks you."

The King kicked his horse, galloping to the front of the column, where the Duke spoke to one of the Generals. The big man had to lean down, since he was riding the tallest and widest horse Tom had ever seen, bred to carry a knight in full plate armor with no difficulty. Tom remembered he was going to ask Rose something and dropped back to where she was listening to Bertram and the red-headed Lady. The wizard was putting a rolled up piece of parchment back in a tube when he rode up beside them.

"We told the wizards to destroy this knowledge," the Lady said. "Don't you packrats ever get rid of anything? People died keeping this out of Lilith's hands. Now this Maynard knows how to make one and Lilith knows where the keystone is. Wizards should develop a little wisdom to go with their knowledge."

Tom motioned to his wife and she left Bertram to his scolding. They angled their horses to where they could speak privately.

"Poor Bert," she said. "He's being yelled at for something the wizards did a thousand years ago. Well, has the King convinced you to join his guard? What is it the recruiters say? A good day's pay for a hard day's work! Sounds tempting to me."

He shook his head. "I'm not tempted by the thought of digging privy holes." He looked around and spoke more softly. "Did you find the other bottle of liniment? Or even better, could you use a healing spell this time? The last potion you used burned like you'd set my pants on fire. I'm going to need it tonight. We haven't stopped for more than a few moments the past two days. I'm in agony and this horse wants to trot. Can you tell this nag to take it easier on me?"

"There's no need to be embarrassed, Tom. A lot of these men will be hurting tonight. You wouldn't get sores if you'd use your legs like I showed you." She paused for a moment, listening as his horse tossed its head and made a snorting sound. "And the horse says if you'll stop kicking, it will stop trotting. You're confusing it."

"I'm trying, but squeezing with my legs just rubs them raw along with my rear. I need your magic."

She put a hand on her husband's arm. "Darling," she said, "It's better to let the body heal itself. You don't need the spells, anyway. Your injuries seem to heal overnight as it is. The only time I've seen you sick was when I first found you. I honestly didn't think you were going to live."

She looked at their shadows, judging how much longer until they'd make camp. "Tell you what, we'll be stopping soon and I'll give

The Weaving

you a good massage for those stiff muscles. But if you do your usual yelling, everyone's going to wonder what I'm doing to you."

Tom grinned at her. "If I do, you can yell back, and I bet nobody has the courage to ask us about it the next day."

They both laughed. For all the discomfort and potential trouble ahead, Tom was glad he'd come along on this quest. This was the woman he loved and, if he had his way, they'd never be apart. He couldn't imagine anything worse than living without her. His humor vanished when the Lady's words intruded on his thoughts.

There was something worse than living without her. It would be living with the knowledge she'd been killed because of his failure.

***

That evening Rose took a stroll with Tom around the camp. She figured the rub down had made him feel much better, considering his reaction to her hands massaging his butt. She sighed and put her arm around his waist, wondering if he'd just wanted some extra attention. Tom had tried to return the favor with a massage on her own sore muscles.

Truth be told, she needed it just as much.

They wandered out to where the camp followers were parked for the night, people who provided services and goods to the soldiers for a fee. They walked past a woman stirring a large kettle that hung, steaming and bubbling, over a fire —a washerwoman, judging from the clothes hanging on a line. The woman looked up, brushed a bit of wet out of her face, and saw Rose and Tom. She motioned to them and they came over to see what she wanted.

"The Lady said a witch would show up soon," the woman told Rose. "You're the first green robe I've seen on this trip. You won't have much competition for your services, that's for sure." She looked at Tom. "I don't believe I've met this man, either. If you're in need of washing or mending, I have good prices and do good work. Just ask for Marge."

Rose looked into the kettle and saw it was full of socks. "We'll remember that," Rose said. "Was there something you needed?"

The woman walked to her wagon, a typical affair of canvas stretched across poles to form a traveling home. She banged on the side. "Miranda! Get out here and bring that bottle. I found a witch for you. We'll soon see what's up!" A girl appeared from inside the wagon and climbed down to join them. She was a plump young thing, wearing a nightshift and clutching a bottle by its neck.

Tom cleared his throat. "Rose, I still need to take the King up on his offer to lend me a sword. Why don't I leave you to conduct your business? I'll see you back at the tent."

She'd been expecting him to duck out as soon as it became apparent this girl needed her services as a healer. The girl handed her mother the bottle and stood, looking down at her bare feet. The woman handed it to Rose.

"Miranda here is what you might call an active girl, always been interested in the boys. She's settled on one young buck lately and I figured they'd be doin' what young folk always do. I picked this up from a witch. It's supposed to keep her from the Mother of All's notice."

Rose looked at the label on the bottle. It had the word 'fertility' scrawled on it in shaky handwriting. Most of the potion was gone. "I see. You need a refill? I didn't bring my stock of potions with me on this trip. Surely it can wait until she returns to her lover? Just make sure you get it refilled before allowing the two alone together."

Rose used a similar potion herself, a recent discovery increasingly used by women who wanted a love life without the Goddess taking notice. She and Tom had decided not to have children, with her career and all.

"No," the woman replied, "I need to settle an argument. Seems Miranda here started missing her monthly. She claims she'd been taking this like I told her, that she wasn't trying to trap the boy into a marriage."

First Rose called Miranda over. The girl jumped when Rose put a hand on her slightly bulging stomach. "Relax, child," she said. "I'm only making sure there's nothing wrong inside." She felt the

The Weaving

spark of new life inside. In fact, there were two sparks. Twins.

"She's with child, all right." Rose looked again at the bottle and removed the stopper. She poured a little bit into the palm of her hand and tasted it, sorting out the ingredients from long practice. The wide availability of something to control pregnancy was still resisted by some of the Mother of All's worshipers. They argued it would lead to widespread debauchery. It was possible someone had played a cruel trick on the girl.

There was something definitely wrong with this potion. She took a closer look at the label. "This isn't supposed to stop fertility, it's a potion for causing it! It's no wonder your daughter is pregnant. Who gave you this? I'll have her robe confiscated!"

Marge swore and looked at the girl, shaking her head. "Don't that beat all? Old Bramble is what we call her and I don't want to cause her grief. It must have been a mistake. The witch is getting on in years, about blind and half deaf. She's all we can afford on our income. Those new witches charge too much!"

"Still, that's no excuse. The next time she might hand out a poison by mistake." Rose made a mental note to bring up the subject of price gouging at the next coven—the tendency to put money over service worried her.

She addressed the girl. "Have you talked marriage with the boy, yet?"

Miranda shrugged, still looking down at her feet. "His Pa is again' it. Says we got no way to earn a livin' and he don't need 'nother mouth to feed."

Marge put her hand on her daughter's shoulder. "We'll just have to change his mind, that's all. By the time we get back, you'll be showing in a big way, and won't be any doubt of the need. We should make enough this trip to help get you started."

Rose sighed. One of the first lessons she'd learned was even the most powerful witch couldn't solve all the problems in the land—but there was one thing she could do in this case. First, she asked a few more questions, finding out exactly where this woman called home. Then she sent a summons to whatever bird might be willing to carry a message in that direction. A hawk interrupted its search for a good roost for the night to come gliding into the campsite, landing on her shoulder.

When the hawk flew off, it was to seek out a witch Rose knew, passing on the message that taking care of this girl during her pregnancy—for free—would be considered a favor to the Witch of the Woods. Refusing to do the power this favor would be considered an insult. Giving birth to twins could be risky and Rose wanted Miranda to have competent care.

The rest of their troubles the mother and daughter would have to handle on their own. She told Marge how to find the witch, and as an afterthought, informed them of the double blessing. She left them staring at each other and repeating the word, "*Twins*?"

Rose looked around for Tom before she left the cluster of wagons, but couldn't see him. She closed her eyes, reached through their bond, and discovered he was fighting for his life against a hoard of elves—*and winning*. She smiled, understanding it was his imagination at work, and he was more likely chopping at a tree with his new toy.

She had a little time by herself. She aimed for another wagon she had noted earlier, this one set away from the others and distinguished by a large red lantern hanging off a post. She made sure nobody was looking, then knocked softly on the wooden side. When there was no answer, she knocked harder. A pretty face finally poked out from the canvas, hair in curlers.

"The lantern ain't lit, can't you see that? Give a girl a night off once in a while, why don't...well, hello." She looked Rose up and down. "Let me guess. You smelled a strange perfume on your man, beat a confession out of him, and now you're here to tell me he's off limits?"

"Excuse me? Oh, Tom had better not—I mean, he would never—well, he doesn't need to—" Rose felt her face redden. This was harder than she had thought. "It's a professional call. I'm willing to pay."

"Hold on..." The woman squinted. "I didn't notice before in the

The Weaving

dark. That's a green robe, isn't it? Some of the other girls have witches as regular customers, but I stay away from that furry transformation stuff."

"Oh! I only want to ask a few questions!" Rose could definitely feel herself blushing.

The woman's head disappeared and a set of steps flopped down from the other end of the wagon. "Come on inside, honey!" the woman called. Rose once again made sure nobody was looking her way, then accepted the invitation, pushing aside the insect screen. She saw an interior with a wide bench and several desks, including a wash basin and toiletries. It was comfortable enough, but she looked around some more, puzzled.

"You're wondering where the bed is?" The woman was sitting on a padded bench, smearing some kind of lotion on her face. She got up and opened a hinged sections of the bench and folded back others. Soon a large, well-padded bed filled half of the wagon.

"Nice, isn't it? I made it myself, from one of my own designs. There's also a hidden privy hole under this bench with a pot you empty from outside. I even have a small water tank built into the side. This is my home for most of the year, after all. I have a little business setup with a cabinetmaker. I'm supplying the income until we start making a profit, and he's putting together a workshop to turn out my ideas. I'm Nellie. What can I do for you, honey? Usually I'm the one asking a witch for a potion."

Rose was impressed by the cleverness behind it all. It reminded her of Bertram's marvels, without the magic. She watched the woman convert it back into a bench and sat down next to her for their discussion.

"I'm Rose, the Witch of the Woods. I just need your experience as a...a professional entertainer. It concerns something my husband has asked me about."

Nellie stopped her lotion application to turn and stare at Rose. "A married witch? That's a first for me. Well, in a world of marvels, one more. And your question is...?"

"Tom knows a song that contains references to...well, certain things a man and woman do together. He doesn't remember—well, let's just say he isn't experienced. He's asked me to...um, demonstrate, but I'm not familiar with the terms, either." She laced her fingers together, trying to illustrate. "Some of the descriptions seem dangerous, if not impossible, and we haven't had much success. I've been dying to find out." There, she'd admitted it, and she hoped the woman didn't burst out laughing.

Nellie smiled sadly. "So you came to an expert for help. Honey, some of that stuff is more wishful thinking than anything a man would actually get done. What's the song?"

"It's *The Maiden and the Dragon*."

"Oh, I know that one! In fact, the Minstrel sang it to me the last time we were together. He said I inspired part of it, but he probably says that to all the girls. Alright, I'll sing it, and you stop me when the Maiden does something you can't figure out. Ready?" Rose nodded, eager for the lesson. The woman began, slightly off key. Apparently her skills didn't extend to this type of entertaining.

"*In days of old, when men were bold and ladies kept their portals closed...a Maiden vowed no man would ever get inside her underclothes...*"

***

By the end of the song, Rose had received a long overdue education. She was a little scandalized at the variety of ways two people could pleasure each other. Most of the methods had never occurred to her and the books she liked to read only hinted instead of giving details. In those stories, some things throbbed and other things thrusted and the rest was left up to the reader's imagination.

She descended from the wagon with a thoughtful expression. It was getting late and Tom would probably be curled up on the cot in their little tent, snoring, expecting her to quietly snuggle in without waking him. She grinned and whistled the tune as she headed back to their tent.

He was going to get a surprise tonight.

The Weaving

With the Ladies involvement, Rose had no doubt Tom would eventually find his missing past. She had promised to help her husband in his search and she would honor her word. But, if some woman out of his past popped up and demanded him back, Rose wanted to make sure Tom thought twice about giving up what he already had.

Sixteen

Keyotie took a deep breath, preparing to do battle once more. His new foe looked to be a grizzled veteran of many conflicts and would be harder to dispatch than the previous two challengers lying at his feet.

"Ready?" he asked. The man wiped the sweat from his brow and nodded. They picked up their tankards. At the signal, both started drinking. Keyotie's head tilted back as he swallowed. Soon he was staring at the ceiling as the last drops ran down his gullet. The crowd urged them on.

He slammed the empty tankard down on the table a bare second before his opponent. The tavern erupted in cheers. His competitor started swaying back and forth, leaning a little more each time, until he toppled over, out for the count.

The crowd cheered again.

Keyotie leaned back, raising his hands. The crowd grew silent. He tucked his chin down and a loud, long belch came from deep within his chest. They cheered once more. Keyotie knew he could have gotten a round of cheers for picking his nose. Give a man enough ale and he'll cheer the end of the world or the sun coming up with equal enthusiasm.

He smiled, accepting the tribute as deserved. He used the winnings to buy another round of drinks for everyone. It was an old game, this tavern contest. People saw his small build and figured they could easily drink him under the table. They didn't know his remarkable shape-shifting body had a much higher tolerance for alcohol than the average person.

He wasn't immune, though. He declined an invitation to another contest when he found it hard to bring the room into focus,

The Weaving

instead relaxed and sipped his refill. He was there to meet someone and wanted to be awake when it happened. *Darn it all, when were those people going to show?*

As if in answer, a commotion stirred at the door, the lookout yelling something about the guards. The dozen or so men in the small room who could still stand bolted for the rear exit, trampling over the guys passed out on the floor. It took only a moment for the tavern to clear out—the patrons of this type of establishment usually had good reason to run from the law.

Two men strolled through the door, but they weren't members of the official guards. Their only identification was a black armband with a stylized spider design stitched in red. The first was a big man—an ugly cuss with a nose that zigzagged down his face, a testament to a history of badly reset breaks. The other man looked half the size of the first, but was probably the one in charge. He seemed a little more alert and flexed his hands like he was itching to grab something. Keyotie slouched at his corner table and waited.

"Slim pickings, boss," the big man said. He walked over and kicked one of the unconscious men. The drunk rolled over and threw up on the man's boots. The leader stopped his companion from stomping the poor fellow for the insult.

Keyotie laughed, catching their attention. The thug squinted his eyes.

"You think this is funny?" he asked. "I'm gonna make you lick it off my boots. You still think it's funny?"

"I'm just delighted at the floor show," he told the bully. "I've seen dancing bears before, but never one that could talk. I must congratulate your trainer. You don't look smart enough to stand on two legs."

It had the desired effect. The giant roared, pulled his knife, and attacked, ignoring his boss's yells to stop. Keyotie waited until the right moment and shoved out with both feet, pushing the bench on the other side of the table into the man's legs. The thug fell forward, burying the knife into the table. The big head came down next to it, bouncing off the hard wood. Keyotie grabbed the man by the hair and

Gerald Ghostlow

added another slam for good measure. The nose received another mortal blow, spraying blood as the man slid onto the floor. Keyotie hadn't even moved from his seat. He picked up his tankard and sipped, watching the twitchy leader for his reaction.

The other man hadn't moved. He looked at his fallen companion without much surprise. "I've warned Yorik time and again," the man said. "All that muscle don't matter if you can't hold your temper." He looked at Keyotie. "I'd hate to have to kill you. I'm recruiting talent like yours, but you're no good to me if you're not going to accept a job offer. I'm Simon the Knife. Wanna try your tricks on me?"

Keyotie had no doubt of the mercenary's abilities. He could tell there was a throwing knife tucked in each sleeve, and probably others stashed in easy to reach places. "No, I'm not stupid," he replied. "I'm more interested in the job you mentioned. I'll listen to your offer." He nodded down at Yorik. "What about this guy? I need to watch my back?"

Simon walked over to look at his companion. The big man was still unconscious. "Not while you're part of my team. Either one of you jumps the other, the winner has to take on me. That good enough?"

Keyotie got up and walked around the table, bending over Yorik. "Just one thing, first," he said. He placed his hands on either side of the mangled nose, grunting with the effort as he squeezed and twisted. There was a grinding sound as he forced the gristle back into place. The two of them studied the result.

"Yorik will never turn a woman's head," Simon remarked, "but it's an improvement." He grabbed the tankard off the table, splashing it in the man's face. It washed off most of the blood and the man awoke with a roar. Keyotie moved out of range of those big hands, watching as Simon helped his companion off the floor and explained what Keyotie had done to fix his face.

Yorik sat down on the bench, feeling his tender nose. "Thab's gread!" he said. He hawked and spit some blood, making a few tentative sniffs. "I can breathe through it again! Ain't been able to do that since I was a kid, when dad busted it 'cause I was messin'

The Weaving

with his new wife." He turned to Keyotie. "I guess I got you to thank. You're lucky I slipped on that puke. You watch your mouth from now on and we'll call it even. Alright with you?"

"Sure," Keyotie replied. He was always willing to let people make excuses for their mistakes—it meant they could be counted on to repeat them. He sat back down at the table and turned to Simon. "So, what's the job?"

"Not so fast. What's your name and where are you from?"

"People call me the Trickster and I've been on the move for so long, I couldn't even point towards my old home. You wouldn't have heard of it."

"The Trickster? That's you?" Simon looked impressed. "I thought those leather fringes reminded me of something I'd seen on a wanted poster. If half the charges are true, we can use you." He looked for the barkeep. "Drinks over here!" Simon yelled, then hunched over the table.

"You'd be working for a dame called Lilith," he said. "She don't like to be called a witch, but that's pretty much what she is, near as I can tell. She rode into town with the Prince, but now she wants to start a gang of her own. She's turned some old mines south of here into a holdout."

"What does she want us to do?"

"All the guards are either marching off to war or hiding inside the castle with the Prince. That pretty much leaves the town to itself. We do the supply runs and tell the shop owner to send the bill to the castle. But that's not all. She wants us to bring her a supply of people, boys and men mostly. She don't care how we get them. She has holding cells in that old mine just waiting to be filled."

"What do we get out of it?" Keyotie already knew the answer from eavesdropping in canine form, but he had to play his part.

"I've got a protection racket going. These townspeople pay me to leave them alone. The ones who can't or won't pay get a trip to the mines. There's more than enough to split three ways—after expenses, of course."

"What does this Lilith do with the people we drag out there?"

Keyotie could still picture the scene in the cave.

Simon shook his head. "None 'a your business. A few of the boys are servants and some of the better looking men are cleaned up and put into special cells. The rest, well...if you don't got the stomach to haul off some barrels full of body parts once in a while, you and me got a problem."

Simon had no intention of letting him turn down this job offer, not after being told the details of their operation. No surprise.

"I'm in," Keyotie said. "When's the next trip to the mine?"

"Not for a couple days," Simon replied. "Now that there's more of us, we can take our time and get a full load. When we hit a tavern, Yorik will go 'round back and make the catch while you and I come in the front to flush them out. We'll take tonight off, do some drinking and maybe find some dames." He dug in his pocket, pulled out an armband and handed it to Keyotie. "Welcome to Lilith's elite guard. You'll be on probation until you can receive her touch."

Simon was still selling what a great job this was, but Keyotie noticed the look on Yorik's face at the mention of Lilith. "This 'touch' something I should worry about?" he asked the big man.

"Nah, just somethin' she does, to make sure you know she's the boss," Yorik replied, too casually. "Might be a while 'fore it happens to you, cause we're in no hurry to meet her again. Once it does, you'll know why it won't be long 'fore she'll run everything. And we'll be right there, helping her do it and gettin' our reward."

Keyotie took the armband, his ticket in and out of the mines where Lilith was hiding. He grinned and slipped it on his arm. The Trickster had once again lived up to his name.

"I'm looking forward to my reward," Keyotie said. "So, are you two in the mood for a drinking contest? Yorik, a big man like you should be able to out-drink little bitty me. Care to make a bet?"

***

The rat was nearsighted, so Beatrice couldn't be sure of anything beyond an arm's length away. The rat was also hungry and could smell food, and she had to stop it from climbing the legs of the dinner cart they were hiding under.

"I think there's a man in the bed and Prince Valant is bending over him," Beatrice said. "Now he's ordering everyone from the room. He's...could the Prince be crying? He's saying something to the man on the bed, but I can't make it out. Shall I have the rat move closer?"

She sat with crossed legs on the straw bed, holding her head in her hands while she maintained her connection with the rat. The Lady sat next to her, the Duchess and the maid giving them plenty of room.

"No," the Lady replied, "Valant might notice and kill the rat. You don't have enough experience to handle being in a borrowed mind when it dies. That must be King Morgan in the bed. It sounds like he's sick, or worse. Can you tell if he's alive? Does the rat smell death?"

Beatrice winced as her head began throbbing again. "The rat doesn't smell anything but food and he's tired of waiting." She grunted and opened her eyes, looking at the Lady. "I couldn't control it. Now I have to eat the slop they serve here with the memory of sausage links on my tongue. Even this small use of my power causes my head to throb. Am I crippled for life?"

The Lady leaned forward, feeling the back of the girl's head. The lump was still tender. "I know it doesn't feel like it, but you're healing. Be patient and remember what you were taught in your College. You're lucky to be alive at all. Without the potion our brave Ilene acquired for you, the infection would have killed you."

The maid started giggling again. Beatrice looked over to where the woman was sitting. The maid was in her customary corner of the cell, arms around her knees. She'd been acting increasingly strange the last few days, with spells of laughter and crying and periods when even the Duchess couldn't get her to respond. Fortunately, the head jailor hadn't visited since the Lady arrived, and the men who brought the daily food and water rations didn't bother to speak. The maid had to be ordered to eat. The Duchess was now reduced to taking care of her servant, but she didn't seem to mind.

Gerald Ghostlow

"I will be forever in your debt," she told Ilene again. "I will begin by making sure the pig who forced himself upon you is punished."

Ilene raised her head, scorn written all over her face. "You mean like this woman has promised to get us out of here? I'll never escape from this nightmare. I'll be old as the Duchess before either of you gets around to helping out one poor maid."

"Hush, now," the Duchess said. "She's doing all she can. If you must be angry, blame me for allowing this unwarranted charge of treason to extend to you." The maid shrugged and put her head back on her knees. The Duchess turned to the Lady. "I'm sorry to hear about our King. He was a wise and noble ruler, before grief for a dead wife twisted his thinking. But now, we must deal with the present. It would ease all our minds to know what you have planned."

"What I have planned depends on our young witch getting better," the Lady replied.

Beatrice got to her feet and went over to the water bucket. She scooped some of the tepid water in her hands, rubbing it on her face. Then she took a deep breath and stood tall. "I am at your service," she said. "While I am not a power, still I am a witch, and I swear this dungeon will not hold me for long!"

***

The Lady was impressed by the witch's speech. Too bad the girl looked like she could be knocked over with a feather. Her condition wasn't as bad as it looked, though. The witch had managed a small healing spell on herself—between that and the potion, she should be strong enough by morning.

"Sit down before you fall," the Lady ordered. "Right now, I only need information. Your sleeves mark you at apprentice level, but how much training have you actually received? When your strength comes back, we might need to move fast." The Lady could picture the gallows in her mind and worried the Prince might get around to deciding these women's fate before she could help them.

Beatrice sank back down on the straw. "I graduated from the

The Weaving

College just last year," she explained. "I was at the top of my class."

"Why aren't you busy working under a Mentor, then? You should have had no trouble finding one."

"It's sort of a tradition to take a year off to celebrate after all that study. Being an apprentice can be an even harder life than going to College." She looked at the Duchess. "Uncle Bud...the Duke...used his connections to get me this post as ambassador for a year. It was supposed to be a paid holiday with nothing much to do but enjoy the social life of a pampered dignitary. I was told to use my talents to do a little spying and let him know if anything interesting happened. Birds and mice can go just about anywhere."

The Duchess spoke. "That's not a huge secret, child. It's expected that ambassadors will be the eyes and ears of their King, but your position was always ceremonial. The Duke sent me a nice letter, asking me to make sure you had someone to escort you to the balls."

The Lady wasn't at all interested in a dignitary's social life. "What transformation spells do you know?" she asked Beatrice. "How small of an animal, and what types?"

Beatrice started rubbing her temples again and reached for the potion. She sipped the last drops from the bottle before replying. "Nothing smaller than, say, a cat," she replied, "and only animals with fur, so far. I can't transform myself into a bird and fly out the window, if that's what you're asking. But if you want a cat or small dog, I can keep the form for as long as I can stay awake, up to several days. I revert back to human in my sleep."

The Lady was again impressed with the girl's talent. Most witches at her stage could hold the spell on themselves for less than a day. She had assumed Beatrice would be limited in her animal forms. Because of the danger involved, an apprentice had to be under the guidance of an established witch—a Mentor—while learning additional shapes.

"You can transform others, too?" the Lady asked. "The school does still require that in order to graduate, doesn't it?"

"Of course," the witch said. "That's part of our final exam. We

Gerald Gostlow

had to pick names out of a hat to see who became our subject and what animal to do." Then Beatrice paused and looked embarrassed. "My test was to turn someone into a warthog. I had no trouble with that, but I couldn't remove the spell afterwards. The standard escape clause should have worked, but the handsome Prince kept on contract for that sort of thing took one look and refused to kiss her. It took three witches working together to get the spell off the student. I thought that would flunk me, but for some reason, it seemed to impress the teachers and I got a pass. But until I learn what I did wrong, anyone I transform is liable to stay that way for good."

Her story sent the maid into one of her laughing fits.

"Well then," the Lady said, "tomorrow morning, if you're strong enough to do three spells, I promise to get everyone out of here."

Seventeen

The King watched his Royal Wizard make adjustments on the strange contraption, turning a wooden wheel a tiny fraction, then measuring the distance between two points before making another turn. Bertram had been fine-tuning for some time.

"Will it take much longer?" the King asked. "I said to send for me when you're ready. Should I leave and come back later? I have a war to run, you know."

Bertram locked the wheel down and straightened. "Sorry, your Highness. The dampness from the river causes the wood to expand, but it's fine now."

King Justin stepped up to the thing, checking it over. Two small, square windows in wooden frames were set at either end of some sliding rails, with the distance between the two windows adjustable through notched gears turned by a crank. This sat on three adjustable legs, with additional gears that allowed it to be aimed by moving a handle. It had taken Bertram the better part of a day to unpack and assemble.

"So this is the famous Far Seeing Window you developed? That money I provided from the treasury wasn't wasted after all." The King looked across the river, at the trees and an occasional glint of sunlight reflecting off metal. He bent down and peered through the windows. Now it only looked like the same scene distorted through several panes of wavy glass.

"I see," the King said. "Or rather, I don't. Bertram, I think you might be overdue for a rest. I've heard about this kind of thing. Those fumes from your work in the tower can do strange things to a man's thinking. Mad Wizard's disease, I think it's called."

The wizard cleared his throat. "Ah, very funny, your Highness.

I still need to add the magic before it'll work." He rummaged in his robe and pulled out a bottle and a cloth. He poured a little of the clear liquid on the cloth and wiped it on the window glass. "It evaporates and has to be reapplied, so I save this step for last," he explained.

The King peered through the Far Seeing Window again. This time, it was as if he was standing on the opposite shore. A man dressed in Morania colors walked into view and the King jerked back, his mind reacting as if he was actually standing that close to the soldier. He stood and looked at the magical device, thinking of how useful it would be to spy on enemy movements.

"Showing off another of your marvels, Bert?" the Witch of the Woods asked, wandering up with her husband in tow. She walked over to look at the magical window. "If I had to guess...a way to capture images on glass? The artists' guild is going to throw a fit, if that's what you're doing."

Bertram started to reply, then got a thoughtful look in his eyes, pulled out a paper and pencil and began scribbling. The King knew to expect another round of requests for funds.

"Look through it and see what you think, Rose," Bertram said, motioning to the thing. She bent and looked, then examined the workings and looked through it again, this time trying to use the steering mechanism. Eventually, she straightened, shaking her head.

"Bert is great at spells, but not so good when it comes to woodworking. There's a...well, *professional* woman in the campsite you should show this to, if you're going to make more. I'll bet she even improves on the design."

"You're talking about Nellie?" the General asked, then got red in the face.

Ah, the King thought, *that profession*. He called over the General. "Hire the woman, but tell her we want furniture made for the Palace. This has to stay our secret. If the Duke says we can trust her, we'll put her to work with Bertram." He turned back to Rose. "I will certainly want more of these made, enough for each outpost. But you don't seem too impressed, Rose."

She shrugged. "Bert is a good friend, but like all wizards,

The Weaving

he does things the hard way. It's not their fault, since the Goddess blesses only women with real talent. Men have to make do with their limited abilities."

"Hey!" Her remark brought Bertram out of his scribbling. "Just because you witches have a different way of working the magic, it doesn't make ours inferior. Wizardry is the future of our people, not witchcraft."

The King motioned for his General to start using the Far Seeing Window. The officer had the same jerking reaction to first looking through it, but was soon dictating what he saw to his aid. He turned to address the Royal Wizard and the Witch of the Woods, each the reigning master of their craft.

"I've wondered about the difference between you two. Don't you have the same talent?"

Rose shrugged. "Not really. Witches tap the magic within our minds. Wizards use the magic outside of their minds. It's not the same thing."

"Nonsense," Bertram replied. "Magic is magic. Everything is made of various combinations of magical elements." He motioned to the windows. "Glass has the property of vision, tied to the magical light element. I change the rules a little and we have this far seeing window. No one can make something from nothing."

The King nodded. "Makes sense. Your reply, Rose?"

The witch cupped her hands and whispered into them. When she opened them again, she was holding a fresh cut rose blossom. She handed it to the King. "Something from nothing," she answered. "Reality is what we imagine it to be. All it takes is the will and the power, and almost anything is possible. I'd also say that probably won't make *sense* to you, because you're only a man, even if you are a King."

Feisty woman. Reminds me of my Queen. The King looked at Tom, who ignored the discussion and was engaged in using his new sword to lop the tops off cattails growing on the riverbank. "Tom," he called, "your wife claims reality isn't really real. What would you say to her?"

Tom looked up from his slaying of the local plant life. "I'd tell her it doesn't matter to me if a pork chop is real or not, as long as my stomach thinks it is."

Rose laughed. "That's my Tom for you, cutting to the heart of the matter. Our meals at home are mostly vegetables and fish, since I don't eat animals I can talk to. He's always on the lookout for a good hunk of meat on our trips. That's his way of saying he can smell supper cooking and I'd better hurry up."

The King looked at the mess tent in the distance. The cook had bought some pigs from a local farmer this morning. Tom must have a good nose. "Alright," he said, "before you go, how would you solve the problem of knowing what your enemy is doing on the other side of this river?"

Rose walked over to the shore and picked out a comfortable log to sit on. She closed her eyes and softly hummed a tune, something that sounded like it could only come from her lips. Then she spoke.

"There are patrols riding up and down the river path just beyond sight, a dozen men in each and armed with crossbows. There are sentries posted along the riverbank, with horns to alert the patrols of any movement. About…yes, an hour's walk upstream. a spot will soon be unguarded—the men there have found a small fortune in gold coins someone left on the ground and are talking about deserting. Other guards are talking about a Prince that's going to be showing up soon, along with an army, and how they don't understand what this war is all about in the first place."

She gave a little shake and stood, walking back over to the King. "That's how I'd do it, by using the eyes and ears of the animals."

The King turned to his General, paused in his viewing to listen. "Did you get that?" The old soldier nodded, then went back to doing his own spying. The King made his apologies, saying there was other business to take care of. Rose and Tom went in search of a meal, accompanied by the wizard, who also expressed an interest in pork chops.

***

The Weaving

Tom was a fast eater, usually attacking his food as if it might get away. He finished long before his wife and Bertram, who split their time between food and conversation. Rose and Bert were old friends, drawn together during their College days because both were superior to the other students and shunned by their classmates for their talents.

He left his wife extolling the virtues of Nellie and went in search of the guard who was supposed to teach him how to handle his sword. He found the Captain supervising the digging of another round of privy pits. The King had a fixation with privy holes and insisted a whole ring of them be dug around the camp, even though most of the others were still unused. The Captain was talking to an unhappy man holding a shovel.

"I warned you, Stewart," the Captain said. "I told you that woman was stringing you along. She wasn't worth you threatening another officer. Your own *brother*, on top of that! You're lucky the General only busted you down in rank, especially after you went over his head with that letter to the King. Now, I want this trench finished and the screens in place when I get back."

The Captain took Tom over to where other men sparred with wooden imitations of the deadly weapon. He picked through a pile of chipped spares, handing one to Tom. "So you want to learn the sword?" the Captain asked. "You've come to the right man. Combat, armed or unarmed, is what I teach. Sword fighting isn't easy, you know. Anyone can hack away with one of these, but facing a man who knows how to use one properly is different. It's like a dance, where the object is to stomp on the other's feet while keeping your own toes from getting flattened."

He picked up a weapon of his own and stood in front of Tom. "Let's see what you can do, first. Try to hit me."

"But won't you get hurt?" Tom asked.

"Trust me," the Captain replied, "I know what I'm doing. Don't hold back. I'm a big, bad elf out for your blood. Hit me." He stepped forward and poked Tom in the chest with the wooden sword.

Gerald Ghostlow

Tom did as instructed. The Captain picked himself up off the ground. The rest of the men around them had stopped their own activity to stare. "Why you little...Tom, was it? Tom, when I said hit me, I meant swing the sword, not punch my lights out with your other hand." He got to his feet, rubbing his jaw. "That's some punch you've got. Fast, too. So, you're left handed? Why are you holding your weapon in the right hand, then?"

Tom looked down at his fist like it was something he'd never seen before. "I don't understand what you mean. Most everyone else holds their sword in the right hand, so I figured that's how it's done. Either way feels the same to me. What's the difference?"

The Captain had Tom try using either hand on the sword, choosing one of the other guards to be the victim this time. The guard had no problem blocking Tom's attack, knocking the wooden sword away no matter which hand was used. The Captain called it off after a short time. "It really doesn't make a difference to you, does it? You're one of those rare people who can use both hands for anything, only in this case, you're equally bad with both of them. Use the left hand to hold your weapon until you can learn to switch in the middle of a fight. It'll confuse the enemy."

The Captain told the men to get back to their practice and pulled Tom off to one side. "You've got strong arms but weak hands," he explained. "I've seen it before. I can show you some exercises to improve your grip. Let's see how bad it is. Squeeze my hand as hard as you can."

The Captain's yelling stopped the practice again as he tried to pull out of Tom's grip. "Let go, you—stop squeezing!" he shouted. The Captain yanked back his hand and examined it. "You almost broke it, you stupid ox! Nothing should be able to knock a sword out of your hand. It's like you're letting go on purpose. I don't know what your problem is. Go away. The King can put me to digging privy holes, for all I care. You're more dangerous without a sword than with one. I'll tell the King that to his face, I swear I will!"

The public humiliation was too much for Tom and something inside of him snapped. He noted with some satisfaction as he drew

The Weaving

back his fist that the other hand fit neatly around the Captain's neck, and his grip was in no danger of slipping this time.

***

The King relaxed in his tent, enjoying a private meal and trying to sort out what he'd learned by the river. He'd always thought of witches as midwives and healers, dangerous only if you ended up on the receiving end of their ability to turn you into a lower life form. Witches played a vital role in the land, but wizards were the weapon makers, the ones he kept an eye on and recruited to his service.

He smelled the rose the witch had given him. She *could* make something from nothing. Or was Rose trying to say there wasn't any difference between something and nothing? He agreed only a woman could understand such nonsense, true or not.

But that wasn't what disturbed him. The Witch of the Woods had casually given a demonstration of the one thing any King would trade half his army for—information. It was the ultimate weapon. Know where your enemies are hiding and what they're going to do, and you've won the war. Bertram could produce wonders from his tower workshop, but Rose was a walking miracle. When this was over, one way or another, there was going to be a Royal Witch in residence at the Palace. He'd get the Duke to work on it. His Advisor might even figure out a way to get Rose to accept the position.

Maybe it would help change her mind if he offered Tom a position of some sort. He'd ordered his Captain in charge of training to give the man instruction on how to use the sword and write an evaluation. The King was confident the report would show only praise for Tom.

After all, anyone Rose married must be special.

Eighteen

The Duke spent a great deal of time, effort and money to create a web of agents to provide him with a steady flow of information. When he needed to know something, there was either a source already on his payroll or an agent who could find one on short notice. Rarely did he have to get personally involved in field work.

Right now, he was engaged in a campaign to extract information from its only known source. He moved his bishop and sat back, studying the source. She was hunched over the board, elbows on the table and frowning in concentration. He tried to figure out what the Lady was thinking and failed. There was no way of getting inside her lovely head to see how the linked minds of the three Ladies actually worked.

Her mind wasn't the only fascinating thing about the Lady. He'd always been partial to redheads, particularly ones with freckles, and especially redheads with freckles that trailed beneath the front of her blouse. He wanted to explore for more. If he was ten years younger and a hundred pounds lighter, he would try to strike up a romance with her, even if she was a power in the land and possibly immortal. That she was easily the most intelligent woman he'd ever met only increased her esteem in his eyes.

She moved her knight and captured the bishop, as expected. He closed his eyes, visualizing the board and moving the pieces in his head, trying various gambits against the counter-responses a player of her skill would bring to bear. There would be only one conclusion.

"Lady, we have another stalemate. We'll go on like this and devastate the remaining pieces on the board, but I see no other outcome unless you conveniently forget how to play the game. I offer a draw. Do you accept? We could start a new game."

The Weaving

She sat back and smiled and he decided even five years and fifty pounds ago would have been enough.

"You knew it was a stalemate when we traded queens, as did I," she said. "I won't win unless *you* conveniently forget how to play the game. I'd rather just sit and enjoy your company, if you don't mind."

Someone clapped from outside the tent. "Enter," the Duke yelled. A guard came in and handed him a letter. The Duke read the message. It said, *Got it*, in familiar handwriting.

"Escort the man who handed you this letter to me, but take your time doing it," he told the sentry. "Stop at the mess tent first. You look like you could use a good meal and our visitor might be hungry." He stopped the guard before the man left to carry out his orders. "Lady, would you like something to eat? I can have it brought here. Plain food, but filling. Pork today, if I'm not mistaken."

"No, thank you, but don't let that stop you from eating," she replied. She stretched, arching her back and putting her arms behind her neck. The Duke waved the guard out without looking away from the figure on display. He felt stirrings he thought a thing of the past. *Age and weight be damned.*

"I've gotten too used to sitting around the Palace and stuffing myself with the fine cooking," he said. "I'm determined to lose a little weight—my poor horse would certainly agree on the need. I've been neglecting the physical side of life too much. You intrigue me, Lady. Perhaps when this is over I could persuade you to visit? If you'd prefer privacy, I'm told I have an estate somewhere that came along with the title of Duke. We could get better acquainted, and do some... exploring of the countryside."

She laughed and picked up one of the chess pieces, running her fingers over the fine carving. "You are a big man, with big appetites and a huge intellect to go along with it. I like all that in a man. You intrigue me, as well. Perhaps when this is all over you'll get in some exercise by visiting *our* home. I promise the view of my... *countryside*...will be worth the trouble. But for now, let's stick to the business at hand. That messenger brought you word about the gifts you promised, and from your reaction, it isn't bad news. What do you want to know about, in return?"

"I know you don't usually answer questions about the past. I'd like for you to make an exception. I believe the gifts are worth the price. Your Sisterself out there talks much but says little. You are the smart one. You talk seldom but say much when you do speak. I was hoping for a little more directness in the answers from you."

She cocked her head as if listening to another voice, then chuckled. "My Sisterself thinks she should be offended by your comment, but we agree to your request. We only ask that anything you learn here stay between us. So, you weren't satisfied with the information your wizard provided. Anything specific?"

"It concerns the woman of two natures. It's a shame such a champion does not have the recognition she deserves."

The Lady looked at the carved piece of bone she was holding. "Her name was Ilian and she wouldn't agree with you on the need for fame. She was the most gentle of spirits. In spite of our warning, she insisted Lilith could be reasoned with. What our champion was forced to do in the end, she considered a failing on her part."

"That's a shame," he remarked. "Such innocence rarely survives the reality of the world. So, the two natures?"

"It refers to a shapeshifter," she explained, "a being born with two natures who can take on either form at will. A shapeshifter that is both man and dog, for instance, will have both the intelligence of a human and the instincts and behavior of a dog."

The Duke nodded. "Two natures and two forms. What was her other form?"

The Lady held up the chess piece. "Have you ever wondered why this is called a knight but often carved as a unicorn? It's the only tribute to Ilian that has survived. She was born and raised a unicorn, discovering her human side late in life. Unicorns live in a world of their own. They aren't capable of worry or fear, don't concern themselves with what has been or might be. It is the definition of innocence. The world she experienced as a human was simply too confusing after her unicorn upbringing. She came to us for help."

The Weaving

The Duke looked at the chess piece, considering this information. "So when your champion faced the monster?"

The Lady sighed. "Lilith attacks by reaching into your mind and finding your worst fears. Ilian never had a doubt or fear in her life. She just stood there, lecturing a demon on the benefits of a moral life. Lilith made the mistake we were hoping for. She physically assaulted the girl."

"And Ilian shifted to unicorn, to defend herself? But—ah yes, the horn."

"Lilith is strong enough to tear a big man like you apart, and it's almost impossible to sneak up on her with a weapon. A unicorn's horn can cut stone. Lilith was badly wounded and fled to what she believed was a secret retreat. The rest you know."

The Lady put the chess piece back on the board. "The human side of Ilian knew what fear was, after that. She was afraid she might be used to hurt someone else and was disgusted by the way people treat each other. She vowed never to be human again. We used to see her occasionally in our mountain valley, but eventually she just left and never came back."

"Well," the Duke replied, "she lived out the rest of her life in peace, at least. That's more than most champions manage."

"Oh, she might still be out there somewhere, since shapeshifters are immune to disease and the ravages of old age. All she wanted was to be left alone and be allowed to forget, and we honor that wish. We promised her we wouldn't even use our scrying pool to check on her. She earned her privacy."

Their conversation turned to small talk and she told him about her mountain valley, how this time of year she could see the dragons performing their mating flight against the backdrop of the setting sun, how it broke her heart that each year there were fewer of them. He listened, hanging on every word.

Eventually, another clap came from outside the tent, and the same guard stuck his head inside. "Your visitor is here, sir. Shall I allow him in?"

"By all means," the Duke replied. He hesitantly took the

Lady's hand in his. "I hope there will always be a place in this world for innocent unicorns and dragons to dance in the skies. You know better than I that the future isn't always what we want it to be."

The guard allowed a stranger to enter. He was a big, scruffy looking fellow. "It's about time," the man said, looking around the tent. "I've got better things ta do than wait around while ye put the moves on some dame, even if ye are paying me well." He took another look at the Lady. "Although I can see why ye felt it was so important. My apologies, yer Ladyship. I hope my rough talk didn't offend ye."

She pulled back her hand and looked at the stranger, then at the Duke, and back to the stranger. "This is our guide?" she asked.

"Don't let his manners fool you," the Duke replied. "Ambrosius is one of my trusted agents, and he'll get your party across the river and where you need to go." He turned back to the man. "You have what we need?"

The man nodded, pulling a small package and a folded piece of paper out of his pocket. "Yer own package reached me just in time. There's an old maid working in the castle that's got a daughter was thrown in the dungeon, so she helped me out. Valant likes ta take long baths so she had plenty of time ta swap the fake for the real keystone. As for where the folks I came for need ta go, no secret there. It's the mines. There's been a lot of work on the place lately, mostly clearing and widening the tunnels." He handed the package and paper to the Lady. "I've marked a back entrance on the map that doesn't seem ta be blocked."

The Lady looked in the package, then unfolded and studied the map. "This is everything you promised. We'll pack light, leave this evening, and head straight for the mines once we're across. Every moment we delay allows Lilith to grow stronger. My Sisterself will let Rose and Tom know, momentarily. Right now, Rose is explaining to some guards that they are certainly *not* going to arrest Tom for assaulting one of their officers. Tom is sulking behind her and claiming the man started it while my Sisterself is trying her best not to laugh. I wish the King hadn't given Tom that sword."

The Weaving

***

Ambrosius watched the Lady leave. "Budrich," he remarked, "am I wrong, or did that dame see right through my hired riverman act?"

"Dame?"

"It's a term of endearment the locals use. Short for damsel, as in distress," he explained.

The Duke shook his head. "Save it for when you're in character. She noticed the resemblance, of course. If you shaved and cleaned up a bit, and I lost a lot of weight, we'd both look like our father. Her reaction was more than that, though. She recognized you as the man who captured her Sisterself. In turn, the Lady in the dungeon is now aware you are my agent, and the Ladies are trying to anticipate our next move and planning their own surprises. You must always keep in mind that what one Lady knows, they all know. That's a remarkably useful ability. So, Ambrosius, where's the other item I asked for?"

"Your suspicions were correct. Valant probably didn't kill his brother." He handed the Duke another small package and sat down in the vacant chair, looking at the chessboard. "You'll have to tell me some day how you knew where to look for the missing Lady. You won't believe how close I came to getting her killed. She's the bravest woman I've ever seen. She knows how to inspire loyalty, too. There was a man with her, some fella she tried her best to convince me was only hired help. He was going to throw himself into a hail of arrows to save her."

He leaned in, studying the board. "Now, this is an interesting puzzle. An unfinished game neither of you were looking at, and neither king is knocked over, so you've called it a draw. I could hold you off for another ten moves at least, but you'll win in the end, as always. I can't believe you'd pretend to lose or draw, no matter how pretty the opponent. This Lady must be remarkable, indeed."

The Duke snorted and sat back, folding his hands across his stomach in a familiar manner. "No, I didn't throw the game. She really is that good. Or should I say *they* are really that good? And as

Gerald Gostlow

it stands, I could beat you in eight moves, and that's using our private rules of play. Your move. We have time enough, while our band of heroes make ready. You like puzzles? Then answer me this—how do you beat someone in a game if that person can see your every move before you decide to make it?"

Ambrosius moved the knight back to a safe corner, and when he took his hand away, a pawn previously taken off the board somehow reappeared next to its king. "You might play so well, the Lady still couldn't counter your moves, even if she knew what you were going to do."

The Duke moved his remaining rook and when his big hand withdrew the resurrected white pawn had been changed to a black piece, threatening the king it once guarded.

"Not if the Lady is a skilled player in her own right," the Duke said in return. "First, it occurred to me that the Ladies must not be able to see their own futures. No one could have that ability and remain human, and the Lady you just met is very much a woman. That means as long as every move I make involves a Lady, I can stay in their blind spot. Then I redefine what it means to win our game with Valant. My goal is to use the Ladies to force a stalemate, with the fewest pieces lost from the board on either side."

The Duke looked up at his younger brother. "Be careful out there, Ambrosius. This game involves real people. I'd hate it if something happened to you or that Lady, and our niece is still in that dungeon. I hope the Ladies can help her, but I've done all I can from here."

"If it comes down to it, I'll bust my cover wide open to help Bea. She's my niece, too, you know." Ambrosius rubbed his eyes and yawned. "This running back and forth is wearing me out. I'm getting too old for this. I might let someone else save the world next time. By the way, you look like you've lost a few pounds. Maybe you're trying to impress a certain Lady?"

Ambrosius was only kidding his older brother, and was amazed to see the man reduced to stammering like a boy with his first crush. Who would have thought the great Duke had finally fallen in love?

Nineteen

"They're gone, sir!"

"Shut up! Can't you see I'm busy?" The jailor didn't look to see who was talking. He was keeping a close eye on the guard holding the dice. "Will you roll, already?" he asked the man. "You'll wear the spots off with all that shaking!" The cup made a final rattle before being slammed open-end down on the table. The men leaned in, holding their breaths. The cup was removed.

"Dragon eyes, by the Gods!" There were groans all around as the cup holder scooped up his winnings, the last of the jailor's monthly pay in the pile. He finally looked up to see who had dared interrupt the game. It was the new recruit, sent down to work the dungeons after being caught stealing.

"Now what are you talking about?" he yelled. "Who's gone? Aren't you supposed to be feeding the prisoners?"

"It's the women, sir," the guard said. "When I went to slide the food in just now, I saw—they're gone!"

"Gone? They're dead? All of them?" Suicide was not unheard of, but he'd expect that from men facing torture—not from a bunch of pampered skirts who might be released one day.

"No, sir, I mean *gone*, as in not here. Well, most of them. That scary one with the dark hair is still there, the one you call Princess."

The jailor sighed and got to his feet. Of course they weren't gone. The only key to the cell was hanging on his belt

None of the other crew volunteered to come along, their attention still on the all important dice and the money they were winning or losing. The jailor followed the guard back to the women's cell. He'd stayed away from this section the past few days, not even peeking in to watch the women using the slop bucket. It had been made clear by his bosses that these dames were not to be molested.

After his little adventure with the maid, he started having second thoughts about the wisdom of his actions. It wasn't really rape, since the girl had—however reluctantly—agreed, but his superiors might not see it that way. The other men would not hesitate to tell on him, not if they thought there might be something in it for them. It was better to just keep away for now and protest his innocence if accused.

He came to the cell and looked through the opening in the door. It did appear there was only one woman in there, the nameless prisoner he'd dubbed Princess. She was standing in the center of the room, looking back at him.

"You women in there!" he yelled. "Get out where I can see you. Now! Or you'll get no food!"

The woman just stood there, staring off into space. He told the guard to stand back while he unlocked the cell. The missing women would be pressed up against the wall on either side of the door. It was a trick other prisoners had tried, each one thinking it was original and would fool an experienced jailor. They'd try to jump him when he walked in.

He was going to enjoy this.

One dame was older than his mother, another half dead from getting her head caved in. That left Princess and the maid, neither one strong enough to worry about. The stupid skirts didn't even think to use the buckets as weapons—those were still sitting in plain sight. He'd show them who was boss.

He opened the door and jumped in, past where they'd expect to attack. He turned, seeing no one else standing in the cell. He looked around, not believing his eyes. The room only contained buckets and several small piles of straw and thin blankets, nothing big enough to hide even one woman. The little window set near the ceiling still had its bars and was barely big enough to fit a head through. He turned back to the woman.

"Where did they go? Someone had to sneak them out. Who was it? One of the guards? Someone on the outside bribe him?" His

The Weaving

hands were clenched as he struggled to hold back his temper. He'd killed prisoners for less.

She continued to stare past him like he was beneath her notice. Good. He had his excuse to beat it out of her. His superiors couldn't blame him for doing his job. He struck out, backhanding her across the face with enough force to snap her head back.

She put her finger to her lip, wiping off a drop of blood. She looked at him and something changed in her eyes. He'd gotten her attention, finally.

"I was not to be hurt in any way, by the Prince or his men," she said. "The deal is broken. I am no longer bound by my oath."

Not what he wanted to hear. If a little slap didn't make her cooperate, he'd use his fist. This time he missed as she picked that moment to lean just a little to one side.

He staggered forward, thrown off balance by the force behind his punch. She grabbed him by the wrist, stuck out her leg, and he was upside down in the air. He landed on his back, pain lancing up his arm as she twisted and something popped. The room started spinning, and it felt like every muscle in his body turned to liquid. He was covered by some sort of heavy cloth. The jailor struggled out from under it and looked up at the woman standing over him. He tried to ask her what she'd done.

"*Ribbit?*" was all he could get out.

***

The three skunks huddling under the straw and blankets burst out of their hiding place. One pounced on the frog, the amphibian trying to squirm out of a pile of clothes. It only had time for a startled croak before sharp teeth ended its life. The skunk tore at the small carcass, not stopping until it was a pile of green bits. The Lady waited until the skunk was stomping the bits into tiny smears before speaking.

"That's enough. You have your revenge. Go join the Duchess. And don't you dare point that tail at me, girl!"

Gerald Ghostlow

The maid had been getting ready to let loose with a spray as a parting gift to the hated prison cell. The skunk walked over to join the other two, who had the guard outside backed up against the wall opposite the cell door. He had witnessed the jailor's fate and was frozen in place, trembling and staring at the skunks. His sword shook as he held it out, pointing it back and forth between the animals as they hissed and made little hops just out of range. The Lady walked out of the cell and he shook even more as he tried to divide his attention between all four threats.

She glared at him and held out her arms. "Ooga booga!" she intoned dramatically, wiggling her fingers. The man's eyes rolled up as he fainted.

One of the skunks blurred and became Beatrice. She bent and picked up the fallen sword, then went back into the cell and rummaged through the pile of clothes the jailor had worn, finding the ring full of keys. When she straightened up to face the Lady, she was shaking with laughter.

"Ooga booga? They never taught that spell in class. Remarkably effective, though." She pointed the sword at the unconscious guard. "What do we do with him?"

"Help me drag him into the cell." The two women finished their chore and stood, catching their breaths, while the Duchess and maid kept an eye out for other guards.

Beatrice examined the keys. "This big one must be to the outside door. Are you sure you won't go with us? For that matter, I still have a score to settle with the Prince. I'll get my two skunks to a safe hiding place and come join you."

"No, you follow my plan," the Lady replied. "Use your talents to find your uncle Ambrosius and he'll take it from there. If a witch named Rose is still with him, she can remove your spells from the other women. If not, they'll just have to remain skunks for a while longer. I doubt anyone will bother them in that form."

"Rose? The Witch of the Woods?" Beatrice looked pleased, then worried. "I met her before, briefly. I think I left a good impression, but she's not going to think highly of a witch who can't remove her own spells."

"You might be surprised. Tell her the Ladies are in your debt, then listen to her reply."

"Wait—you're one of *those* Ladies?" Beatrice looked stunned. "But there has to be three of you—don't there? Not that I don't believe you...um, Lady. I thought you were...I don't know what I thought. Lady, please excuse me for laughing at you. I mean, I didn't laugh at you, only at your silly...I mean..."

"That's enough of that," the Lady cut in. "We'd rather have Rose yelling at us again than listen to, potentially, the second most powerful witch in the land gush over the honor of meeting us. If you've finished bowing before our greatness, could we get started? We're not out of the dungeon, yet."

***

Beatrice spelled herself back to skunk form and led her troops down the corridor, tail at attention, making sure the guards got a good look at the trouble coming their way. The men decided they weren't about to battle skunks that magically appear in dungeons or the powerful woman behind them. Since the missing jailor had the only keys to the outside, they retreated to the office and barred the door.

Once outside, Beatrice took a deep breath in the clean air and drew upon the strength of the life around her. She was relieved to be out of that place, but the humiliation of needing to be rescued still burned. "I swear by the Goddess, I will never again let myself be locked away from the open sky! Never! I will practice, and learn, and grow stronger. I will become such a power in the land that no one will dare lay a hand on me!"

The Lady nodded. "One day, if you wish, come to us in our mountain home. I will teach you a way of fighting that uses your enemy's strength against them. Combined with your other talents, you will be able to teach anyone who dares lay a hand on you a lesson in manners."

"I...thank you, Lady," Beatrice replied. She felt like bowing, but instead clasped the woman's hand in parting, remembering the Lady's attitude about worship. The great power had just volunteered to teach her! She marched off with her two skunks. First, she had to get as far away from the castle as possible, and then use her magic to find Uncle Ambry and make her way to him without being seen by anyone. She couldn't wait to tell him her story.

Wait...the Lady said...second most powerful witch? Beatrice decided she must have misheard in the excitement.

***

The Lady stood enjoying the fresh air and sunshine. Her Sisterselfs paused in what they were doing to give her a mental hug, sharing her joy at being out of that place of misery. They were slightly behind schedule, but would be joining her soon. Ambrosius was with them and would be notified his niece was safe and on her way.

Then she walked back into the dungeon and locked the outer door behind her, causing panic again in the men who were just emerging from the office. The young guard had recovered and joined his comrades, telling them about the jailor's fate at the hands of this woman. She searched through the keys for the one that would open the door to the stairs, then climbed up to the castle proper, emerging into the kitchen. The Lady helped herself to the food sitting on the counter. She hadn't been able to bring herself to eat much the past few days. Even the toad stew from the forest was preferable to prison slop.

The kitchen staff didn't know what to make of her, but the cook finally decided to let her do what she wanted until a guard arrived, just to be on the safe side. It wasn't long before they set a table in the corner and furnished it with a plate full of steaming food and glass of wine, just to get her out of their way.

She took her time eating, and at one point, saw a head poke out of the open stairway to the dungeon. She waved a fork in that direction and it disappeared. From the loud banging that followed,

The Weaving

the guards were trying to break down the outer door. By the time they managed to do so and spread the alarm, Beatrice and friends would be across the moat and long gone.

Satisfied, the Lady handed out complements all around, then strolled out of the kitchen, munching on a roll. She followed the servants carrying fancy silver dinner trays, figuring Valant would be at the receiving end. She was going to have a serious discussion with that man about monsters and keystones and the proper way to treat a Lady.

Twenty

The small band of would-be heroes stood on the riverbank, waiting for the sun to touch the treetops in its journey across the sky. Their guide was concerned that, even at nightfall, the moon would be so bright a sentry might spot them on the open water. They needed additional cover and the two Ladies volunteered to provide it.

One of the Ladies casted doubtful looks at the bottle Bertram pulled out of his robe. "It will work," he insisted. "Once you do your part, my spell will keep the magic bottled up. It'll keep repeating itself until I let it go."

She shrugged, walked over to join her Sisterself. They held hands and looked at the river. The air was cooling, causing a slight mist to form over the warmer water. Bertram watched the Ladies at work, a rare opportunity he didn't want to miss. They started humming, but unlike Rose's song of power, their pure harmony somehow carried the smell of rain showers. Gradually, the air grew damper, the mist rising from the water. Eventually, Bertram was surrounded by a fog so thick it was impossible to see beyond the little clearing.

The guide, a man introduced as Ambrosius, spoke. "Ah, m'Ladies, I believe that's plenty. A patch of fog along the river is not unheard of this time 'a year, but best not overdo it. The other rivermen would know it ain't natural, but they won't talk. Anything more might cause the sentries ta get suspicious."

The Ladies released each other's hands. The wizard rattled off a trap spell and reached out with his power, watching a tiny bit of the fog swirl as it was sucked into the bottle. He put the stopper in and grunted with satisfaction.

"That's it," he said. "Now, every evening at this time, it will get

The Weaving

foggy like this for as long as I need it. I wish I knew how you Ladies do that, make such a huge change in the magic of the world without effort. It's an unbreakable rule that large effects require strong spells. I didn't feel any spellcasting at all."

The Lady shrugged again. "Water enjoys changing form. You just have to get its attention and know how to speak its language."

Bertram shook his head. First Rose claims magic is all in her mind, then the Ladies tell him they can talk to a glass of water. He understood all about professional secrets, but if they didn't want to tell him, they should just say so.

"I'll let the King know you're on your way," he said. "Good luck. I hate not coming along, but I have my orders. If word gets back that you've failed, I'll take it upon myself to rescue any survivors from Lilith."

The guide snorted. "If we fail, I don't think ye'll find anyone left ta rescue where we be a'going. But if ye happen to spot someone runnin' as far and fast as he can away from that place, it'll be me."

***

"Tom, you are staying on this side of the river, like it or not." Rose was through with arguing. It was time for her to put her foot down.

"You can't change your mind now!" Tom insisted. "I'm packed and ready to go."

"I never intended on letting you get this far," she insisted back. "I've been waiting for you to come to your senses on your own. There is no reason for you to put yourself in danger, and nothing you could do to help me. You're going back to the camp."

"Honey, I'm going with you, and that's final," Tom replied. "I have to."

"You keep saying that. Why do you have to go? At least tell me that much."

He stood there holding their packs, looking stubborn. "I can't tell you why," was all he said. "You'll just have to trust me. I won't get in your way." He looked over at the Ladies, his glance telling her who to blame. She turned to confront the one who'd started this mess.

"So, my husband's missing past can be found over there? What did you see in the water? Is Tom going to discover he's a bastard son of King Morgan and inherit the throne? Well, his quest can wait until later. Tell him!"

"Rose, you should know better," the Lady said. "The questions and answers are private. Your husband asked you to trust him. If you're not smart enough to do this, that's your fault, not mine. Your marital problems are not my concern."

Rose walked over to the Lady, waving off Tom's protest. "I'm tired of your mouth," Rose spat, glaring at the woman, "and I won't take marital advice from a woman with no man of her own. Your reputation might make other people put up with your attitude, but not me. When this is over, I will teach you proper respect for the Witch of the Woods, even if I have to take on all three of you."

The Lady started to reply, but then stopped, getting the blank stare that told Rose the other Ladies were stepping in. "We apologize, Witch of the Woods," said the other Lady. "For what it's worth, two of us agree you have cause to complain. If you still want a duel with this Sisterself after our journey is over, we agree, and will not interfere."

Then the blonde Lady took a deep breath, and Rose saw what she could swear was sadness, maybe even pity, in the woman's face. "I am speaking for myself, now," the Lady said. "I hold you no ill will, Rose. I did have a husband, a very long time ago. I'd forgotten what it was like. I ask you to accept my apology, even though my comments were inexcusable. I consider you to be the greatest Witch of the Woods that has ever lived, and I've met them all. I'd rather be your friend than your enemy."

The Lady's apology seemed heartfelt and the praise was a definite change in attitude. Mollified, Rose looked back at Tom, who was down at the boat engaged in conversation with their guide. "I guess I can't force him to stay," she said. She watched Tom buckle a sword around his waist, wearing it in such a way it was sure to get tangled in his legs. She shook her head. "He's trying so hard to be a

The Weaving

warrior. He doesn't need to prove anything to me. I see strength in Tom that is hidden to most people, including himself. I can't stand the thought of him being hurt."

"I know how you feel," the Lady said. "In my case, I was the leader of my clan and there were always more battles to fight. I put my husband in charge of protecting the camp while I was gone. One day I came back...well, as I said, that was a long time ago."

Rose sighed and went to get in the boat with Tom. She had to hide these people from a hostile Prince and his army, defeat a monster that can't be killed, all while making sure Tom didn't get himself or the group killed by trying to help.

It's going to be an exhausting trip.

***

Tom handed the last pack to the guide. The boat shifted under him when he stepped into it, making him lose his balance. He was about to fall backwards into the river when the guide grabbed the front of his shirt, which unfortunately included a handful of the chest hair underneath.

"Careful, fella," the man said. "Taking a swim right now would give your wife another excuse to leave you behind. The name's Ambrosius, by the way."

"Thanks for the save," Tom replied, rubbing his sore chest and blinking away tears. He sat down in the center of the boat. "I'm Tom, pleased to meet you. Rose will settle down once I prove to her that I'm not going to do anything stupid and get us all killed."

Ambrosius chuckled. "Don't count on it. I've never met a wife yet who wasn't sure she knew her man inside and out."

Tom glanced over to where Rose and the Lady were still going at it. "Those two have been at each other's throats since all this started. I wish I knew why."

Ambrosius shrugged. "Women can be fighting one moment and best friends the next. I've learned not to get involved. I doubt those two will let their differences get in the way of our mission."

Gerald Gostlow

Tom listened to Ambrosius speaking and realized there was something different. "Didn't you talk funny before?" he asked.

"Ye mean ta say where's the crusty riverman?" He grinned. "He's not needed anymore, now that it's just the five of us."

The women finally came over, acting as if nothing had happened. Ambrosius raised an eyebrow, as if to say, 'I told you so'. Rose didn't mention her objections to Tom coming along, accepting his help without comment while getting into the boat. He received a peck on the cheek before she sat down next to him. Neither Lady needed help, barely rocking the craft as they boarded. Tom would bet the river was afraid to let these two get wet against their wishes.

The boat was long and narrow, designed to move swiftly, with one man at the oars. Their guide seemed confident of where he was going. They glided through the fog, his strokes barely making a splash in the slow current. Tom was starting to get chilled, his shirt soaking up the dampness. Rose noticed and picked up her pack, rummaging around and pulling out a jacket. He pulled it on and jammed his hands into the deep side pockets to warm them, wondering how the others could get by with so little covering against their skin. Soon he could smell the pine trees and hear the lapping of waves against the opposite riverbank, along with something else that should concern them. As usual, none of the others seemed to notice what was increasingly obvious to his senses.

"Psst!" he whispered. No one paid any attention. Not wanting to make any noise, he tapped Ambrosius on the knee to get his attention. He pointed toward the shore and tried to imitate someone sleeping. Ambrosius looked puzzled and stopped his rowing and listened for what had alarmed Tom. Then he shrugged, shook his head, and was about to continue when Rose stopped him again. She shut her eyes, doing her reaching out business. Then she nodded her head and pointed to where they were heading, doing a much better acting job to let their guide know someone was out there.

Ambrosius nodded his understanding. He let the boat glide the rest of the way in, silently putting the oars away and taking out his boot knife. The blonde Lady stopped him just as he was about to

The Weaving

climb out of the boat to deal with the threat. Frustrated, he sat back and watched her leap gracefully onto shore.

The Lady disappeared into the fog. Tom heard a muffled grunt and the snoring stopped. The Lady reappeared, holding a kicking frog by the legs. She held it up, whispered something in its ear. It stopped struggling and she set it down. It hopped into the river and swam away.

"He had a small campfire on the other side of those bushes," she explained. "I told him he'd return to human once he reached the opposite shore. He doesn't know he'll be captured by the King's guards soon after."

"It's safe now," Rose said. "That was the only sentry anywhere within hearing range. Let's go get warm while our guide hides the boat and brings the horses. The raccoon clan will warn me if anyone else comes this way."

The women disappeared into the fog, leaving the men to fetch the supplies. Tom and Ambrosius sat and looked at each other.

"You know," Ambrosius said, "I've never felt so useless in my life. Between your hearing, Rose's seeing, and the Ladies doing whatever it is they do, I might as well be a pack mule."

Tom got to his feet and stumbled when his legs got tangled in his sword, stepping into the water instead of on solid ground. His foot sank into deep mud, leaving him up to his knee in the river and with the other leg twisted helplessly under the seat. The edge of the boat was pressed painfully between his legs, keeping him trapped in that position.

He looked at Ambrosius. "Stop snickering and help me out of this muck. I think sometimes Rose only keeps me around because I make her laugh. I bet she gets the hiccups again over this one."

***

The Ladies had only smiled upon seeing Tom squishing his way into the little sheltered campsite, carrying the waterlogged boot. Rose didn't quite get the hiccups, but she didn't hold back her laughter, either, as she came over to help.

Ambrosius left to get the horses, leaving Tom to dry by the fire. He thought about what he'd learned about his group so far. He needed to know their limits, if he could trust them with his life, if need be.

It was hard to imagine any limits to this bunch.

Since he'd already met the first Lady, he was expecting to be equally impressed by the other two and wasn't disappointed. He figured this Lilith was in for trouble when all three women finally arrived.

Rose was easy to understand. She was an agent of her Goddess and had survived this long because she was good at walking into a dangerous situation and coming out alive.

Then there was Tom. Ambrosius arrived at the riverman's house, wondering what the Ladies could be thinking by dragging the man along. Tom was a mystery, in more ways than one. He could be oblivious to the worst commotion going on under his nose and then spot someone sleeping in the distance by hearing a quiet snore. Tom seemed as dangerous as a little lost kitten, but Ambrosius had heard all about the beating he'd given a combat officer. It was an interesting puzzle.

Ambrosius whistled, letting the people in the house know he was outside. Their boy came out to help him saddle the horses. Puzzle or not, his band of heroes had to dodge the patrols until daylight and then make their run for the mines. It would only get more dangerous the further along they traveled. He climbed into his saddle, gathered the reins of the other horses, and risked a whoop as he rode off.

This was the most excitement he'd had in years.

Twenty-One

Maynard inspected the doorway to nowhere he'd built in a corner of Lilith's throne room. It was nothing fancy, just two upright wood beams set in the floor with a shorter beam spanning the distance across the top, large enough for one person to walk through. He consulted his sketch again, made back in the forbidden library of the Wizard's Council. He pulled out a string and made some measurements of the beams, checking if the height and width were of the proportions the scroll said were necessary. When it came to wizardry, precision was everything.

Satisfied, he took up a brush and a jar of white paint and began drawing the runes—arcane symbols that would shape the magic force when someone with the talent and a keystone powered it up. He stopped his work when he felt Lilith's touch in his mind, making his hand twitch enough to ruin one of the complex drawings. He turned to see her striding into the chamber, making her usual appearance now that the sun was going down. He fell to his knees, as she'd insisted on being greeted. Lilith seemed in a good mood for a change, was even singing.

"...*You giving up, the Maiden asked, admit I've won the bet...I'll make it fit, the Dragon spit, I'm not defeated yet*...Hello, Maynard. Let's see what you've done." She stood over him, inspecting his work.

"Not finished?" she asked. "You're certainly taking your sweet time about it." She yawned, picking up his notes and looking at the drawings. "You wizards have such a strange way of working with magic. Useful to have around, though. The one who poked his head through to my world managed to kill himself before I could enslave him." She stroked the hair on his head. "I'm glad the wizards of this age are more realistic in their desire for survival."

"It's almost d-d-done, M-Mistress," he replied, "b-but there's a p-problem."

The hand stopped stroking and grabbed his hair, pulling up his head so she could see his face. "Problem? What sort of problem could my pet wizard possibly have when it comes to carrying out my desires?"

"It's the s-spell. The p-p-p..." His speech became entirely stuck and she shook him by her grip on his hair. The pain helped clear his mind. "The portal spell," he managed. "The magic needs the k-k...the amulet to work."

"The keystone?" Lilith shrugged. "Oh, I'd planned on taking that away from my dear Prince, anyway. He hasn't come to visit since I moved out, so it's obvious I can't count on his undying love."

"B-but the keystone protects its owner from you!"

She smiled at him, smoothing his hair back down. "But it doesn't protect him from *you*, my pet. Go see your old employer. Find some excuse to get him in a room by himself—I'd suggest you drive a knife into his back. Surely you have some little spell to overpower one little Prince. Act like a wizard for once. When you get the keystone, bring it to me."

Maynard had never hurt anyone in his life, although he'd received plenty of beatings, first from his father and, later, the children who picked on the skinny, stuttering kid. He thought of the oh-so-confident Prince, who casually tied him up and left him alone back at the cave. He should kill the man for that, if nothing else.

He received another pat on the head. "Such tasty images," Lilith said. "You're coming along nicely. Yes, you might prove worthy to be my High Priest when I establish my temple. What you lack in skill, you make up for in devotion. Finish the portal and get a night's sleep. Then be a good pet and go fetch my keystone, and I might have my elite guard bring you a female slave to share your cold bed. I want you to put it in my hands when I get up tomorrow night. Don't disappoint me."

She withdrew from his mind, satisfied for now. "I'm heading

The Weaving

over to check the larder. My bedslave failed to rise to the occasion yesterday, so I'll need a new one. It's been a few days since I've eaten, anyway."

The larder? Maynard came to his senses with a shudder. This was a monster, not a woman. He needed some way of making sure her new Priest would never end up on the menu, and she had just ordered him to acquire the one object that could provide safety.

***

Lilith returned after changing her bedslaves, noticed Maynard had finished and left. She wiped the blood off her hands and face, tossing the towel to a slave boy and telling him she wasn't to be disturbed. She gave the portal a closer inspection. The one she'd stepped through so long ago was bigger, made of etched and polished metal, but there was no doubt it was the same design.

Lilith walked over to her throne to continue her own construction. What she built there was invisible, but even more important than the portal. She sat and closed her eyes, withdrawing her spirit from the physical world. The body she was wearing slowed its breathing, the heartbeat growing fainter, until anyone checking would swear she was dead.

In fact, the real Lilith was never more alive. She was inside the empty mind of her host body, her spirit's hollow chamber. Only here could she take her true form, that of a woman's head on a spider's body. Lilith reached beneath her swollen abdomen with her front legs, taking the silk emerging from her rear spinners and began weaving. She cast the strands out into space, watching them pass through the shell of a mind and reach out across the land. The strands were composed of digested terror, the tasty fear human minds were so good at producing. Each one was carefully anchored at the center, where she perched.

Once her spinners were again empty, Lilith sat and checked her web. Her many legs lightly caressed the strands, playing them like an impossibly complex musical instrument and reading what they had to say. She saw the world touched by her weaving as a landscape of emotion, one that grew larger as she continued to feed and spin. There was the strong, steady pulse from the slaves in her nearby tunnels, and the more subtle flavor of those people still walking free, their daily fears and nightly terrors betraying their presence. All of the fear flowing into her throne room through the strands was ingested and turned into power. Most was simply stored, called upon when needed to attack. Eventually, there would be enough to start thinking about laying eggs.

But for now, she simply sat in the center of her web and fed. She was finally strong enough to reach the castle, a place where fear came in a thousand varieties. She could pick out the old King, along with other people she'd sunk her fangs into. There was a strong vibration from someplace in the castle, a group of people sharing a common fear. She identified it as a dungeon from the flavor of hopeless despair. For a moment she paused, thinking she'd tasted magic. When some searching of the area didn't bring anything unusual, she remembered the young witch confined to the dungeon when the Prince took over. If the girl hadn't escaped and made it out of the kingdom by now, she wasn't much of a witch.

Before Lilith withdrew, she revisited the King. She reversed the flow, sending more terror into his feeble mind. There was a brief flare of emotion and the strand went dead. Scratch one King off the list. She did it out of spite, only because Valant had insisted the old man not be killed.

Lilith brought her host body back to life. She felt invigorated, ready to take on the world. Life was good in this world of plenty. A thousand years of darkness had taught her patience. She'd taken precautions in case the Ladies showed up looking for another fight, but Lilith preferred they stay in their little mountain valley for now. She'd sit in her place of power, growing steadily stronger as her web grew ever larger. They'd have their rematch once she became so powerful not even the Gods could defeat her.

She stood and stretched. There was still a busy night ahead, starting with a visit to the kitchen. She'd decided to experiment with

The Weaving

having her meat cooked for a change. The kitchen slaves might balk and need some discipline. She'd have them begin with the remains of the used-up slave she'd just butchered. Maybe a simple rib platter, lightly seasoned and a side garnish.

Lilith strolled out of her throne room, singing the tune her old bedslave had taught her. She'd love to meet this Minstrel who wrote it. She could show this writer of ballads some tricks unmentioned in the song and have him compose a tune in her honor. It was about time people appreciated her finer qualities.

***

Valant sat in his war room, receiving the final readiness report from the Generals about his special army units. He was about to call a lunch break when a commotion in the outer office disturbed them. He ordered the guard standing at the door to find out what was going on and returned to going over lists. The guard opened the door and walked out, yelling for silence. There was a brief pause in the thumping and banging, then the shouting and noise became worse. The meeting was interrupted again when bits and pieces of hardware began to sail back into the room, beginning with a broken spear and ending with a dented helmet.

Valant reacted quickly, gripping the edge of the heavy table and upending it. He crouched behind the cover and drew his sword, shouting orders for his men to form a line. The old soldiers ignored him, huddling in the farthest corner of the room and yelling for help of their own. He watched the doorway and waited for the assassins to make their rush.

So this is how it ends. He decided there was no point in delaying the inevitable. "You out there!" he yelled, standing up and walking around the table. "Come and get me, if you dare!" He gripped the sword tighter. It would be told in the history books that Prince Valant went down fighting for his destiny to the bitter end. Let that Prince Valiant guy top this.

The noise from outside stopped and a woman walked into the

room, dusting off her hands. She had the same long black hair as Lilith, but this young woman was much shorter and had a slight tan. Did Lilith have offspring?

That was a scary thought.

He circled around, keeping his distance, and peeked through the doorway. There were several guards moaning and twitching on the floor, their arms and legs twisted in unnatural positions. This must be some kin to the Lilith monster. He pulled the keystone out from under his shirt, just in case it had power over this one and prepared to take on the demon.

"My apologies for the rude entrance," the woman said. "Your men refused to convey my message requesting an immediate audience, then became forceful in their insistence I leave. It's not my place to criticize, but your staff is being derelict. I assume the only reason you didn't call on me in the dungeon was because they forgot to tell you of my arrival."

The Ladies. Ambrosius had sent word of a partially successful mission. He'd put off dealing with the Lady when told of her arrival at the dungeon, since she obviously wasn't going anywhere. He was wrong on that count. Apparently, this woman was in the habit of going wherever she wanted, when she wanted.

"My sincere apologies," he said, sheathing his sword. "In this case, the dereliction was my fault. There is just so much to do when a new administration steps in and I'm trying to get an army built. On top of that my father, the King, died last night in his sleep, so now I have a funeral to plan. I hope my forgetfulness didn't cause you too much discomfort. Excuse me while I take care of this." A guard was groaning and crying, blubbering something about his leg. Valant told his Generals to come out of the corner, get help for the wounded and send in some staff to straighten things.

The Lady stood in the center of the room, waiting for something. Maybe an invitation to sit? He looked around at the overturned table and chairs. "Why don't we go to my private quarters for our chat?" he asked. "It's time for lunch, anyway. I'll have the staff bring another place setting."

The Weaving

She followed him back out of the room, stepping over the fallen men. "Their shoulders are only dislocated," she said in passing. "I did break this one's leg when he made an unnecessary insult about my parentage. There was no need to get personal. I've already eaten, thank you, but some tea would be nice. My Sisterselfs have been enjoying a special blend lately, so I've acquired the taste."

Valant led her down the hall to his personal suite, trying to remember everything Lilith had told him about these Ladies. One thing he did recall. "I've heard your touch can turn people into frogs. If that's true, then wasn't your assault on my guards doing things the hard way?"

"Perhaps," she replied, "but I'd rather not use my magic if at all possible. I can feel Lilith's web all around us, although she's probably asleep right now."

They reached his quarters, where the food was already laid out on the sideboard. The chamberlain was sent for tea, then sent out again to round up a maid and have a room prepared for the Lady when he discovered she'd be staying a night or two.

"Do you mind if I eat while we get acquainted?" Valant asked. She shook her head, spooning sugar into her cup. The Lady had a sweet tooth. He liked this woman. She was cultured, from the upper class, perhaps even nobility. It showed in the little things, like how she responded to the servants and knowing proper manners without hesitation.

"You do know there's a certain...someone...who would prefer to have you slowly and painfully executed?" he said. "I'm taking a chance hiding you. I know what she's capable of and would rather not have to face her wrath while I'm trying to gain an Empire."

"Her name is Lilith," the Lady replied. "You can say it. She can't hear you. No, you don't want to face her wrath, but you will. Sooner than you'd like, unless you listen to what I have to say."

They were interrupted by the chamberlain barging in, saying there was an emergency. A mighty wizard had showed up and turned the jailor and half the prisoners in the dungeon into skunks, and the castle was in an uproar as sightings of the animals were coming

Gerald Ghostlow

in from staff on every floor. The castle might have to be evacuated. Valant looked at the Lady who was sitting quietly, nibbling on a biscuit and sipping her tea. "Lady, could you tell me to what extent this is true?" he asked. "I remember we did have a deal about you not escaping. To my knowledge, my end of the bargain was kept."

The Lady confirmed several prisoners were now absent, advised him the jailor was dead, and denied any skunks or wizards were wandering the halls. He told the chamberlain to pass this information on and restore order, then sat back and listened to the Lady tell him about the jailor's conduct. She left out the whereabouts of the escaped women.

"You have my sincere apologies," he said when she'd finished. "Please believe me when I say if you hadn't killed the jailor, I would have sent him to the gallows for what he did. I don't allow rape under any circumstance. That sort of behavior cannot be tolerated if a King is to maintain order among his subjects. As for the man striking you, I'd have to say he was doing his job. I admire how you brought that about. I should have issued more exact orders about your treatment."

He dabbed his mouth with a napkin, then sat back and poured a cup of tea for himself, although it wasn't his favorite drink. "Now, you're here about Lilith. It's true I want her gone. Reports indicate an alarming growth in missing persons since she arrived, but so far it's mostly confined to men who would probably end up in my dungeon, anyway. Still, those subjects belong to me and I should be the one deciding their fate. Why would you help me? Aren't you working for King Justin?"

The Lady leaned forward. "First of all," she said, "we Ladies don't care if you or Justin or the town idiot rules this land. Kingdoms and rulers come and go, and you're neither the best nor worst of the people who have assumed authority over the centuries. This squabble between Kings is not our concern. You did free Lilith from her prison, but the wizard Maynard is the one responsible and will soon get what he deserves."

Valant was taken aback by the change in the Lady. It was easy to forget this slight woman sipping tea was some sort of immortal

The Weaving

demigod equal to Lilith. "Alright," he said. "So I've done enough damage and I'll behave now." He pulled out the keystone again. "If you're going to fight Lilith, you'll want this. That must be why you took the risk of allowing yourself to be captured. What will you offer me in exchange for my only protection against the demon?"

She laughed. "Being captured was not part of my plans, believe me. Nor do I have to bargain for what doesn't belong to you in the first place. I was going to sneak into the castle and take it from you by force. It turns out, we already have the keystone. You're wearing a copy. The Duke managed to get his hands on a forgery and his agent performed a switch while I was locked away."

The Lady frowned at the sugar left in the bottom of the now empty cup and reached for a spoon. "The deal we Ladies offer is only this—a hot bath and lodging until I'm ready to join my Sisterselfs, along with the return of my horses and supplies. In exchange, we will do our best to remove Lilith from your kingdom. I'll even throw in some advice. Don't let Lilith catch you without the real keystone. That thing wouldn't fool her for a moment."

Valant looked at the amulet he'd placed so much faith in. Yes, someone in housekeeping could have performed the switch while he was taking a bath. Should he believe the Lady? He'd studied the thing soon after acquiring it and it didn't look any different. He held it to the light and looked closer, noticing the absence of slight wear marks and scratches he knew were present before. This was, indeed, a fake.

He set the useless charm on the table in front of the Lady. "It's a deal. I would have given you this for the promise of destroying Lilith, anyway. If she wants it bad enough, all she has to do is send assassins to get it for her. There should be a maid waiting in the hall and she'll take care of all your needs. I wish you luck in your coming battle with the monster."

He stood and tossed his napkin on the plate. "Now, if our business is finished, I'll escort you to the door and be on my way. I still have a lot of work to do, starting with rounding up the Generals and having them all hanged. Cowardice will never be tolerated in my army, no matter the rank. This will serve as a warning to the next set of Generals I promote."

***

"Sorry, sir. The Prince isn't in his rooms. He just left. You might be able to catch him before he leaves the residential wing."

Maynard looked up and down the long hallway, but all he saw was a girl standing next to the mouthy old maid. The girl was staring at him and smiling, looking pleased. Then she said something to the maid and was escorted on down the hall. Must be someone just hired. He felt like he should know this young lady. Maybe she was one of the girls he'd picked up in a tavern with his fake jewelry scam.

He turned back to the guard, wondering if anything else would delay his finding the Prince. He'd arrived at the castle to find the drawbridge raised and new security measures in effect because the old King had died. When he did get inside, it was to discover everyone running around, yelling about wizards and skunks. The mention of an invading wizard made him hide in his old room, but it turned out to be a false alarm. Then some General grabbed him and started yelling about a monster running loose, killing guards left and right. Maynard had escaped from the madman, but now the Prince had finished eating and there was no telling where he was. The knife tucked inside his robe was a constant reminder of his mission and Lilith had been specific about wanting it done today.

"Look," he told the guard, "I can't chase him all over the castle. Why don't I just wait here for a while in case he comes back?"

The guard looked inside the open door, where the staff was cleaning up the room. "Well, I guess you can go in," he said, "but only until the maids get done. After that, I gotta lock the door again and you can't be in there."

Maynard walked in, looking for a place to get comfortable and be out of the way. He saw the dishes from lunch hadn't yet been cleared, and went over to see if there was anything left to eat.

Then he saw the keystone sitting on the table. Valant must have taken it off and forgotten to put it back on.

The Weaving

He stood and stared at it, not believing his good fortune.

He looked around for witnesses. The two maids were dusting and chatting on the other side of the room, paying no attention. He glanced back at the door, but the guard had his back turned.

Maynard scooped up the keystone and stuffed it in the hidden pocket next to the knife. He whistled as he walked back out the door, telling the guard he'd changed his mind about waiting. All he had to do was get out of the castle before the Prince discovered the theft.

It was that easy.

He'd kill Valant later. Come to think of it, why should he take the risk? A High Priest with a protective amulet could tell Lilith to do her own dirty work.

Tonight, when the demon strutted into her thrown room, she'd find him wearing the keystone. He'd present a list of demands, from getting a harem of women slaves to her stopping her irritating habit of calling him a pet.

Fate had finally chosen to smile upon him. At long last, Maynard the mighty wizard was going to get what he deserved.

Twenty-Two

Rose's animal friends warned her of a patrol coming their way. Since one missing sentry might not raise an alarm, Ambrosius had the group erase all sign of their visit and tried to make it look like the man fell into the river, complete with empty wineskin on the bank. He led them to a more secure campsite, not far from the river, where they could spend the night in relative comfort.

The next morning, Ambrosius watched the witch perform some magic she claimed would allow them safe travel for the second stage of their journey. Rose hummed a soft tune as she walked up to each person in turn, waving her hands around as if she was covering everyone with an invisible blanket. Then she stood back and whispered something into her cupped hands. When she threw up her arms, the Ladies, Tom and Rose shimmered in the bright sun and were replaced by members of a guard patrol. He examined his companions with a critical eye. It was impressive enough he was startled to hear a Lady's voice coming out of a bearded man's mouth.

Instead of slinking around in the shadows, looking suspicious and being noticed, they were just another guard patrol on their way back from the front line. Ambrosius had papers showing he worked for the Prince and was known on these roads, so if they met someone, he did the talking. The rest of the band just acted unfriendly and were left alone.

They reached the vicinity of the castle on the second day and Ambrosius decided to make camp well before nightfall. Rose hadn't complained, but Tom had taken Ambrosius aside and told him she needed a break. Her illusion spells required constant attention, unlike a permanent change. It would have been easier for her to transform the people into horses for the trip. Rose gave a sigh of relief as they

The Weaving

turned back into themselves after Ambrosius led them to a secluded hideaway.

Everyone was hungry, so eating was first on the list.

***

Tom finished stacking wood for the fire and examined the hard lump of something he'd been handed. "I give up," he said. "What is it?"

"Meal, complete, one each. Just add water," Ambrosius said. "Standard rations for soldiers on the march. Guaranteed to take up little space in your pack, stay edible for months as long as it doesn't get wet, and provide enough nourishment you can march another day."

Tom sniffed the thing. It smelled vile and had the consistency of a rock. There was no way it was going near his stomach. "The King still has an army after handing out these?"

"Well, I said they were standard rations, not that anyone willingly eats the stuff. You scrounge what you can off the land. The men call them bricks. Saying 'time to eat the brick' is army slang for going into a desperate situation. I know of one garrison besieged by a raiding party that ran out of arrows and held out until help arrived by throwing these at the enemy. More than one bandit met his death that day, felled by a brick!"

This last was too much to believe, and Tom tucked the thing in his pocket. "Next you'll be telling me the men build their garrisons out of them. Alright, you've had your fun." He reached into his own pack, and pulled out a small cooking pot. Inside were some of Rose's journey cakes, sealed by cloth wrappings dipped in beeswax. He broke one open and the nut and honey aroma made his mouth water. He looked at Ambrosius, seeing the same reaction.

"Here," he said, breaking it in two and handing Ambrosius a piece. "This is what the better half eats when we're on the march. It'll take the edge off your appetite until supper's ready. I'll go back down to the stream and get some fresh water." He gathered up the canteens and waved to Rose and the Ladies, who were strolling back into the campsite. They were carrying armloads of roots, mushrooms, and other plants to be cooked into one of Rose's vegetable stews.

"Happy Samhain, dear!" Rose called. All three women giggled and whispered to each other.

Was it that time of year again? Samhain was the harvest celebration. The one last year involved a community feast with Rose giving a benediction, ending with the Chase. It took Rose no time at all to catch him in the night. Tom really enjoyed *that* part of the celebration. So did the other couples, judging by the number of wives giving birth about the same time the following summer. He started whistling a tune. It might be a nice night to take a walk with Rose, get away from the group, enjoy a little privacy on their trip.

Tom reached the stream and dumped his load of canteens. He squatted and started filling one, looking around for something to sit on. Then he caught a whiff of something, a smell he hadn't encountered before. He kept still, looking in the direction of the scent. The slight blurring in the bushes bothered him, like a fuzzy surface the color of the leaves. *Green fur?* Rose had told him about magical beings like pixies inhabiting this world, but those were rare and stayed away from humans. He shifted to his Sight, hoping to see one of them. The world became a jumble of glowing shapes, each type of life having its own particular magical color. The bushes had an unusual lavender hue, but he still couldn't see a tiny little person-shaped creature lurking in them.

He blinked and dropped the Sight. Using it for more than a brief time made his eyes water. There was still no movement and even the scent was gone, only the normal smell of the woods remaining. It was probably his imagination. He was tired and hungry, and because of his worry about Rose, hadn't been sleeping well.

His listening did pick up someone walking down the path from the campsite, so it was no surprise when Ambrosius showed up. "Rose said get a move on," he told Tom. "Return the ones you've filled, and I'll do the rest. I had to answer the call of nature, anyway." He walked downstream to the bushes, unbuttoned his trousers and

The Weaving

started urinating.

That was when the bushes jumped them.

***

Rose dumped the chopped wild onions in the pot. She was wondering what was taking Tom so long when his distress hit her through their bond. "Tom!" she screamed, jumping up and knocking over the pot. She took a step toward the stream and was tackled from behind, going down under her attacker. She twisted and started shouting a spell that would turn her into a bear, her preferred form for close fighting, until she recognized a Lady sitting on top of her. "Are you insane?" Rose yelled. "Let me up! Tom needs me!"

"He doesn't need you dead," the Lady said. "Look!" She pointed to where Rose had just been sitting and she saw an arrow sticking out of the log. She looked toward where the arrow had to have come from, somewhere in the treetops past the horses.

Then she saw the blonde Lady standing in the center of the campsite. The woman was balanced on the balls of her feet, legs slightly bent and arms moving slowly in a complex pattern. There was a faint twang and a blur of motion. The Lady held an arrow in her hand, the point almost touching her eye. She dropped the arrow and returned to her stance, looking relaxed and unconcerned about someone trying to turn her into a pincushion. Several arrows lay at her feet.

"She's drawing their fire. She can't keep that up forever, so move!" The Lady dove behind the log and Rose scrambled after her, sliding down behind its protection just as a *whiz-thunk* told her the archer had remembered the other targets.

"I don't understand," Rose said. "None of the wood life alerted me. Even the birds say there's no one—damn! *Elves!*" Rose started weaving magic into an invisible ball. "Tell your Sisterself to cover her eyes," she said. She threw the magic spell in a high arc while sending out a warning for surrounding animal life to duck and cover. The Lady did some sort of backflip, bringing her over to join them in their shelter. There was a brilliant flash of light, so bright that even with eyes closed and hands covering them, Rose could tell the spell had worked. A scream came from the trees, answered by another scream from the direction of the men.

"I added an unbinding spell," she said, getting to her feet. "Even if they can see, everything from their clothes to their bowstrings are coming untied. You handle what's out there." She ran for the stream. At least her bond was telling her Tom still lived.

***

Tom glanced up just in time to catch the action. Ambrosius was standing on top of the bushes with both hands occupied, so he had no time to react when an elf popped up between his legs. They went down in a tangle. Then two more bushes further upstream turned into men, both easy to identify as elves because of the white hair and pointy ears. One started running his way while the other stood looking back and forth, trying to decide who might be more of a challenge. He sneered at Tom and turned toward Ambrosius.

Smart elf, thought Tom, dropping the canteen and fumbling for his sword. He yanked it from the scabbard, only to watch it slip from his wet hand, flying through the air past his opponent's head. The elf had a knife in his hand and a snarl on his face, so Tom did the only thing that came to mind and pulled the field ration out of his pocket. He stepped forward, snatching for the knife while putting everything he had into cramming the brick down the elf's throat.

To his surprise, it worked. He held the knife while his attacker twitched on the ground, his mouth a bloody mess while he choked to death. He'd been lucky with this one, but he had to help Ambrosius. Tom gripped his weapons tightly and looked for the third elf, sure he was in for a life and death struggle this time.

***

"Grab me by the privates, will you?" Ambrosius finally

managed to get his boot knife out, sticking it in the nearest body part and hoping it wasn't his own. The elf he was wrestling screamed, rolled off and clutched his stomach as blood seeped out from under his hands. Ambrosius leaned over and drove his knife into the elf's throat, ending the screaming. He sat up, checking to see if Tom needed help. There was a body crumpled on the ground, but Tom was standing and holding a knife. He was staring at a dead elf floating in the stream about halfway between them, this one with a sword sticking out of his back.

Ambrosius wiped off his knife on the dead elf and slid it back into his boot. "A sorry state of affairs, when a man can't even relieve himself without checking the bushes for elves first. What happened over there?"

Tom started to reply, still staring down at the floating elf, then jerked his head up as both had the same thought at once. "Rose!" Tom shouted, while Ambrosius yelled "The women!" and scrambled to his feet.

Then Rose came running, colliding with Tom. They clung to each other. Ambrosius started up the path to see about the Ladies, only to be stopped by Rose's hand on his arm.

"They're safe," she said. "There was an archer, but not anymore. Best to stay here for now." She stepped back from Tom, checking him over. She gasped when she saw his bloody hand, then looked puzzled when she held up a mangled field ration embedded with broken teeth. Tom ignored her pawing over him, staring at the dead bodies.

Ambrosius checked the surrounding trees, even though he knew there could be a dozen elves standing in plain sight and he'd never know. "I doubt there's any more," he said. "Once they spring an ambush, they don't stop until one side or the other is left standing. Can your magic help make sure?"

"I'm sure there are no humans around, but most animals have a hard time seeing an elf when he doesn't want to be noticed. I'm waking up the bats right now and we'll have a patrol that doesn't need to use their eyes." She looked around. "What happened here?"

Ambrosius walked over for a closer examination of the elf he'd gutted. "This one apparently took exception to being piddled on and jumped me before the others were in position. By the time I won my battle, Tom had taken care of the other two. Your husband is a skilled fighter, but he hides it well. Is it supposed to be a secret?"

"Skilled, nothing," Tom said. He rinsed his hands in the stream, then pulled the sword from the elf, looking sick. "I was lucky, that's all. I disarmed myself. The sword flew out of my hand and this elf happened to be in the way. I was desperate enough to feed the other one my fist."

"Being lucky is a good part of surviving any battle," Ambrosius replied. "So is being desperate. The important thing is, you didn't freeze or panic. You kept a clear head. That's the sign of a warrior, my friend. That sword looks familiar. Can I see it?"

Ambrosius checked the etching on the blade, that of a fierce mountain cat. He handed it back. "I thought so. This is Cat's Claw, the Duke's sword. There's not another like it. How did you get it?"

Tom slid it back into the scabbard. "A guard came running up just before we left the camp, saying it was a present from the Duke."

Rose interrupted. "Before you two continue congratulating each other, may I make a suggestion?" She pointed to Ambrosius's pants. "Unless you're planning to see if any more elves are hiding as bushes, I think you can put that weapon back in its scabbard."

Ambrosius blushed and turned away to button his trousers. "My apologies. I've been in many a knife fight, but this is a first for me. Having it hanging out in the breeze, a ready target for your enemy to slice off, sure motivates a man to fight harder."

***

Rose searched the surrounding area using the bat's echo sight, confirming it was safe to rejoin the Ladies. When they returned to the campsite, she saw one Lady picking through the scattered vegetables that hadn't been trampled, while the other one sat on the ground, looking at a rip in her long skirt. The only thing out of place was the

The Weaving

naked elf trussed and propped against a tree next to a pile of clothes and an unstrung bow.

"I can't wait to hear what happened here," Ambrosius said, looking at the arrows scattered around. "How did an elf manage to miss every shot?"

"He didn't," the blonde Lady said, pulling up her skirt. She was sitting in a puddle of blood with more running down her leg. "Rose, I could use your services."

Rose had already paused to check on the elf. She grabbed her pack and came over, pulling out her traveling aid kit. "There's nothing I can do for that one," she told Ambrosius. "The spell went off in his face. He's blind for life." She spread a blanket and had the Lady roll over on her side, skirt pulled high. "I'll need the canteen," she called over her shoulder. Tom handed her one, then left her alone to work.

She held the canteen in both hands and poured magic into it, bringing it to boiling before pulling the heat back out. The witches had long since learned that untreated water increased the chance of infection, although they still didn't know why. She rinsed her hands, then rinsed and examined the wound. It was a clean slice to the thigh from an arrow barb, deep but no arteries cut. She placed a hand on the wound, concentrating. The flow of blood stopped. "I need to sew this," she said. "I've used a spell that will speed the healing, but you should take it easy on the leg for a few days. No rolling backflips, if you can help it."

She pulled out her needle and thread, along with a container of powder to numb the wound. "That thing you did with catching the arrows was amazing, by the way," Rose remarked. "Even the shot that caused this could be counted as a near miss. I don't think anyone would believe me if I told them what I'd seen."

The Lady grunted as the powder was applied. "That stings. I don't know if enduring the needle wouldn't have been better. Thank you, Rose, but a miss of any type does not bleed all over the place. My backflip was slow, and if it wasn't for this thick skirt she insists on wearing, you'd be digging the arrow out of bone. This body is out of shape."

Rose looked up from her sewing, recognizing what was happening. "You're the other Lady right now, aren't you? The one waiting for us? What did you do, take over her mind?"

"More like a swap this time. My Sisterself is currently enjoying a hot bath in my body. She's explaining to the maid why a naked, wet Lady would suddenly start yelling about elves. I've taught this Sisterself some of my fighting art, but she's never faced a sustained barrage of arrows. Acquiring that level of skill takes a teacher who can beat discipline into the student. She would hardly stand for that. This was the best way to handle it."

Rose finished her stitching in silence and began bandaging the wound. Finally, curiosity got the better of her. "I've wondered what it would be like, never having any privacy," she said. "My wedding bond with Tom is a constant comfort even when we're apart, but it's not the same as having someone else present. Say when he and I, um..."

The Lady smiled. "You want to know if we share our love life? Of course we do. It does take a certain spirit of...adventure, I suppose, on the part of the man." She lay back and put her hands behind her head, looking up at the clouds while Rose worked. "The affairs do tend to be brief. For all their fantasies, most men of any worth seek the love of one woman. The men you least expect it from will turn out to have a romantic streak." The Lady suddenly sat up. "I'm going back to that bath. See you soon, Rose."

The Lady took a deep breath and stood, testing the leg. "Oh, that bath felt good," she continued. "I disagree with my Sisterself. This body is in fine shape—I'm just not built to place my feet next to my ears. As to your question, in my old clan there was precious little privacy, since entire families would huddle together in one large hall over the long winter. You accept lovemaking as a public performance. If not, you miss out on one of the joys in life." The Lady picked up her pack and limped away to change out of the bloody skirt, leaving Rose to put her tools away and try to imagine the Ladies' love life in action. She supposed the biggest problem would be finding a man

The Weaving

who didn't mind an audience—and how critical the audience was of his performance.

**

Ambrosius handed the red-haired Lady the other canteen and helped her put the stew on the fire while she filled him in on their fight with the archer. Then he went over to interrogate their captive. "Tom, I think you might find this interesting," he said. "Have you ever met an elf before?"

"No, but Rose spent some time with them," Tom said. "She told me what they're like and I've heard stories about the wars. It seems to me they're nothing but brutal savages."

Ambrosius knelt and examined the clothes. The clan markings had been removed. A Shaman had woven the magic into the fabric, allowing the elves to hide in plain sight.

Fortunately, hiding an entire Elven army at one time seemed beyond the Shaman's ability. Still, the border guards in particular suffered a lot of casualties because of their ability to blend, and the wizards hadn't yet figured out how to counter it. The thing Rose did with the bats was new to him, something he'd have to pass on to the Duke.

Ambrosius spoke to the elf in his own language while Tom stood nearby and watched. "You, there," he said, "do you know our speech, or must I translate? Will you bargain, or does your contract include not talking unless tortured?"

The elf shrugged. "No," he said in human speech, "there is no need to translate, and no, the one who sent us did not think to include such details in the contract. I am free to bargain."

"What do you have to bargain with?"

The elf squirmed against the rough bark of the tree, trying to get a little more comfortable. "I have the story of how my brothers and I came to be here, waiting in ambush. What do you offer? Your healer already said my blindness cannot be removed. A quick death is only worth the name of your true enemy."

Ambrosius made sure Tom was listening. "I can tell you our names and promise you that this will get you and your brothers past the guardians of the bragging hall, when you join them."

"Truly?" The elf looked interested. "For that, I will give you everything. The woman who caught my arrows must be a great champion. I am glad my last sight was of her dance. Her name will allow me through the door, but my brothers must have their own brag. If you know this, then we have a deal."

Ambrosius took out his knife and began cutting the elf's bonds, explaining what was going on to Tom. "The elves believe when they die, the warriors go to a place where there's a great party hosted by Death and only the very best braggers are allowed in. You can brag about how great of a warrior you are and how many people you've killed and end up a guest of honor. But, if a great warrior kills you in battle, instead, you can still brag about what a great fight you put up and how brave you were to face such a mighty warrior in the first place. If Death is impressed with your name dropping, she might let you stay."

"I don't see getting myself killed as something I'd want to brag about," Tom said, "no matter who killed me. It's still a picture of the afterlife only a brutal savage could come up with."

"Of course Death is brutal," the elf said. "Life is brutal, so why should Death be different?"

Ambrosius turned back to the elf. "Who are you and why are you outside of your borders? Were you exiled or sent here on a mission?"

"I am Climbs Tree of what used to be the Mountain Clan. My brothers and I had a disagreement with our King some years ago. That pimple on a pig's nose decided we were no longer fit company for the rest of his subjects. The details are none of your concern."

"Abolished the clan?" Ambrosius shook his head. "You must have really ticked him off. So you've been hiding out here for years. You didn't take the chance of attacking us without reason. Who hired you?"

"The Spider Woman, a demon we remember from our stories,

The Weaving

a name used to frighten our children into behaving. We were stealing supplies from the humans who work the mines when I encountered the demon. She said we would be safe from her appetite if we agreed to a contract. We were to watch for three women traveling together and capture or kill them. You are the second group we tracked down. She was disappointed with the first three we brought her, pointing out two of them were younglings. If she had told us from the beginning all the women had to be full grown, we would not have wasted our time."

The two Ladies had come over to listen, joined by Rose. *Yes,* Ambrosius thought, *three women, just not the three Lilith expected.* "Are there more of your brothers out there, still hunting?"

"You will not have to worry about more attacks from my brothers. We were the last of our clan. Now, what are the names of these important enemies of such a powerful demon?"

Ambrosius looked at the blonde Lady examining the bow. She nodded her permission. "The woman who dances with arrows is one of the Ladies, known to you as the Three Terrors. The woman who blinded and defeated you is the Witch of the Woods, someone your King honors. She has just finished treating the wound you inflicted on the Lady."

The elf started laughing. "Of course! I should have known Spider Woman was once again warring against the Three Terrors, her ancient enemy. So I took on one of the Three *and* the famous Thorny Rose—and managed to draw blood? I will indeed have something to brag about. What of my brothers?"

"I am Ambrosius, leader of the band of men that captured your King, forcing an end to our last war. One of your brothers died under my knife. The other two..." He looked at Tom, who shrugged. "The last two were defeated by a mighty warrior named Tom, the husband of Rose. The Duke himself considered that man a great enough warrior to gift with his own sword, the one you call Cat's Claw."

The elf laughed again, finding all this wonderful. "I know of you, Ambrosius, and this Tom must be a champion as well, for the Duke is the wisest of humans. We will astonish Death herself with our tale." He stood up, leaning against the tree to steady himself. "I have told you all I know. Now, I choose not to linger in a realm of darkness. If I can pick, may it be the Lady? It would be a final honor."

The Lady had already restrung the bow, anticipating this, and with a fluid motion, sent an arrow directly through the elf's heart, pinning him to the tree. She threw the bow away and walked over to join the other women, who were dishing out hot stew onto plates. Ambrosius pulled down the body, covered it with the clothes, and went to join them.

***

Tom delayed leaving the dead elf, thinking about the education he'd received. This elf was savage, but so were his companions when they needed to be. Still, the elf had confessed with no remorse to sending innocent women and children to certain death. The line had to be drawn somewhere.

He snorted, suddenly struck by the image of the two elves he'd killed, standing in the Bragging Hall and trying to convince Death to let them stay. They were telling her all about this lucky man named Tom who had defeated them in battle with a thrown sword and a hunk of field ration. They better hope Death has a sense of humor.

He went to get his own plate. If he ate fast enough, he might be first in line for seconds.

Twenty-Three

The group took their time eating and lingered over cups of tea while debating what to do with the dead elves. They couldn't just leave the bodies scattered around, since it was possible one of Lilith's minions would stumble across this site tomorrow. Ambrosius would have liked to bury them, the usual way of tidying up a battlefield, but Tom protested it would take all night to dig a big enough hole in the rocky soil. The elves normally cremated their dead, but a huge bonfire was out of the question.

Rose finally told the men to just drag the bodies deeper into the woods, strip them, bury anything not edible, and she'd summon the scavengers to a feast. Once the unpleasant chore was over, Ambrosius pulled a bottle of wine out of his pack. They sat around the campfire unwinding and trying not to think about how close they'd come to being the ones lying cold and stiff on the ground.

***

Ambrosius accepted the storytelling cup with the right hand of friendship—an Elvin tradition, one Ambrosius had asked them to honor in tribute to the dead warriors. Whoever sipped from the cup was required to recite a tale to the best of his or her ability, and everyone else was required to shut up and listen, no matter how badly the teller mangled the story. They'd been passing the cup back and forth and it was almost empty, signaling the end of the night's entertainment.

"I have friends among the elves," Ambrosius began this time. "In spite of our wars, they are gracious hosts when circumstances allow. A year ago, I heard their version of what happened when the

Elf King sent a message to Rose, requesting a meeting. It seems fitting to this occasion." He took a drink to wet his throat and began.

"The King of Elves swallowed his pride and begged Thorny Rose of the human witches for help. It seemed the King's youngest son was undergoing the trials of adulthood and had been sent on the first of the ordeals, the spirit quest. When the three days and nights passed and the son did not return, it was assumed the spirits had rejected the young man for some hidden fault. The cremation team was sent to retrieve the body. This was cause for weeping, but not alarm.

"The men returned, unable to find the boy, alive or dead. They sent for the best Shaman in the land. This man went to the spirit field and found where the boy had eaten the wrong kind of mind-altering mushroom. Instead of sleeping the sleep of death, either to stay that way or return with wisdom from the spirit word, the King's son had wandered off into the countryside buzzed out of his skull. The Shaman lost the trail after that, but could smell human magic involved. All of this the King of Elves explained to Thorny Rose and offered her the pick of her choice from his treasure room, if she would find his son.

"Thorny Rose went to the spirit field and asked the birds and beasts if they'd seen this boy. She followed the trail of witnesses until it became clear what had happened—he had wandered into the Ice Queen's domain, been captured, and then taken to her tower stronghold. Thorny Rose then turned herself into the tiniest of mice to slip into the tower unnoticed. She approached the boy in secret to steal him back, only to discover the young man was anything but a prisoner. The elf refused to leave, saying a soft bed and a sexy, experienced woman beat the rough life of a young elf hands down.

"Thorny Rose confronted the Ice Queen and challenged her to a duel for the boy, and to her surprise, was told to take him. The Ice Queen explained she'd been using the elf to provide an ingredient for one of her potions, a new kind of skin cream. More than enough of the substance had been collected from the young elf due to his enthusiastic cooperation. Now, the elf had taken to following her

The Weaving

around the tower like a lost puppy, whining for further attention.

"*The young elf was heartbroken when his captor told him to leave with Thorny Rose, but returned to his home, having gained some wisdom about the strange ways of humans and much confidence in his dealings with women. He stood before the elders and told them of his ordeal. It was decided this qualified as a successful spirit quest, even if it was the most unusual one ever recounted.*"

"And that is the end of the tale," Ambrosius said, putting down the cup.

"That sounds like the Ice Queen," the blonde Lady remarked. "She makes top quality potions, but you don't always want to know what's in them."

"How accurate is the story?" Ambrosius asked Rose. "The boy must have quite a reputation by now. Do you know what name he eventually picked for himself?"

Rose reached for the cup and drained the last of the wine. "Gushing Fountain," she replied and had to wait for Ambrosius to stop laughing. "It's accurate enough," she continued. "I mean the story, not the name—you'd have to ask the Ice Queen about *that*. You know elves don't value modesty, and the boy goes around bragging that his performance at the...ahem...*hands*...of the Ice Queen was of epic proportions. What isn't included in the story is how he tried to use his *fountain* on me and spent most of the return trip in the form of a rabbit. The boy takes after his father. It was the Elf King who first named me Thorny, after I taught him to keep his hands to himself."

***

Tom had heard Rose's version of the story before and was scarcely paying attention, sitting and examining his sword instead. He turned it over and over in front of his eyes, watching the polished blade reflect the firelight. The etchings of a fierce cat fascinated him.

"It's a beautiful piece of work, isn't it?" Ambrosius remarked, noticing Tom playing with the sword. "The elves have a legend that their final battle with humans will involve a cat in some way. The Duke made quite a stir when he showed up during the last outbreak of hostilities waving that thing around. You've been staring at it for a while. Looking for anything in particular?"

"Magic," Tom said. "Rose has books where people own special swords like this, ones with names like Stormbringer or Elfsbane or Slamding. They always do things like warn of danger or return to their true owner. This one jumped out of my hand and saved your life. The Duke must have commanded the sword to protect his brother. My Sight has never failed me before, but I can't see a bit of magic in Cat's Claw."

Ambrosius came over. "I've been around weapons all my life," he said, "and I've never found one yet that did anything but turn a live enemy into a dead one. May I see it again?"

Tom handed Ambrosius the sword. Ambrosius made a few quick passes in the air with it, saying, "My brother was presented with this by the men in his old squad, back when he was promoted from Captain to King's Advisor. A friend of his made it, a soldier who'd been wounded in action and found a new calling as a master blacksmith. He lives somewhere near your home, so you've probably seen his shop. His forge turns out the best blades in the land. He's only made a few of this quality, though."

Ambrosius whipped his arm around, letting go of the handle, and the sword sang through the air across the camp, slicing into a tree trunk point first and vibrating from the force. Rose was startled, distracted her from showing off her own brand of homemade skin cream to the blonde Lady. The sword had sounded enough like an arrow in flight to make her think they were under attack again. She jumped to her feet and glared at Tom, who pointed to Ambrosius, who pointed back to Tom. Rose muttered something about boys playing with toys, and went back to testing the Lady's skin care formula, spreading a bit on her hand and remarking about the pleasant scent.

Ambrosius walked over and yanked the sword from the tree. "You shouldn't take those stories too seriously, Tom. They're all make-believe worlds where anything is possible. The elves love stories like that and stuck this sword with a name. You'd be better off having Rose read you a history book. The truth is fascinating enough." He handed the sword back. "Cat's Claw is as finely balanced as a throwing blade, the steel highly tempered without being brittle. Any soldier would give a year's pay to buy it and refuse to sell it for twice that amount. But it's only a sword."

"Both of you are wrong."

Tom turned to see the quiet, redheaded Lady looking their way. She'd been sitting cross-legged in front of the fire doing her usual meditation. She hadn't said anything or moved from the spot since serving the stew, only shaking her head when the storytelling cup was offered.

"Ambrosius, your history books are a mixture of guesswork and lies," the Lady continued. "Take the war with the dragons that ended the age of knighthood. The historians would have you believe a mighty wizard enslaved the father of all dragons and then threatened to kill the ancient beast unless the Dragon Queen accepted a truce. The wizard took all the credit, but it was actually a small girl who woke the Eldest Dragon—and he became her friend, not her slave. The Eldest isn't the father of all dragons, but he is the oldest surviving, hatched when this world was nothing but swamps and giant lizards. And no one can make Fiona, the Dragon Queen, back down from anything, then or now. She took one look at the handsome male and decided the Eldest was going to fertilize her next egg. She lost interest in the campaign against humans after that. Dragons tend to be easily distracted during mating season."

She got to her feet and came over, pointing to the sword. "May I see that?" Tom handed it out again, and she ran her hands down the blade, then did a series of passes with it that were just as impressive as Ambrosius' demonstration. Tom wondered if everyone but himself was an expert with a sword. He'd never seen Rose touch one, but he expected her to step up next for a turn.

The Lady held up the sword, doing her own close examination. The hilt was capped with the head of a wild cat, chased in gold and with small rubies for the eyes. "The Duke definitely intrigues me," she said. "I hope he does come to visit. He keeps his promise to both help Tom and remain silent at the same time."

She handed it back to Tom. "In all fairness, I must tell you this sword is a message. It also contains something deeper than magic. Once in a while, a master swordsmith manages to put a little of his spirit into the metal. Over time, the sword will take on a mind of its own. Cat's Claw has a destiny, but not here and now. It must pass through other hands, first. For you, it is as Ambrosius said—only a sword."

The Lady returned to her quiet contemplation by the fire, leaving Tom wondering what to make of her outburst. That was the most talking she had done the entire trip, and she might not speak again for the rest of the night. He put Cat's Claw in the scabbard, unbuckled the belt and handed it to Ambrosius.

"Here," he said. "Please give this back to your brother, with my thanks for the loan."

Ambrosius looked at the sword but didn't take it. "It wasn't a loan," he said. "It was a gift from the Duke. My brother is without doubt the smartest man I know and he has a reason for everything he does. The Lady's right. He might be trying to tell you something."

Tom thought about the discussion he'd had with the Duke. "If it's a message, I'm too stupid to figure it out," he said. "All I know is, I can get myself killed trying to use a weapon I don't have the skill for. After all, no one here wears one. I'd do better carrying a rock into battle. Apparently, I'm good at beating people to death."

Ambrosius took Cat's Claw, buckling it around his own waist. Then he reached down and took out his boot knife, sheath and all. "If that's what you want," he replied, "then please accept this gift from me. I've watched you move and thought about what you did to that elf at the stream, and I think I know what your problem is—you're a born infighter. Your natural instinct is to get up close and personal, grabbing an enemy instead of standing off and swinging at him. Nothing wrong with that, since you're quick and strong, but it requires a different weapon."

Tom accepted the knife, checking to see how the sheath

The Weaving

clipped onto the boot. He pulled out the knife and made a few practice slashes. "It does feel more natural. Won't you need it?"

"I'll get another. I'm leaving the group in the morning, anyway, right after Beatrice and her furry friends get here. I have to get back to the Prince and make sure he doesn't upset our plans. Now, let's find out how good you are with a knife. When you see me start to draw my sword, reach down and pull your weapon out. Don't think about it, just react." He smiled crookedly and held up a hand. "Considering what happened to that officer back at the camp, I'll add that I'm not asking you to actually stab me."

They stood several arm's length apart, legs planted and flexing their hands. Ambrosius went for the sword. Before it cleared the scabbard Tom had stooped, pulled the knife, taken a step closer, and had the point pressing against Ambrosius' stomach.

"See?" Ambrosius said, backing away from the point. "A smaller weapon makes up in speed what it loses in power. This knife is also balanced for throwing, so I can show—"

Tom didn't wait for Ambrosius to finish, instead rearing back and throwing the knife the same way he'd seen Ambrosius throw the sword, at the same tree. It hit handle first and took off again, sailing back into the clearing. It finally struck the ground between Rose and the Lady, who were sitting practically knee to knee. Tom turned to ask what he'd done wrong, only to find himself standing alone.

Ambrosius' voice came from the darkness. "Run, you fool!"

***

Rose jumped to her feet again, but the men had already disappeared into the night, not waiting around for the explosion.

The blonde Lady looked up at Rose. "You really got a good look at it?" she asked. Rose grinned and held up her hands, measuring off a span of distance between them. The Lady grinned back. "This I have to see for myself. It appears the Samhain chase is on, after all. Help me up, grab some blankets, and let's catch them!" The giggling women ran after the men, or in the Lady's case, limped.

Gerald Ghostlow

The quiet Lady watched from her seat next to the fire, but preferred not to join the playful goings-ons. She was still anticipating sharing in the pleasure, of course. She had no doubt her Sisterself would soon find Ambrosius in the dark woods in spite of the handicap. It was obvious to her, from before they crossed the river, the man would welcome an opportunity.

For now, she preferred to sit and watch the dancing flames and relive a time long ago, when a huge, golden-scaled dragon had shown a little orphan girl with freckles and red hair what it was like to finally have a friend.

Twenty-Four

Beatrice woke at first light on her bed of pine needles, one furry bundle across her legs and the other draped across her neck. She was cold everywhere else, the blanket she'd stolen from a clothesline being too thin to keep her warm. Her stomach ached with hunger. She'd kept on the lookout for food as they had snuck around the past few days, but there are never any pies cooling on windowsills when you really need one. All she'd managed to forage for them the day before were a few late season apples left in an orchard.

She was careful to move slowly, waking the transformed women without startling them. Accidents *do* happen in the world of skunks, and Beatrice was trying to avoid another after tripping over Ilene yesterday. Fortunately, the spray had only struck the bottom of her robe, so a cleaning spell removed most of it. If Ilene's scent gland had gone off in the witch's face—well, she didn't even want to imagine what that would have been like.

"I'm hungry!" Ilene said, as soon as her feet hit the ground. She was starting to get on Beatrice's nerves.

"We're all hungry, child," the Duchess replied. The old skunk rolled over on her back between Beatrice's legs, pulling up her tail and picking at some burs. "I wonder how other skunks get by without a comb?"

On the other hand, Beatrice enjoyed talking to the Duchess. They hadn't had much contact before the dungeon. Beatrice had spent most of her days riding and hiking and finding rare flowers for her collection. The nights had been reserved for social gatherings with people more her own age. When the Prince called his meeting, she was on her way back from an all-night party and had a little too much to drink, and that's why someone was able to sneak up and bash her over the head. That's what she told herself, anyway. Beatrice vowed to never touch alcohol again.

"Well, when are we going to eat? And stop calling me a child!" Ilene was definitely getting on Beatrice's nerves.

The Duchess walked over to her maid, tail curled up, looking like a skunk that'd had enough. "Then stop acting like one," she said. "Beatrice can't conjure up a feast out of thin air. If you get hungry enough, eat a bug like I did. That's what skunks do, you know. The beetles taste like chicken salad on crackers, but I'd stay away from the millipedes. The legs stick in your throat going down."

This ended predictably with Ilene going into one of her sulks. At least she wouldn't be pestering them with complaints for a while.

"Well, it won't be long now," Beatrice said. She wrapped the blanket around her as protection against the chill morning air and started walking down an old miner's path, following the directions of the forest animals. "There's another Lady with Uncle Ambry, so they know we're coming. I'm sure they'll have something for us to eat."

This motivated Ilene to move faster, and she even ran ahead for once, her tail bobbing as she hopped over the trees that had fallen across this abandoned trail. It was still morning when the animals inhabiting the area told Beatrice the camp was not far ahead. She stopped, sensing another mind in the woods—a very powerful mind watching their every move.

"I greet you, Witch of the Woods, High Priestess of the Great Mother," Beatrice said, careful not to extend her own mind without invitation, as protocol demanded. "I ask your permission to enter your presence."

A woodpecker flew over, landed on a nearby tree and performed a series of complicated rap patterns. Then it settled down to digging out the grubs exposed.

"That sounded interesting," the Duchess said. "What's going on?"

Beatrice started walking again. "It's a code witches have worked out over the years to pass messages back and forth. We learn it in our College. In the feathered world, only the big hunters are intelligent enough to think in words. This way, complicated messages can be sent and understood."

"That's delightful! Just think how it would change the world if ordinary people could talk over distance like that. What did the Witch of the Woods say?"

"She said stop that nonsense and get over here, and don't be worried about the four somethings lying in the path ahead. I couldn't remember what that one code meant."

Then the aroma of startled skunk reached them and Ilene ran back down the path, yelling about half-eaten naked bodies.

"Oh, that's right. *Rap-rap-pause-diddle-diddle-rap*. It stands for elf, with the modifier that means used to be. I'll be glad when Ilene is human again. We'll have to find a wide detour around that smell."

***

The witch and her two skunks arrived at the campsite with no more surprises, and Beatrice ran over to hug her Uncle Ambry.

"Bea, you're looking better than I expected," he told her. "I heard you were hurt. Are you all right?" He felt the back of her head.

"I'm fine," she replied, pulling away. She looked at the woman who was standing next to him, a freckled redhead. "I greet you, Lady," she said. "Your other...the Lady I met before told me...well, you'd know that already, wouldn't you?" she ended awkwardly, not knowing what to say to the legendary power.

The woman stood and studied the young witch for a moment. Then the Lady smiled. "My Sisterself is correct, both in your potential and need for guidance. If you find yourself without a Mentor, come to us." Then the woman walked away, leaving Beatrice astonished.

Ambrosius chuckled. "Takes some getting used to, doesn't she? That one rarely says anything, but when she does speak, you know it's important. Best remember it." He wrinkled his nose and looked down at the skunk sitting patiently at her feet. "Tom smelled you coming last night, and even I knew you'd stumbled across the elves. There's nothing quite like a skunk announcing its opinion of the world. I thought there were two of them. Did one get lost?"

Beatrice looked for Ilene and saw the girl had torn open someone's pack and was gorging on what looked like cake. A man was watching the skunk, standing at a safe distance and looking upset. "That's Ilene, the maid that...well, you have to make allowances for what she's been through. I'll take care of it."

"No, I'll do it. You go see Rose." Ambrosius walked over and pulled the rest of the cakes away, shaking his finger under the skunk's nose when Ilene started stomping her feet. Beatrice looked around for the Witch of the Woods and spotted her on the other side of the camp, working on something behind a fallen log. Beatrice had been both looking forward to and dreading this meeting with the famous power. She went over and discovered there was a half-undressed woman lying on a blanket behind the log. Rose was inspecting a nasty wound on the woman's leg.

"Running around the woods last night caused some bleeding," Rose was saying. "The healing spell is working fine, but I'd better leave a few of the stitches in for another day or so, just to make sure. I'll take the rest out now. Hand me that bag, will you?" This last was addressed to Beatrice, who picked up the small aid pack sitting on the log and handed it over.

"I greet you, Witch of the Woods," Beatrice said. "This is the second time I've been honored to speak with you."

"So formal," Rose remarked. She looked at the woman getting her wound treated. "Reminds me of you, when you came riding up to my cottage. I don't remember hearing it was an honor to speak with me, though." The woman stuck out her tongue at Rose, who responded by yanking out a stitch. The woman grimaced, but suffered in silence. "I remember you from my last visit to the College," Rose continued. "You stood out from the usual handful of young witches eager to take on the world. The Ladies say you have a problem for me to solve. Tell me what I need to know."

Beatrice told Rose about turning the two women into skunks on the Lady's orders and her problem with not being able to change them back now. "She said you'd be able to do it for me," Beatrice concluded. "Oh, she also said to tell you the Ladies were in my debt, and then listen to your response."

"My response is, so what?" Rose replied. "If you continue your path to power, there will be many people in your debt. Are you planning on keeping track?"

"Of course not," Beatrice answered. "I help people because it's the right thing to do, not because I expect something in return."

Rose turned and gave Beatrice her full attention. "You don't want the fame and respect that comes with being a witch?"

Beatrice hesitated, but decided honesty was best. "I do dream of being famous. I'd love to have people tell stories of my great deeds, like they do yours. But that's not why I studied so hard. My talent is a gift from the Goddess and I believe it should be used in her service." Beatrice was beginning to feel like she was back in College, being given an oral exam.

"What about the people you feel a debt to?" Rose asked, not finished with the grilling. "Suppose Ambrosius or the Duke asked you to do something you felt was wrong? Come over here and finish bandaging while you're deciding what answer will impress me again."

This last question was even harder, since she couldn't imagine either of her uncles asking her to do something wrong. But what if they did? She considered her answer while performing a cleaning spell on her hands, then rummaged in the bag and found some ointment that would keep the wound from itching as it healed.

"I guess I'd also have to say, so what?" Beatrice finally answered as she worked. "My first loyalty is to the Goddess. I think the Ladies...lift your leg, please...are stupid for getting so bound up in their promises. If someone forces me to make a deal at the end of a crossbow, you can bet this witch will have no problem breaking it. If my uncles can't accept a refusal, I might have to...well, teach them better manners. There, does that feel too tight?"

Beatrice put the supplies back in the pack as the woman stood, straightening the heavy skirt. Rose was standing over them, watching the young witch at work. "Fine words, and I'd make you live up to them, if that's what you decide," she said, as Beatrice handed her the aid pack. "Let's see about your two skunks. Call them over here."

The Duchess was sitting with her tail wrapped around Tom's leg, nibbling on a piece of cake and sipping from a cup placed on the ground while the man repacked his belongings. Ilene was sulking nearby, Uncle Ambry standing over her with arms folded, daring the skunk to try something. Beatrice whistled and motioned for them to come over.

"You'll have to excuse Ilene's behavior. I was injured, you see, and the jailor—"

"Yes, I can see Ilene's problem," Rose interrupted. "You feel a debt to her, don't you? So you treat her special?"

This brought Beatrice up short. She realized the maid had been getting away with behavior that would have earned Beatrice a whipping from her father. Even now, if her father was still alive.

The woman in the long skirt finally spoke. "A light dawns on our young witch. You're not doing Ilene any good by indulging her self-pity. Ilene has never learned to look beyond her own needs. Being raped is a terrible injury, but you cannot heal the damage to her spirit unless she wants to change."

Beatrice stopped watching Rose and looked at the tall, well-built woman next to her with a sinking feeling. She'd assumed this one to be a Duke's agent, like her uncle. "You're the third Lady, aren't you? I apologize for the remark about...well, I hope I didn't say anything that caused offense."

"Since Rose neglected to introduce us, we can hardly take offense," the Lady said.

Rose straightened up, finished with her examination. "Tom, I need your eyes," she called. The man came over, handed Beatrice one of the cakes before stooping over the skunks. She mumbled her thanks. So this was Tom, the husband of Rose. He was the subject of much speculation among the girls in the College. Being unbonded was a price the girls had assumed came with the career. Everyone agreed Tom had to be special, but he didn't look special. She came over to see what Rose was doing, cramming the cake in her mouth

The Weaving

and eating as fast as she could.

"Look for a tangle," Rose instructed him. "It could be anywhere."

Tom squinted at a skunk, then pointed to a spot between its ears. "This looks like it," he said. "The lines are so heavy. It's all twisted in a knot."

Rose turned to Beatrice. "You're pouring too much magic into the weaving," she said. "I had the same problem at first, but the previous Witch of the Woods straightened me out. Practice using as little magic as possible in your work. You must develop a delicate touch. There's enough magic here to bind a dragon." She bent down, placed a finger at the spot Tom had identified, and the Duchess stood before them.

"Let me try that," she said, wiping crumbs off her hands and stepping up to the remaining skunk. The witch placed her fingers on the same area, feeling around her weaving. Now that Rose had pointed it out, the problem was obvious. The strands were too tight, too strong and definitely tangled. She picked at the offending knot and the spell came apart, returning to nothing. Beatrice stepped back and looked at Ilene. The girl remained a sulking skunk. "What did I do wrong?" Beatrice asked.

Rose addressed the skunk. "Young woman, why don't you want to let go of what you are now? That's the only thing keeping you from changing."

"I like being a skunk," Ilene replied. "Nobody can force me to do anything while I'm in this body. I don't have to be afraid of people. They're afraid of me. I'm not going back to being a maid."

The Duchess stepped up. "If you want to remain a skunk, that's your choice, but you're still in my employ and will follow my orders. You'll start by not using that squirt gland unless I give permission. If you want to resign from my service, you can go live in the woods. I'm sure the other skunks will show you the best bugs to eat. Now, we've delayed these people long enough. They have more important things to do."

Gerald Costlow

***

After the horses were saddled, everyone said their goodbyes. There were more people than horses, now, but the Ladies insisted they would be fine doubling up since they actually didn't have much farther to go. Ambrosius told the Duchess to ride his horse and hold Ilene while he and his niece shared the remaining mount. The Duchess had the good sense not to argue.

Rose and Tom left first, heading toward the mountain that loomed over their camp. Beatrice helped the Duchess adjust the stirrups while her uncle had a last whispered conversation with the Ladies. She stopped in shock when the conversation ended with Ambrosius grabbing the blonde Lady and engaging in a passionate kiss.

"It's not polite to stare, dear," the Duchess whispered. "Watch without being obvious."

"But...a Lady? Uncle Ambry?"

The Duchess shook her head. "I see only a man and woman enjoying a bit of happiness. Would it shock your youthful sensibilities to learn that even I have a lovelife?"

It was more than Beatrice she wanted to know about the Duchess. She helped the woman into the saddle, then handed Ilene up before walking over to her uncle, who was leaning across his own horse, watching the two Ladies ride off.

"What a woman," he said. "I hope we meet again." He looked at Beatrice. "I spent an inordinate amount of effort finding an unguarded opening into the mines and the Ladies are going in the front door, instead."

Beatrice picked up the last of the packs and helped her uncle finish saddling his horse. "That's why they didn't leave with Rose and her husband? I suppose they made another of those deals with someone. I'll never understand why they insist on living by those rules."

Ambrosius started shifting the packs so Beatrice would have room to sit. "Bea, did you learn what a paradox was at the College?"

he asked.

"A paradox?" Beatrice wondered if her uncle was deliberately changing the subject. "Sure, when we're taught about the limitations of magic. A paradox is something that can't happen. Like, I can use my magic to make you see two of me standing here, but one would have to be illusion. I can't actually be in two places at the same time."

Ambrosius swung into the saddle and held his hand out for his niece, pulling her up behind him. "The Lady and I had a long talk last night, after—after we made camp. She found out I like puzzles and presented me with one. As I understand it, the Ladies looked into their water and saw only three possible futures for tomorrow: either nobody uses that secret entrance, or only Rose, or Rose and Tom together. No one else ever shows up. Now, suppose the Ladies show up there. A paradox, right?"

"So there's no possible future where the Ladies use that entrance? If they try, something will happen to prevent it. It explains why they're staying away, but it's not a paradox."

"That was my first response. She disagreed. To quote the Lady, *'The ability to change what must be is a terrible burden.'* According to her, the only reason the Ladies aren't using that entrance is because they decided not to do so, even though they made the decision after they found out it was what they were going to decide. My mind just goes in circles when I try to think about it."

Beatrice thought about the puzzle for a moment. "The Lady is saying the laws of destiny don't apply to them, and they *could* create a paradox if they aren't careful. That's...scary. I wonder what would happen then?"

"She lost me completely there. Something about torn anchor lines and irreparable damage to a web. I got the impression it isn't the kind of mistake they can make twice. So, if you think about it, there might be a good reason the Ladies are so strict about the rules they follow." Ambrosius turned around, shaking his head while he looked at his new little band of companions.

"A Duchess, a witch and a skunk," he said. "I'll drop you off at a safehouse on the edge of town. The people who live there don't normally ask questions, but this might need some explaining. Then I've got a day of hard riding ahead of me. The Ladies told me Valant and his army are on their way to meet our King and I need to be there before it happens."

They spurred the horses, picking their way through the trees. "Uncle Ambry," Beatrice said, "do you think the Witch of the Woods will give me another chance? I didn't make a very good impression. I arrived reeking of skunk, told a Lady she was stupid, had to be shown how to remove my own spell, and was scolded for letting my emotions get in the way of my duties. She must think I'm a sorry excuse for a witch."

Her uncle laughed along with the Duchess, who was riding close behind and listening. "My niece is growing up—I overheard that comment about teaching me manners—but she has a ways to go. Duchess, do you want to tell her?"

"I'm tempted to make her guess," the Duchess said, "but I suppose that would be cruel. Beatrice, dear girl, I listened in on the whole conversation. That was a job interview. Weren't you paying attention? The Witch of the Woods indicated she was willing to accept you as her apprentice. She's letting you think it over first. Once her current quest is over, she'll be expecting you to formally apply for the position and begin your training. That means you'll be the next Witch of the Woods, if you study and practice and live up to her expectations. Congratulations."

Eventually Ambrosius had to call a brief halt. "Bea," he said, "I'm happy for you, but if you don't stop squealing 'No way!' and 'Thank you, Goddess!' in my ear, I'll make you get down and walk. I'm sure the Goddess has heard you by now."

Twenty-Five

The nightly fog was just what Valant needed.

His spies had kept track of the King's movements on the other side of the river and insisted there were no more than several hundred soldiers in the camp. They also told him an army of several thousand was converging on this spot from the main roads and would arrive tomorrow. With that many men, King Justin could build a small fleet of rafts and send his entire army across the river. It was now or never

If only the other nobles in the vassal kingdoms land hadn't turned out to be such cowards. Even the Ice Queen had sent a letter saying King Justin had promised her a substantial bribe not to get involved and thanked him for it.

The rivermen paid to ferry his raiding party across proved expert at their task, quietly loading his men. Ambrosius and his thugs were already across, their mission to secure the landing area. He squatted in the boat, heart pounding as the shore became visible through the mist. He listened for signs of alarm, hearing nothing.

A vision of horror appeared out of the fog as Valant stepped onto the riverbank. It was Ambrosius. Blood dripped from the man's sword and the shifty looking strangers with him were soaked in it. Valant raised one eyebrow and Ambrosius nodded before slipping off to continue his butchery. Even a guard making a late night visit to the privy could raise an alarm. The first step was completed.

Valant waited for the other boats to silently slip in, directing his soldiers to line up in columns. It took several trips, but eventually the raiding party was ready. The fog thinned as he marched his men away from the river. He came to the small hill his enemy had chosen as a campsite and spent a moment checking it out from the shelter of the trees. Judging from what he could see in the full moon, his

Gerald Gostlow

spy's map was accurate. It was laid out in a standard circle, with the larger tents of the officers in the middle and the regular guard's tents forming a series of rings around the center. The ground around the camp was dotted with enough screened privy holes for a camp twice that size. There were smoldering campfires, but not a single guard was visible. Ambrosius and his men had taken out the sentries as promised.

Valant reached the first tent and raised his sword. The battle yell he tried to give sounded weak coming from his dry throat, but the men picked it up and ran into the enemy camp with a roar, shooting their crossbows into the tents. He ran with his personal guard for the center pavilion with the royal standard. As he reached it and entered to capture the King, the sounds behind him began to register. There were no screams of pain or clang of sword meeting sword, only puzzled shouts from his men.

He stumbled to a halt in the tent, his men piling into him. Several lamps were lit, and in the center there was only a folding table with several benches, the table holding a chessboard. A man sat on a bench, facing him, but it wasn't the King. This was a huge man, hunched over the table and studying the chessboard.

It could only be the famous Duke.

Two guards in full armor stood behind the fat man, helmets down and hands on swords, but not yet attacking.

"Prince Valant!" One of his men ran into the tent, gasping for breath. "We've been tricked! There's no one in the camp!"

Valant motioned for the man to be silent. "I know. Tell the men to form a ring around this tent and sound an alarm if there's any sign of the enemy. At least we'll have the high ground. You two behind me, stay here and wait for my command." He turned back to the Duke and gestured at the chessboard. "So I didn't capture the King. You're worth almost as much."

The Duke laced his fingers over his stomach and leaned back. "Capturing me is only useful if you can carry me back across the river and demand ransom. Since I'll refuse to move from this bench, I hope you brought a block and tackle. You can kill me, of course. My

The Weaving

only protection is you knowing that doing so would also mean *your* certain death. We both have a stake in our negotiations here."

Valant tensed as the Duke reached under the table, but it was only to bring out a bottle and a couple of glasses. Valant sheathed his sword and pulled off his helmet, sitting down on the empty bench. He picked up the glass closest to the Duke and held it out to be filled.

"I hope it's a good vintage," Valant said. "It might be my last drink. You first, of course."

"Of course." The Duke poured the wine and took a drink. "It's from my own vineyards," he added. "I think you'll enjoy it. I don't believe we've met. The few times your father came to the Palace, he didn't bring you along. So, Valant, how do you like running a kingdom?"

"I'm beginning to wonder if owning a kingdom is worth it. You wouldn't believe the stack of reports I have to go through each day, mostly stuff I consider a waste of time. I'm thinking of taking the biggest waste of my time off the stack once in a while and treat the idiot responsible to a stay in the dungeon."

One of the guards chuckled. "You're at attention, soldier!" the Duke barked, glaring at the man. He turned back to Valant. "If my King came up with that idea, I'd advise against it. You'll eventually scare people away from reporting the really important things you need to know."

"To get back to more pressing issues, why *are* you here?" Valant leaned in, studying this man. "I assume I won't make it back across the river. I'll be forced to fight your King and his full army tomorrow?"

"Oh, your retreat is cut off, certainly. Our Royal Wizard was hiding in the fog and is now capturing the boats and any men you left to guard them. If you're thinking of leaving in any other direction, be advised our men have spent the last week digging a line of privy holes in the ground surrounding this camp to hide in, and are waiting with crossbows ready. You'll lose at least half your men escaping and still be on the run. But you labor under a misconception. I want you to return and rule Morania."

Gerald Costlow

Valant nodded. "To be a figurehead? The condition being I agree to the occupation of your forces?"

"Not at all. I want you to reopen your border and then issue a public apology for your treatment of our ambassador. We'll insist you reduce your army back to peacetime levels, of course. Let your Advisor handle the details. King Justin won't be happy about it, but I can talk him into going along."

"That's it? We just shake hands, call off the war, and everyone goes home?" Valant sat back, thinking about the offer. He looked closely at the Duke sitting across the table, issuing orders and ultimatums in the name of the Empire. He realized what this meant and started to stand.

"Would you like for me to read your mind?" the Duke asked. This caught Valant off guard and he sat back down.

"Right now," the Duke continued, "you're thinking I'm the one actually running the Empire and must have a network of spies and agents. You're picturing a life of jumping at my command or being murdered in your sleep, and won't live like that. You've decided to kill me and take the chance of escaping."

That was exactly what Valant had been thinking and it only firmed his resolve. "I'm wrong?" he asked.

The Duke sighed and shook his head. "Prince Valant, if I'd wanted you dead, I would have ordered my agents to kill you a month ago and saved us all a lot of trouble. Let me show you something." A guard handed the Duke a small box, which he opened and placed on the table. "Look inside and tell me what you see."

Valant looked. "It's an arrowhead, with the shaft broken off."

"Can you guess where it came from?"

Valant shook his head. "I'm too tired to play guessing games. I'll sit here and listen to what you have to say until my men sound an alarm or I get bored."

The Duke nodded. "Very well. When this all started, I became curious about events in your past. I had my agent break into your royal crypt. This was removed from the body of your brother. It's the arrow that killed him."

The Weaving

Valant began to get angry. "Will that accident haunt me for the rest of my life? Alright, I killed my brother, daddy's pride and joy. If you want to believe I did it on purpose, go ahead. What possible reason would you have for showing me this?"

"Look closer at the arrow, Valant."

He picked up the box, taking the contents out to examine. No rust, stained black..."This isn't mine!" he exclaimed. "I'd never use a barbed arrow for hunting deer in a forest. If you miss with this thing, you'll never dig it out of a tree!"

"I thought as much, but needed your confirmation. We had the metal tested by our wizard. It's a silver alloy, used only by the elves."

Valant started to speak several times, then put the arrow back and took another drink of the wine. He needed time to sort through his emotions but there was still an army bearing down on him. "Why do me this favor?"

"To show you why I need you alive. Our population is growing and we need more farmland. We've already reached the point where a few years of bad harvest would mean famine. It's time to expand our borders again and the elves know it." The Duke refilled both their glasses. "This little campaign was a test. I pushed you to see what you could do. You created an army from scratch, complete with weapons, training and supply lines, in less than a month. That's a remarkable talent for organizing. I'll want you in charge of logistics when we next march against the elves."

"Allies against a common enemy?" Valant felt a bit of hope he'd survive the night, after all. "I can agree to that. You must have some other conditions. It can't be this easy."

"Well, there is one other thing," the Duke said.

Valant tensed again. Now would come the real cost of walking out of the trap.

"The Duchess is due for retirement, so I'd like you to pension her off and consider my brother as your official Advisor." One of the guards lifted the faceplate on his helmet to reveal a familiar face.

"Ambrosius! You traitor!" Valant realized how much he'd

been manipulated. "I'm supposed to keep listening to this man?"

The Duke pulled a medallion out of his pocket. "Do you know what this is?" he asked.

"More guessing games? Well, I do know this one. That's an Advisor's Medallion. The Duchess wore one when she was acting in her official capacity. I had hers confiscated. It's supposed to..." He looked at Ambrosius. "It contains magic that forces the Advisors to always speak truth to their King when wearing it. You'd wear one? You'd swear loyalty to me?" Another suspicion began to form. "I've had one medallion switched for a fake already. You won't fool me twice."

Ambrosius came over and picked up the bottle of wine, taking a healthy gulp. "Test your medallion all you want," he said, wiping his mouth with the back of his hand. "If it's a fake, I didn't have anything to do with it. My loyalty has always been to the good of the people over my brother or even King Justin. I would do my best to forge Morania into a strong kingdom. Should you ignore my advice and engage in conduct I can't accept, I'll resign. My only demand is that you don't ask questions about work I've already done for the Duke. I won't answer those questions, and I'll keep your confidences the same way. That's the best I can offer. I'll wear whatever you want and swear this is true."

Valant considered it. Yes, Ambrosius was a man who'd lived in the shadow of his famous brother and might want to make a name for himself. At the very least, the Duke's brother would make a nice hostage.

"I agree, since I don't have a choice," Valant told the Duke. He picked up his glass. "Let's drink a toast to a successful peace negotiation—and to the end of a war in which the battles were all fought before the armies met on the field."

He looked back at his men, seeing relief in their faces. "I only hope I have a kingdom left to rule when I get back. There's a big problem there by the name of Lilith. A Lady has promised to take care of that monster, but if she fails, I might need your King and his army to secure my throne. Who would have thought?"

The Weaving

The Duke picked up his glass. "You should have known better. Being blinded by ambition is a common failing of our nobility. Should the Ladies fail, the elves will be the least of our worries. Let's drink a toast to their success, as well. We'll wait here until you issue the order that reopens the border. If it doesn't happen within a week, our army will pay you a visit and see what the problem might be."

***

Prince Valant, soon to be crowned King Valant, left with Ambrosius to start their journey back to Morania. Ambrosius would be needed to give the signal to let King Justin's forces know the battle had been canceled.

Once they were gone, the remaining guard pulled off his helmet and wiped sweat from his brow. "Budrich," he said, "you are the most devious man I know." The King sat down on the bench and started unlacing his armor, pulling his crown from under his shirt and placing it back on his head. "That was brilliant. Ambrosius told me you'd arranged a supply of pig's blood to make it look like our sentries were slaughtered, but I missed learning about the arrow. Was Valant's brother really assassinated by the elves? That's disturbing. How safe is my own family? Or was it a fake?"

The Duke shrugged. "As it happens, Ambrosius and our champions had a run-in with some elves that had been using that area for years as a hideout. It's likely the Prince's brother stumbled across one of the outlaws. Those particular elves won't be bothering us again. I would have used a fake arrow, if need be. I had to see his face when I told him."

"So now he knows he didn't kill his brother. Why go through all that?"

"To observe his reaction. It was mostly relief. I knew then he really did love his brother. The thought that he'd killed the man, even by accident, had been eating at him. Valant always had a ruthless streak, but it wasn't until his father turned against him that he turned vicious. I believe he's going to make a strict but fair ruler, in the end."

Gerald Costlow

The King moved a piece on the chessboard, trying to anticipate where his Advisor was going to attack from next. "And if he'd shown no emotion? What then?"

The Duke looked up at his King. "Then he'd never have made it back across the river. A man incapable of feeling guilt sitting on a throne? That will never happen while I'm around." He moved a knight to the center of the board.

Justin studied the board for a moment and then knocked over his king, conceding defeat. "Valant thinks you're the real ruler of this land, the one running things. If I was a suspicious King, I'd begin to wonder if that's why you keep my days occupied with endless reports."

The Duke put his hand on his heart. "Sire! I am shocked, shocked I say, that you would ever think such a thing! You are the King, while I am only your lowly Advisor. Should I put on the medallion and answer the charges? Would that ease your mind?"

Justin laughed. "Budrich, I told you never to wear that thing around me. You're more than my Advisor—you're my friend. My father taught me that the second biggest mistake a King could make was to not trust his friends." He got to his feet. "Of course, he also said the biggest mistake was picking the wrong friends, so one day I just might have a need for that medallion." He yawned and stretched, looking out at the night. "Why don't we round up a cook and get something to eat? This is the first time I've felt hungry since the Lady arrived at the Palace. I wonder how she's doing."

The Duke accompanied his King, looking at the sun about to rise as they left the tent. "Sire," he said, "everything we've just accomplished doesn't mean a thing if Rose and the Ladies don't succeed. Your army doesn't stand a chance against something those women can't handle."

The King wished his friend hadn't spoke. His appetite was gone again.

Twenty-Six

Rose slipped out from under the blankets before dawn, taking care not to disturb Tom. She took the special robe out of the pack, the one she was wearing upon her return from the realm of the Goddess. She pulled it over her head, tying the sash and running her hands down the material. Rose never tired of the sensation, and would often reach into the chest where it was kept at home just to marvel at how it felt against her skin. Even the softest fur couldn't compare to the lightweight and tightly woven fabric. The air felt cold enough to frost, yet already Rose was comfortably warm. The robe was irreplaceable, and Rose had kept it safely tucked away until now.

She held out her hand, whispered a word, and a ball of light appeared in her palm. The daylife in the woods was not even stirring as Rose walked far enough into the trees for privacy. She asked around, and a yawning sparrow led her to a suitable spot, fluttering from branch to branch, until she reached a break in the trees. The ground sloped away from the mountain, giving a view of the stars where a faint glow on the horizon showed the sun would soon rise. There was even a flat stone, perfect for her needs.

Rose whispered another word and the ball of light rose in the air to illuminate the makeshift altar. She knelt and pulled the small icon from her pack, propping it up on the stone. She touched the pendant on her crystal necklace and opened to the life around and about, the countless offspring of the Goddess. The animals responded, pausing in their daily struggle for survival to take notice. Rose could feel the Goddess watching through the eyes and ears of her children.

"Mother of All," she said, "your servant kneels before you once more, seeking guidance at the start of a new day..." Then she paused, knowing the rote prayer would not serve this time.

"We need to talk," she continued. "There's something I have to say. I know, Goddess. I finally figured it out. Not why I used the portal in the first place, or what went on in your realm, but I feel the connection to what's happened since. There is a monster loose on your world that even the Ladies fear, and...it's my fault. I know this."

Rose looked at the icon, the little scrap of wood with a figure of the Goddess carved into it. She'd labored over it as a young witch, proving if nothing else, she wasn't an artist. The image was of a middle-aged woman, tired and pregnant, with a sad smile. Rose had tried to make it look like the last memory of her mother, before Mama died trying to give birth to what would have been her younger brother.

"I've tried and tried to remember, to understand what I did wrong," she said. "I want to make it right. I'll take my punishment. But all the deaths, the suffering this creature has caused. I can't—how can I forgive myself for being responsible? I failed you. And Tom, somehow he's involved. That worries me more than anything."

She picked up the icon, running her fingers over the swollen belly. "I remember only two things for certain from my visit—being hugged and being told you were proud of me. It felt so much like Mama...nothing could make me forget that. I'm not proud of myself right now, though. If you'll only let me remember the rest, perhaps I can undo the harm I've caused without anyone else being hurt."

She turned over the image. On the other side was a carving she'd added soon after the trip through the portal. It was of a different woman, this one slim, younger looking, not smiling at all. There was a resemblance between the two faces, like they were portraits of sisters. It was an image Rose carried in her head since returning from the realm of the Goddess. It seemed right that these two figures would be on opposite sides of the same piece. Rose looked at the eyes and it seemed she fell into them, a single memory coming back with a rush. She was sitting at a desk of some sort, in a small room with pictures hanging on the wall. The taste of herbal tea was in her mouth and this Goddess was holding her hand and asking a question.

The Weaving

"Do you regret the path of power you have chosen, then?"

Rose looked up to see a great white owl perched on a branch overhead, watching and waiting for an answer. The automatic denial died on her lips. "Sometimes," she admitted. "I never have enough time to spend with my husband. I worry about what will happen to him if I don't return from one of my quests. Yet, being the Witch of the Woods is as much a part of me as being a wife. Do I choose one or the other? Is that what you require? Tell me what I should do!"

Another bit of memory came back. Rose was still in the little room, preparing to return home after receiving her answer. But what was the answer, and to what question?

"I can't tell you what to do. You must work out your own life, child, and accept the consequences of your actions."

The Goddess went silent. When no more memories were revealed, Rose tucked the icon away, looking back up at the owl. "Very well. Thank you for listening to my plea. I picked an apprentice yesterday and told the young witch to live up to her words. It's time I did the same. My duty to you will always come first, but I still deserve a love of my own. I am sorry for whatever mistake I made, but it happened. I can't change the past, but I can try to make it a better future for everyone."

The owl managed to look amused at her reply, then tucked its head beneath its wing to roost for the day. The audience was at an end and the answer to Rose's request was hardly satisfying.

So be it.

She left to get the day started. One thing Rose was sure of—in spite of what Tom wanted, he was not following her into the mines.

***

Tom was having a strange dream. A woman was speaking to him, telling him something important. He'd met this woman before and knew he should listen carefully, but the sound of his wife calling his name woke him. Rose was puttering around the campfire, up before dawn as usual. The dream faded as he pushed away the blankets to start his day. It was still dark out and there was a chill to the air, but it didn't look like daylight was far off.

"I wish we didn't have to get such an early start," Rose said. "You look like you need the rest. I know you haven't been sleeping well lately. You tossed and turned all night."

"I can say the same thing about you," he replied. "When this is over, I'm going to hang a 'Do not disturb' sign on the path to our home and keep you with me in bed for at least a month."

"We'll do that, and woe to anyone who ignores the sign. We deserve a holiday once in a while." Rose stirred something in a pot she was heating over the fire, pouring it into two cups. She put a pinch of something into one of the cups, bringing it over. "Here, I made you some tea. I even put the last of the sugar in yours, as a treat."

Tom set down the cup while he pulled on his boots. The argument they'd had last night was fresh on his mind. He had to get their feelings settled before anything else. "Rose," he said, "I've thought about it, and you're right. I shouldn't go in there. You could have been killed when the elves attacked, trying to rescue me instead of looking out for yourself. I can't take that chance again. I'll stay here and wait."

Rose looked surprised, since nothing she'd said on this trip had shaken his resolve to be her shadow. "What about your quest?" she asked. "So far, there's no sign you've ever been to this little kingdom before. You still have no idea of who you were."

"Your safety is more important for now. I'd rather have a future with you than a few memories of my childhood." He reached for the tea, but Rose picked that moment to step in front of him, knocking over the cup. She ignored his squawk at the loss and bent down, taking his head in her hands and looking into his eyes.

"My love," she said, "I think only today have I understood your frustration at not remembering. Once this is over, I promise to use all my power to help you find your past, no matter what means to our marriage. You don't need the Ladies while I'm around."

Tom pulled Rose down on his lap, falling back on the blanket

The Weaving

with her in his arms. "A little jealous, maybe?" he asked. "The blonde is too tall, and the freckled one too serious. You're just right for me. Besides, from what I've seen, I'd have to take on all three. Even the mighty Tom isn't up to that. But don't change the subject. You just spilled my tea and there's no more sugar. I demand a duel!"

"I'll give you a duel," she replied. "Take that..." She slid a cold hand down his pants, but it didn't stay cold for long.

"Ahhh...you cheat, woman! When did the maiden do that?"

"She didn't. This was my idea. Now kiss me. Your fair maiden would reward her mighty warrior for admitting he was wrong."

***

Rose eventually fixed Tom another cup of tea while he pulled on his other boot. This time she didn't add the sleeping powder to the sugar, enough of a dose to keep him out for a whole day. She'd hated doing it, but it was the only way she could think of to keep Tom from following. Rose had been afraid her husband would never forgive her. His change of mind was a huge relief.

"I found a hidden stash of sugar," she said. "We weren't out, after all." She handed him the cup, then slung the small aid bag over one shoulder and a canteen over the other. "I have to go. The Ladies told me I need to be in the tunnels before full daylight. Apparently, once Lilith settles in somewhere, she stays up all night and sleeps during the day. This is the best time to catch her without a lot of guards and slaves running around. I don't know how long this will take, but we rescued enough journey cakes from Ilene to last for several days. If I'm gone longer than that...well, I won't be gone more than that."

Tom came over and they hugged while she did her little scratch behind his ear. He didn't make his purring noise. She left him standing by the fire drinking his tea, watching her march off to battle. She inspected the old mine shaft again, clearing out some cobwebs and conjuring up a ball of light. The Witch of the Woods walked into the maze of tunnels, guided by the map Ambrosius had provided.

Gerald Ghostlow

***

Tom watched Rose disappear into the mine, then began cleaning up the camp. He stashed the packs under a log and covered them with leaves. Tom didn't know what to do with the horses and finally removed their tackle, trusting they could take care of themselves. He selected a couple of sticks from the small pile of firewood and tore a spare shirt into strips. The can of cooking grease was used up by the time he finished, but in the end, he held several torches.

He'd hated deceiving Rose, but this was the only way he could think of to ease her mind. He hadn't lied when he said it worried him she might be fatally distracted if she knew he was in danger. This way, Rose could concentrate on saving her own skin.

Tom lit a torch from the campfire and kicked dirt over the coals. He poked his torch into the mine entrance, seeing footsteps leading off into the darkness. He heard nothing and smelled only the sour droppings from the bats that roosted here during the day. He'd studied the map Rose carried and hoped his memory was good enough. The Ladies had told Tom to follow his wife into the maze, and that certainly meant the mine tunnels. Now he had to meet the beast within, armed with only a torch and a boot knife.

What was it Ambrosius had claimed soldiers say when doing something stupid like this? *Time to eat the brick.* Tom walked into the mines to find his lost memories.

***

The two Ladies took a different path from Rose and Tom, making their final camp several hours' walk from the main entrance to the mines, the closest they dared approach. The third Lady was already there and they spent some time just holding hands and merged in a celebration. Then they waited for Keyotie.

Dawn approached the next morning with Keyotie still not

The Weaving

there. The Ladies debated taking the risk of using their scrying to find his location when he finally showed up in animal form. The reason for his tardiness was evident when they saw he was limping along on three legs, holding a front paw off the ground and panting heavily. He collapsed, then shifted to human, lying on the ground and gasping for breath.

"Hello, Ladies," he said. "Sorry it took so long. Could I bother one of you to remove this knife from my back? The darn thing's stuck where I can't pull it out."

***

The Ladies swarmed over Keyotie, something he would have enjoyed if he'd been in less pain. "Brace yourself," he was told, and the irritating blade was yanked free from his shoulder bone. He yelped and shifted back to coyote in reaction. His own Lady knelt next to him and held on to his neck. He sighed, putting his head in her lap and wagging his tail, adding a few whimpers for good effect as her scent filled his nostrils.

"Ahem," another Lady said. "As much as we hate to break up this tender moment, we really must be going. We're behind schedule, and I'm sure whatever plan you've come up with is going to take time. When will you be able to travel?"

Keyotie whimpered again and shifted. He stood and rubbed his shoulder. "It'll be sore for a while, but the wound is already closing. I could have traveled better on two legs, but had to stay in true form to track you three. I spent the whole night dragging myself around the countryside, my only thought to meet my Lady here as promised, even if it killed me." He helped his Lady to her feet. "I'd almost given up hope of finding you. 'Someplace near the entrance, at the full moon' isn't much to go on, you know."

His Lady took over the massage. "My knight in shining fur. I couldn't hold a war council with Ambrosius and his men about to take me away. Does the knife mean Lilith is after you?"

Keyotie grinned and pulled an armband from his pocket,

putting it on. "Say hello to a duly authorized member of Lilith's elite guard. As for my plan to get you into the mines, it's a little complicated, so I'll explain it on the way."

He escorted the Ladies back the way he'd came. Just behind a screen of trees was a road. The wagon was parked where he'd left it. "Here's our transportation, Ladies," he said. "We'll be in the mines well before dawn. My plan is, you tie your horses to the back, climb in, pretend I've captured you, and we'll drive right past—what, too complicated?"

All three Ladies stood glaring at him. "Desperately dragging yourself all over the countryside?" his Lady asked. "Searching on three legs all night long, even if it killed you? I'll bet you didn't have a bit of trouble finding us. I should have known better than to fall for your habit of stretching the truth. I suppose you stole the wagon from some poor homesteader?"

Keyotie dropped the tailgate and pulled Simon the Knife out by the legs, dragging the body over to hide in the bushes. "No," he said, "this wagon is payment for putting up with these two thugs the last couple of days. Simon here knifed me in the back when I insisted we let the human cargo return to their homes. Sorry about all the blood, but that happens when I rip out someone's throat. The guy who looks like he was trampled to death is Yorik. I asked the released cargo to keep him occupied while I dealt with Simon. I'd appreciate some help dragging that big ox over here."

***

The Ladies rode to the mines in the back of the wagon, hands loosely tied behind their backs. Keyotie had no trouble with the guards, who had seen him several times before on regular delivery runs. They'd even knew of Lilith's interest in collecting women in groups of three, so they allowed Keyotie to escort the captives inside on his own, knowing the man would want to take all the credit and collect a reward. One guard asked about Keyotie's two missing comrades and was told a wild story involving the local brothel, a disease often found

The Weaving

in such places, and a failed attempt at a remedy that left both men unable to walk. His audience was laughing too hard to notice the Ladies glaring at Keyotie for taking so long. Keyotie finally marched the women through an outer temple under construction and into the mine.

Once the four were inside, Keyotie led them to an unused tunnel where the Ladies slipped out of their ropes and dropped the scared captive act.

"Now, we're counting on your skills as a thief," his Lady said. "We need to avoid being discovered and find her throne room, or whatever she's calling it this time."

"That's what she calls it," Keyotie said. "It's in the middle of the mountain. I spent some time in here nosing around. She thinks being at the center of a maze is clever, but this one is pathetic. Not a single hidden death trap."

The Ladies walked into the maze, guided by Keyotie. After this, they would owe him a great debt. While all three were looking forward to giving this man a reward he would appreciate, two of them were wondering if putting up with the Trickster again was worth his help.

Twenty-Seven

Keyotie led the Ladies to the center of the maze, made sure no one was around, and then left to make sure Rose was in the mine and on her way to battle Lilith. He found Rose's scent and then literally ran into her as he trotted around a corner, nose pressed to the ground, and failed to notice she was standing right in front of him, studying a map. She was startled enough to throw a magic spell his way. He started shrinking with a *"Yikes!"* before she made another motion and he ended up in human form.

"That tickled," he said, rubbing his arms. "Not like my natural shifting at all."

Rose looked ready to try something more effective. "Keyotie, if I hadn't recognized you, I'd be looking at a groundhog right now. What's happening in there? These tunnels seem to go on forever and this map is next to useless."

"The Ladies are at the center, getting ready for Lilith. Our unknowing host is visiting her private prison, encouraging the captives to new heights of terror. The next big passage on your right will take you there. What do you plan to do?"

Rose wadded the map up and tossed it. "The Ladies want me to stand back and lob spells at her. That will cause Lilith to retreat and keep the demon so focused on me she won't notice their ambush. I still don't think that's necessary. What does the demon have, some magic and the ability to cause fear? I've been afraid before and it never stopped me."

Keyotie stepped closer, taking her hand and looking up at this brave woman's determined face. "Rose, please listen. The Ladies know what they're doing. Lilith needs to actually touch a witch of your power to infect your mind. If you get close enough for a real fight, anything might happen."

"Even if you're right, it doesn't matter. I caused this, so it's my responsibility and my risk to fix." Rose put her hand on top of his. "Just do me one favor. If something happens to me, could you take care of Tom? He'll be at our campsite on the east side of the mountain."

Keyotie looked back down the passage in that direction. "Of course I will. Well, let's get to it. May Old Man Creator grant you strength, my friend."

"And may the Goddess watch over your life, my friend." Rose outstretched her hand again and the glowing light reappeared in it. She marched down the tunnel.

Keyotie watched her go, knowing the Ladies were right and his warning would make no difference. Her warrior's pride would allow nothing but a true test of strength. *I've been afraid before and it never stopped me.* Like all the other heroes he'd known in his long life, Rose didn't understand why that made her special. He shifted and left in the opposite direction. So, she thought Tom was waiting at a campsite? Strange, since he'd caught a stray whiff of the man's scent back in the tunnels. He'd almost told her, but decided she didn't need the additional worry.

Keyotie caught up with Tom in a remote section of the old mine, heading in the wrong direction down some tunnels. He found the man with a spent torch in his hand, squatted next to a dark hole blocking the passage and trying to see how deep it was. The dim illumination Lilith had created with her magic was barely enough for Keyotie to see by, so he supposed Tom would be nearly blind.

Keyotie grinned. This was too good an opportunity to pass up, and they were too far away from anyone else to be heard. He crept up behind the man, then when he was close enough to bite, let out with an earsplitting howl. Tom made an impressively high jump, bouncing him off the roof of the tunnel and bringing him down squarely in the center of the hole, cursing the whole time.

Keyotie watched Tom twist and fall feet first into the pit, shocked when the man disappeared completely. Keyotie knew from previous travels that the hole barely came to his knees. For one panicked moment, he doubted his memory and thought he'd killed his drinking buddy, but the cursing was still going on inside the pit. He poked his head over the edge.

"You notch-eared candidate for castration! You roller in offal and beggar of scraps! You...you...*canine*!"

The insults were coming from a black cat! It was the only thing in the shallow pit, so mad it was spitting and dancing around. Keyotie prepared to run if it came after him. He tried to avoid tangling with cats, especially one this ticked off.

"Tom?" It had to be Tom, transformed somehow. But there were no witches around. So that meant..."Hello, little cousin." he said. "Sorry about that prank. You're a shapeshifter, like me, aren't you?"

"Of course I am, you mangy mutt. But I'm no cousin of yours." The tomcat was starting to settle down, but Keyotie jumped back when it popped up out of the pit. It only sat and started cleaning itself.

"Relax, Keyotie," it said. "It was your warped sense of humor that finally shocked my human side into letting me back out, so I won't hold a grudge."

"Tom didn't know he was born with a dual spirit?"

The cat sniffed, sneezed, and stretched. "I'm the original Tom, you stupid dog. I was the last of seven kittens, born the usual way in a barn loft by the best mouser on the farm."

Keyotie sat and studied him. "Why didn't you remember what you were, then? I've never heard of a shapeshifter whose forms didn't share memories."

"I don't have time to satisfy your curiosity." Tom started walking back down the tunnel. "I need to find Rose."

Keyotie got up and followed. "I don't think that's smart. She's going to have enough trouble without you showing up."

Tom sniffed the floor, looking down a small side branch, trying to decide which way to go. "I have to. It's what the Lady said. She said I'd remember who I was if I followed Rose into the maze and

The Weaving

encountered the beast within. Beast within, my furry—*humph*. Then the Lady said Rose would die if she didn't find out. I can't take the chance on waiting."

Keyotie shook his head. "Figures. Well, come on. I'll lead you to your wife if you'll tell me what happened."

Tom followed Keyotie as they picked up speed. "I told Rose I had a bad feeling about her plan to use the Portal," Tom explained. "I was minding my own business, waiting for Rose to come back, when the Goddess popped out instead. She told me about my dual nature and offered me a chance to court my mistress in human form."

"You didn't discover you were a shapeshifter on your own?"

Tom harrumphed again. "Well, I had to wish to be human for it to kick in, didn't I? Why would I ever wish that? Oh, I was in love with Rose. I fantasized about her having whiskers and fur, not the other way around."

Keyotie laughed. "You're a cat, all right. And then?"

"The next thing I knew, it felt like I was being squeezed headfirst down a mouse hole and it hurt so bad I blacked out. I awoke back in time, when I first found Rose. Only I was in human form this time, and sick as a...as a dog. I'd never been sick in my life. I thought shapeshifters didn't get sick. My human side dismissed memories of being a cat as fever dreams. Now we're finally in touch and he needs to stop reminding me about Rose and let me work."

Keyotie stopped, Tom almost running into him. "The Goddess erased part of your life? Tom, shapeshifters like us are tough to kill, but we're still mortal. I wouldn't want to chance what you went through."

Tom sniffed the ground, rubbed his cheek against a spot on the floor and purred. "Rose has been here recently. I can take it from here, dog."

"I've told you before, Tom. I'm not a dog, I'm a coyote."

"I've been meaning to ask you about that. What *is* a coyote, anyway?"

"Like...a dog, only better."

"Well, it would have to be, wouldn't it?" Tom grunted and

Gerald Crostlow

followed the scent, then stopped and shifted back to human. "When we get out of here, we'll have to go drinking again," he said. "Don't think I forgot I still owe you a punch in the nose for what happened back at the conference, though."

"Heh. We did have a wild time, didn't we? We'll do that. Take care."

Keyotie watched Tom shift back to cat and disappear into the gloom. He left in a different direction, using a shortcut to the center of the maze. He had his hiding place picked out behind the throne and had to be there before Lilith arrived. The Trickster grinned once more and began running. This was the most fun he'd had in ages.

***

Rose was well aware of the dangers of overconfidence, and in spite of her words to Keyotie, was not taking her coming battle with Lilith lightly. Rose had fought renegade witches, evil wizards, rogue dragons—even the last remaining Old One. Yet the Ladies insisted this monster was in a class by itself. Perhaps it was because Lilith came from another world, like Keyotie. In that case, Rose was a game warden, and Lilith was a trespasser caught poaching. Rose figured she had the homeworld advantage, and that would make a difference.

She came to the tunnel Keyotie had mentioned and peeked around the corner. This one did look different—wider, with a more finished look. It was even lit better. She extinguished her globe. Rose saw no movement, but there were dark rectangles at regular intervals on both sides of the tunnel. She slipped over to the first one, keeping against the wall, and discovered a heavy iron door. The prison. Lilith had to be in one of these cells. She could hear something that sounded like muffled crying on the other side. There was a small window with heavy bars, and she stood on tiptoe to look in.

It was hard to make out details in the gloom, but it looked like a child—a girl—sat against the far wall, sobbing quietly. Probably one of the women the elves brought in. Rose looked up and down the tunnel, biting her lip and trying to decide what to do. She couldn't

The Weaving

check every cell, but if she continued down the tunnel, Lilith might end up behind her.

"Mistress?" the crying stopped, replaced by a plaintive voice. "Is that you? I'm sorry. I really am. I won't steal food anymore, no matter how hungry I am. Please let me out? I'll behave this time. Hello! Who's there?"

The girl was getting louder and showed no sign of quitting. Rose had to shut her up. She started to pull the heavy bolt and discovered the cell wasn't even locked. This girl was too terrified to escape. She entered, conjuring another ball of light and holding a finger to her lips for silence when the girl jumped up.

"Quiet, little one," Rose whispered. "Nobody must know I'm here. I'll make sure Lilith doesn't hurt you anymore."

The girl ran past her to look out the door, checking both directions. "All clear," she said. "You wear a green robe, so you're a witch, aren't you? Grandma said witches could do anything. You're here to save us, right? Are you alone? Who's with you? Where's everyone else?"

Rose tried to put her hand on the girl's shoulder, but the poor thing flinched and pulled away. Judging by the bruises on her arms and legs, the child had grown to expect an outstretched hand to mean punishment. She let her arm drop. "I'm all that's needed to stop Lilith. You'll have to stay here until I come back for you."

"I can do better than that." The girl leaned forward, whispering. "I can lead you to her. She came by here just a short time ago but told me I wasn't sorry enough and she'd be back tomorrow. She'll still be at the larder. I'd have to sneak through there, anyway." The girl ran out the door and motioned for Rose to follow.

Rose was impressed with this girl's bravery, but more so with her caution. The girl moved quietly, checking around every corner, and made sure she didn't get too far ahead of the woman she was leading. Still, Rose decided this was too much risk. She motioned for the girl to stop, but before she could say anything, the girl turned and held up her finger for silence.

"She'll be in that last cell on the left," she whispered. "The one with an open door. That's where she keeps her pretty-boys. She likes to play with them before she goes to bed. Now you can kill the monster and we can all go home."

Rose motioned for the girl to stay put, then started walking quickly down the center of the tunnel. This cat and mouse game had gone on long enough. It was indeed time for Rose to face the monster so everyone could go home.

Twenty-Eight

Rose tapped the magic in her mind as she approached the open door, allowing it to flow down her arms and weaving several spells. She threw up her hands as she entered the cell, releasing a burst of magic. Anyone in front of her would be too dizzy to stand and be violently sick at the same time. While Lilith was trying to figure out what hit her, Rose would be weaving magic shackles on the monster a dragon couldn't break.

Rose walked into an empty room. Sudden comprehension came, and she tried to jump forward, away from the girl. Too late! There was a touch on her back and her magical defenses were ripped open. Her heart raced and she felt like she was suffocating. Rose stumbled to her hands and knees as her mind became flooded with terror. She looked up and saw the girl standing there, gloating. Rose gasped for breath, trying to form a spell in the confusion and pounding in her chest.

"Pitiful," the girl said. Her features blurred, and a pale-skinned woman with black hair stood before Rose. "Tricked by a simple glamour. This is my place of power, witch, and I tasted your magic. Did you think I wouldn't notice a transformation spell in these tunnels?"

Rose was barely listening, struggling to eject the panic burrowing into her mind. "You! Face me...duel!" she gasped.

Lilith squatted and grabbed Rose by the chin, pulling up her head to get a good look at the crystal necklace. "You're one of those powers Maynard told me about. A Goddess worshiper. Witch of the Something-or-other. You go around sticking your nose where it doesn't belong."

Rose managed to form a coherent thought. She began

whispering a spell to throw Lilith across the room. "No, we can't have that," Lilith said, clamping a hand over Rose's mouth. "I butchered my wizard yesterday, so I need you to replace him. Let's rummage around a bit to see what you're afraid of."

The last bit of control was swept away as Lilith walked into Rose's mind.

***

Rose pulled Lars along by the hand. "You'll see. It's a surprise," she said. Lars looked reluctant but followed. She found a secluded spot in the woods and turned to face him. Looking at Lars always made her weak at the knees. Blond hair, tall and muscled—all the girls in the village wanted him, and he knew it, picking the prettiest to take walks with at night. Rose was late to develop, and so far, he'd ignored the flat-chested kid who was always hanging around. She was sure after today he'd pick her.

He stood and looked around, puzzled. "So where's this big surprise? I don't have time for games, Rosalina. I'm supposed to help Pa stack the hay."

"Watch me," Rose said. She took a deep breath, closed her eyes, and repeated the trick she'd learned. She reached out with her mind and touched the life around them. Normally, the birds would flock to her, but now they didn't want to get near Lars. He had killed several of them throwing rocks this year. She insisted, and finally one came fluttering over, landing on her outstretched palm. It was a robin.

She opened her eyes, expecting to see the same wonder in his face she felt. He was staring at the bird. "It's all right," she said. "If you're real quiet, maybe I can get it to sit on your shoulder."

"You're a witch!" Lars began backing away. "Don't come near me! Pa told me about your kind, how you can read a man's thoughts. Stay out of my mind!" He turned and ran.

She knew then he'd never ask her to take a walk at night in the woods. She knew none of the boys would ever take her out, not

The Weaving

after Lars told them what she was. She stood alone in the woods. She'd always be alone in the woods.

"Stay out of my mind?" Rose thought. Lars had said that... back when she was a young girl just discovering her talent. Stay out of his mind? No, stay out of my mind! This isn't real. Stay out of my mind!

***

"Stay out of my mind!" Rose screamed.

"Oh, how droll," Lilith said. "That's your big childhood fear, that boys won't like you? Let's try for something more current."

***

Rose winced with pain as she tried to open the jar. The swollen joints in her fingers were bad this winter and would only get worse. None of her magic or potions could cure old age.

The lid popped off, making her drop the jar. Tea spilled all over the floor as it shattered. She sighed, reaching for the broom, then thought better of it. She lived alone in her cottage, isolated from the nearest town, so there was no way to get more supplies before the spring thaw. She concentrated, weaving a basic repair spell. The pieces of clay began moving back together while the tea leaves swirled and flowed back into the jar. She bent and picked it up, grunting with the effort, only to watch it fall back apart in her hands.

She sat on her bed, crying. Even the magic was abandoning her. She looked at her reflection in the tarnished mirror on the wall and saw an old, old woman—a crone. Useless and alone. Someone else was now Witch of the Woods, a young woman strong in power. No one came to Rose for help anymore. No one needed her. She was alone. Just another retired witch, living alone with only her mind to keep her company.

Company of her mind? No, she had company in her mind.

Gerald Gostlow

This wasn't right. Tom should be here. Where was Tom? This wasn't real. There was someone in her mind.

***

"Stay...stay out of my mind," Rose pleaded.
"Almost there, my pet. I think we'll go in this direction and see what happens."

***

Rose perched on the branch, using the owl's senses to navigate the darkness. The farmhouse below had to be the right one. Her ears could pick up a mouse squeak, so the voices coming from inside the building were no challenge to overhear. She recognized one voice in particular.

She flew to the ground, letting the owl form go. It had taken days of searching to find this place. Now that she'd found it, she was reluctant to intrude. The people inside sounded happy. She saw light from one of the side windows and walked around to look, spying from the night.

There was Tom. He was sitting on the floor, laughing. Two children were wrestling with him, a small boy and girl. The boy had Tom's curly hair. The girl had his green eyes. He was telling them something, but she couldn't understand the words over the laughter.

Then a woman walked into the room. She was a raven-haired beauty, everything Rose was not. She said something and the children nodded, gave their father a hug, then ran out of the room. Bed time.

Tom got to his feet and took the woman in his arms. He was facing the window and saw Rose standing there. She put her hand on the cold glass, begging him to come out into the night, to walk with her in the woods. Surely there was enough of a bond left for Tom to feel her need.

The Weaving

He only shook his head, turning from the window and whispering to his wife. They left the room, heading for their own bed. Tom had found his past and his family. There was no bond with Rose, not anymore.

She was alone. Tom would never again walk with her in the woods. She would always be alone in the woods, with no one to call her own. Tom was gone. Her Tom, her husband was not here. She needed him to be here. She needed Tom, and he wasn't here.

***

Tom padded through the maze, using his cat senses to navigate the gloom. His nose could pick up Rose's scent and his ears could detect the faint sound of someone talking far ahead. He was a mighty hunter of the night, a killer of rodents and other vermin, and he was on the prowl.

He rounded a corner and stopped, tail twitching nervously. His lips drew back in a hiss. Her scent had changed, tainted with the sour taste of fear. It was coming from directly ahead, where an iron door stood ajar. He stalked toward it, silent as only a cat can be.

He looked through the doorway. Rose was on hands and knees and someone was standing over her. It looked like a woman, but had a scent he'd never encountered before. He shifted to the Sight and discovered the air was thick with strands of magic, their color an oily blackness that somehow managed to glow in the dark. The creature was weaving more lines, wrapping Rose in them like...*like a spider does a fly!* He started to shift, his human side wanting to come forth and beat this monster back from the woman he loved.

But then Rose moaned his name. Her agony reached him through their bond and instinct took over. A furious cat yelled his battle cry and launched himself toward the monster, aiming for the vulnerable face. He scored a direct hit, wrapping his front claws around its head and kicking with his hind legs, going for the eyes and nose. The monster tried to pull him off. It only made his claws dig in deeper as he opened bloody gashes across its cheeks. It beat at him and the pain fueled his anger. He yelled his battle cry again, letting the world know Tom, the mighty warrior, had arrived to save the day.

***

Rose woke from the nightmare, but wondered if she had only entered another, stranger dream. She could swear she heard the mother of all catfights in progress. When she looked up, she couldn't make any sense of what was happening. A black cat had attached itself to Lilith's face and the demon was staggering around the cell, trying to pull it off with one hand while hitting it with the other. Rose tried to get up and join the fight, but was too weak to stand. Wherever it came from, she hoped the brave little beast could grant her time to recover.

But then Lilith seemed to have had enough. She grabbed the cat around its middle with both hands and yanked, doing some yelling of her own as the claws ripped free, taking chunks of flesh with them. She wound up and threw the cat as hard as she could against the rock wall. Its snarls died in the crunch of breaking bones. The cat slid down the wall, leaving a red stain behind. Lilith wiped her hands across her face and looked at the blood smeared on her palms. She ran from the room, slamming the iron door behind her and throwing the bolt.

Rose finally managed to stand, but had to catch herself against a wall. She felt violated and realized the demon had left a gaping wound in her mind. Lilith would use that to even greater effect next time. How could she fight it? She looked at the locked door and tried to come up with a plan.

Change to mouse and squeeze under the door. Dog form to track the smell of blood...no, a cat, she decided. Having another cat show up might confuse Lilith enough for Rose to take the offensive. Her wounded, vulnerable mind would still be in the cat's body, but it was better than nothing.

Rose took another deep breath and drew on her magic reserves, pushing herself away from the wall. Her hands trembled slightly as she took a long drink of water from the canteen. Now she would avenge the poor little cat. The Goddess must have sent it here in her hour of need.

The Witch of the Woods wasn't out of the battle yet.

"Rose..."

She looked down in surprise as the cat spoke her name. Nothing should have survived being thrown like that against the hard stone. She went over and knelt next to it. She could at least end its suffering. Rose touched the fur, then watched the cat groan and change form, stretching to become a man. Tom!

"Oh, Goddess, no!" Rose looked at her husband lying on the ground before her. Blood bubbled from his mouth as he tried to speak. She placed her hands on his chest, desperately weaving her strongest healing spell, concentrating on the punctured lung. A rib shifted under her hand, pulling back into place before she could complete the spell. Somehow his body was mending itself, knitting crushed bone on its own and closing off areas of bleeding.

She probed deeper. There was...*oh, Goddess*...his spine was broken, and that was only the beginning of the damage. She finished the spell and sat back, having done all she could. She pulled her aid pack around, trying to think of any potions that would help.

"Rose...guess what? I remembered. I'm a shapeshifter...born a cat. Do you still love me?"

She looked at his face. He was conscious and watching her. At least he was breathing easier. "Tom, you big idiot, of course I still love you." She wiped some blood off his lips, bent over and kissed them. "So, you were born a cat. I always knew you were special. Now relax and heal. We'll discuss this once I get you to safety."

She watched for signs he was getting better, but instead saw him break out in a clammy sweat. He was growing paler and weaker by the moment. She prayed to the Goddess for strength and held his head in her hands. She closed her eyes and brought their bond to the forefront, sending her spirit to merge with his. Her viewpoint changed and she was looking out of his eyes and feeling the pain of each breath they took together. She struggled to keep his heart beating.

"Fight, Tom," she said with his voice. "You just need a little more time to heal. I'll help."

"You offered me my heart's desire. How could I refuse?" His reply seemed to be directed toward someone else, an invisible presence she could now feel in the room. His spirit started to slip away and she grabbed for it, pulling it back into his body.

"Tom...please..." She could feel her grip slipping.

"Yes, it was worth it," he said. Then she felt him turn his attention back to her. "Darling, I love you, but she says there's too much damage, even for a shapeshifter. I have to go."

"No! We can do it!" She held on tighter, putting all her strength into keeping his body and spirit together. *Just a little more time!*

Then the other presence stepped in and the strongest hands in all creation pulled her from Tom's body, gently separating their spirits. She opened her eyes as Tom took his last breath.

Rose watched him revert to true form in death, becoming a cat again. She picked up the limp little body, hugging him to her chest. She sat, rocking back and forth, too overwhelmed by the loss to cry.

Once dead, forever dead. It kept running through her mind. *Once dead, forever dead.* That was what her old Mentor had taught her. But not Lilith, not that demon. It wasn't fair. Rose remembered the gloating face of the monster and rage swallowed the numbness. She used her will to forge a sword out of her rage. She opened her mouth and her song of power became a scream as she turned the sword on herself, slicing away a lifetime of discipline, allowing the controlled trickle of magic coursing through her mind to become a devastating flood.

She got to her feet, still holding the cat in her arms. Rose went to find the creature responsible for the death of her husband. The wild magic crackling from her body hit the iron door and she walked through a puddle of metal.

Her footprints caused the liquid to vaporize.

Her willpower kept the magic dammed up for now, but when she did let go, the blast would sweep through the mine, cauterizing this evil place. That would happen when she once again confronted Lilith. At that range, even the monster's supposedly immortal spirit would be shredded and thrown to all the corners of the world, never to reform.

Of course, it also meant Rose's own destruction.

She was looking forward to it.

***

The Goddess stood in her realm of past lives, watching the story unfold. She held Tom's spirit in her arms. "Sleep, brave little warrior," she whispered. There was no reason for him to see this. Tom had played his part.

She watched Rose march toward the center of the monster's web, glowing with the magic force she now contained. The witch was dripping magic strong enough to be visible without the Sight, green liquid that ate into the stone underfoot, stronger than any acid. Rose had no idea what such raw power could do. The Mother of All watched and wept for her children. The Keeper of Stories wondered if the book would be closed forever on this particular world.

Two monsters now stalked the tunnels under the mountain. When they met, there would be no monsters left—and no mountain, either.

It was possible there would be no world.

Twenty-Nine

Lilith stumbled through the maze, finding it hard to see through the blood running into her eyes. *A familiar, of all things!* A damned witch's familiar had attacked her. Sneaky witch, keeping something like that in reserve. Her face hurt, and she hated pain—her own, at least. Before this was over, she would carve that witch's face into something no man could look at without getting sick.

She turned the final corner, coming to her thrown room. She threw herself onto the throne, letting the flow of fear along her web soothe the throbbing ache.

"Slave! Attend me!" she yelled. The boy poked his head out of a side chamber, rubbing sleep from his eyes. He stared with mouth open when he saw her condition. "A mirror! Bring me a mirror!" she screamed. "And a bowl of water. And a towel!"

"It looks like you've lost the first round," said a familiar voice. "Cuts like that can get infected, you know."

Lilith wiped her eyes again and saw the Ladies standing on the far side of the chamber. All three of them were present, holding hands and looking just as smug as the last time they'd met.

So the witch was their puppet. She should have known.

As usual, the Ladies sent someone else do their fighting for them. Testing, Lilith spun a line of terror their way. It rebounded against some kind of protective spell. Now was the time for caution while she figured out how to counter it.

"This the best you can do?" Lilith asked. "What, no unicorn this time? You've already lost and you're too foolish to know it. I defeated the mightiest wizards this world had to offer when I first arrived, so one little witch is not even worth my notice. I will hang the head of every witch, cat, and unicorn in this world on my walls before I'm finished."

The Weaving

The Ladies didn't reply as the slave ran back with his arms full. Suddenly suspicious, she reached into the boy's mind as he came within reach, freezing him in place. He stood trembling as a wet spot grew around his feet. She examined him as she took the mirror and cloth, wondering if this was another shapeshifter.

She glanced at the Ladies, seeing only amusement as they watched the great Lilith trying to decide if a small human boy was dangerous.

No, they wouldn't pull the same trick twice.

Lilith released the slave's mind, and he dropped the tray before running from the chamber. She looked in the mirror, exclaiming at the damage. Pieces of her scalp were torn off, and her lower face was a mass of deep cuts, one cheek laid open to the bone. No healing sleep could eliminate all signs of the damage. This body was her greatest artistic creation and now it was ruined. She pressed the wet cloth to her cheek, turned her attention back to the Ladies and saw the keystone hanging from the neck of the middle one.

"So you've made sure of your own safety? I hope you only turned my handsome Prince into a frog instead of killing him outright. Now when I force you to turn him back, Valant will join the ranks of the other true slaves in my bed. You've done me a favor by bringing the keystone to me."

The Ladies marched closer, looking ridiculous as they continued to hold hands, allowing the amulet to protect all three. Lilith addressed the redhead on the left. "You're wearing a different body. Finally decided to dump the ancient crone for a newer model? You know, we don't have to fight. We're both alike in how we survive. There's no reason we can't share the people in this world. You're only being selfish, wanting to keep it all for yourselves."

"Don't you dare claim kinship with us, parasite!" The blonde spat and started to walk closer, but was jerked back by the others. "This mortal is a part of us now," the Lady continued, "but remains in full possession of mind and body. Where is the witch who once owned that hollow shell you're so proud of? You take what is not rightfully yours!"

Gerald Ghostlow

That blonde Lady stopped talking while the other Lady spoke. "The amulet does more than protect us from you," she said. "Your pet wizard failed you. Without the genuine keystone, the portal you had him build won't work. What price did he pay when you found out the one he wore was his own forgery?"

"The same one you'll pay after I tire of playing with you." She licked her lips and laughed. "Poor Maynard was trying to say something in the end, but all he could get out was d-d-d-don't." She walked over and stood just out of reach. "I can't hurt you directly, not while you're wearing that and linked together. You can't hurt me, either, not in my place of power. I *can* keep you from leaving this chamber. We'll play a little waiting game. I can survive without food and water or even sleep. Can you?"

They still refused to look worried, infuriating her. "I'll wait several days, then offer a deal. Give me the amulet and you all get water. Then, if you don't agree, I'll wait several more days and the offer will be two of you get to drink and watch the third die of thirst. You have to keep your deals, don't you? If you're still stubborn, in the end I'll take the damned thing off your dry corpse—what in the worlds was that?" A long wail echoed throughout the caverns, the sound more disturbing than a slave undergoing severe torture.

"What we've been waiting for," the blonde Lady said, hanging her head.

"Tom is dead," the black-haired Lady continued, looking at her Sisterselfs.

"And Rose is still alive," the redhead concluded, looking Lilith in the eye. "No matter what happens now, you lose again. Your mistake this time was killing the cat and not staying to finish the witch. Rose is coming for you."

"Oh, isn't that a shame. Your witch won't give me a bit of trouble. Once I get my fangs into someone, they're mine. She can scream all she wants."

"That is the sound of your doom, Lilith," the Lady insisted. "At her normal level, Rose is more powerful than anyone else in the land. Normal doesn't apply anymore. She's opened her mind to the raw

The Weaving

magic of this world."

Lilith reached through her web to take care of the problem. Locating the witch was easy, but Lilith drew back at what she found. This mind was a blazing inferno! Lilith attempted to take over again, but found no fear to latch onto, only hatred directed at her image. The consuming rage noticed her intrusion and raced back up the connection at the speed of thought. Lilith cut the thread just in time.

"Well, then," she said, "I'll kill her the old fashioned way. I'm strong enough to tear off her arms. You three still won't get out of this chamber alive." She threw down the towel, preparing to confront the witch approaching her lair. Another few moments and Lilith would have revenge for her face.

"You're still not getting the point," the Lady insisted. "Rose has become a door to the primal force of this reality. When she lets go, that door will be thrown wide open. Killing her now would only do the same thing." She pointed to the portal with her free hand. "We know what happened to your last world, why it's now a barren wasteland with dust-filled skies. The people who once lived in that place used machines instead of their minds, but you remember what happened. You need to deal with us for your survival!"

Lilith did remember the all-consuming fires and raging wind that left nothing standing in its wake, the black clouds that would never again allow the stars to shine through. Those humans had made a last stand against her and her offspring, and it had turned into mass suicide. Many of her children had faced their true death in the destruction. For the first time since coming to this little pocket world, she began to worry about her own existence. Lilith turned back to her hated enemy.

"You want to deal?" Lilith asked. "You will perish as well, so you are in no position to barter. I'm not going back into some dark hole again. What do you offer?"

"The deal is simple. We will attempt to stop or at least delay Rose. We will give you the key, so you can use your portal. We only demand in return that you use it to leave our world forever."

Lilith wanted time to consider. The Ladies had tricked her

before, and they were too eager for this. Besides, this was not the outcome she'd planned for the last thousand years. Then her slave came running out of a passage, continuing across the chamber and out the opposite doorway, shouting something unintelligible along the way. A glow began to light up the room, coming from where he'd appeared. Lilith stood in indecision.

"It's now or never," the Lady said. "Agree or prepare to meet the Keeper of Stories." The Ladies sounded desperate, telling Lilith there was true danger approaching. She held out her hand.

"It's a deal. Give me the keystone."

The Ladies let go of each other long enough for the blonde to remove the amulet. Lilith snatched it from her hand and ran over to open her portal. She figured if this walking destruction they called Rose could be delayed just a little bit, she'd be able to make an escape. She'd come back later to see if there was anything left of this world. Lilith hoped the Ladies weren't killed in their battle with the witch.

She wanted that privilege for herself.

**

Rose was beyond thinking. The pressure inside her head was taking all her concentration to contain, and the magic was responding to her slightest wish. She wanted to find the monster, so the magic was pushing her in that direction.

She came across a young boy, but he turned and ran. It barely registered above the image of Lilith fueling her rage. A tiny part of Rose wanted to stop and consider her plan, but the feel of the soft fur against her arms drove out all doubts. If the boy was in the clutches of the monster, he was already doomed. Her actions would give him a quicker, cleaner death.

The tunnel ended in a large torch-lit room and she finally saw Lilith. The monster was on the far side of the chamber, trying to create a portal—not that it would do the creature any good. One shrug of her will and the magic in this room was under *her* control. Lilith looked over her shoulder and Rose saw a satisfying look of

The Weaving

astonished fear in a mutilated face. Another shrug of her will and a fountain of magic sealed every doorway leading out of the room. Lilith could not escape.

But then the Ladies appeared before her. Their hands linked, a white glow radiated from their bodies. Rose felt a slight resistance, as if they were trying to stop her. The magic within her surged and the Ladies fell back a pace, overwhelmed. Rose stopped, struggling to speak against the pounding in her head.

"Ladies, get out of my way," she finally managed. "If you are now slaves of this monster, know your bondage is at an end. If not, use your powers to protect yourselves."

"Rose, we are not slaves," the first Lady said.

"And we can handle this our way," the second Lady continued.

"If you give us a chance," the third Lady finished.

They were sweating from being close to the deadly furnace she had become. The stone under her feet began dissolving, creating a pit that steadily ate deeper into the earth the longer she stood in one spot. Rose noticed and used a tiny fraction of the magic to float in the air, then looked at the blonde Lady, the one she'd thought was her friend.

"You knew all along."

"We knew," the Lady answered. "We let Tom sacrifice his life to save you." And then, in a whisper, the Lady added, "I'm so sorry."

Rose saw tears run down the Lady's face. "Tom once said he felt sorry for you. I'll give you the same chance you gave him and use your own rules. My only question—why should I stop? Three answers, then I do this my way."

The first Lady spoke. "Rose, this will destroy you along with Lilith. Think of what this means to you and to a world that needs your talent."

"Do you think I care? Some other witch will take my place. There's your first try."

The second Lady spoke. "Rose, this mountain will be turned into a smoking pit. Think of the people who will die, and the destruction to the land."

"Would Lilith cause less death and suffering in the end? That's your second try." Rose began walking again, knowing this was pointless and wanting to get it over with. The magic pulsed, growing ever stronger with each step closer to Lilith.

The blonde Lady turned her face away from the burning glow, refusing to back up further. "Rose," she said, "you're carrying Tom's child. You're pregnant. Think of the baby and know you still have something to live for."

This answer hit her as nothing else could have. She stopped and stared at the Lady. "Pregnant? No, that's impossible. Why would you say that? Haven't you hurt me enough?"

"It's true. Check for yourself."

Rose sent a tendril of thought down to her womb and was amazed to discover the tiny spark. It was brand new, perhaps only days old, but unmistakably there. "How...I took care not to..." Rose knew her potions were effective. She and Tom had agreed not to have children.

Then she remembered the washerwoman at the camp and the pregnant girl with the bottle of fertility potion. The potion Rose had tasted. Just a tiny bit, but obviously enough. She looked down at the cat. "Oh, Tom. Our baby!" She closed her eyes and concentrated, trying to shut off the flow of magic. It was like trying to close a floodgate with her bare hands.

"I can't do it!" she cried. "There's too much!"

**

The Ladies could see Rose was trying, but the pent-up magic had no place to go.

"Rose, use your bond with Tom," the first Lady said.

"Send the magic to the Goddess through him," the second Lady continued.

"She can handle it," the third Lady concluded.

They watched Rose hesitate, not wanting to give up her final connection to her husband. Finally, Rose looked down at the body of the cat she clutched. She held it out and began singing her song of power, haltingly at first as she stumbled across the torn sections. By the second time around, it started mending, taking in the pain and grief as part of her song. Soon Rose's voice filled the room and the magic again responded to her will. The cat began to glow as it flowed down her arms and into him. The green curtains sealing the room melted and ran back along the floor, rejoining their source. The glow continued to strengthen until Rose held a small green sun. Then her voice trailed off and the light slowly faded, leaving nothing behind but her empty hands.

The Lady ran to Rose, barely catching her as the witch staggered, almost falling back into the pit her magic had created. Rose clung to the Lady, sobbing. The sound of clapping came from behind them. Lilith was perched on the arm of her throne, watching the show with her usual sneer, applauding.

"Congratulations," she said. "You women really are good. I've never seen raw power being thrown about like that. There was so much static in the room, I couldn't even get the portal to work." She got up and stood in front of the wood frame, checking to make sure it was now powering up. She hung the keystone on the peg reserved for that purpose, then turned back to address them.

"Let's see, the deal was I'd leave, right? Well, the deal's off. Instead, I'm going to open this doorway to my old world and summon my daughters to join Mama in a banquet. They haven't eaten in many thousands of years, stuck in that barren place."

The portal opened behind Lilith. The red-haired Lady spoke. "It doesn't look like a wasteland to me. Quite a nice place, in fact."

"Jesting in the face of defeat? I've enjoyed our little game, but all good things come to an end." Lilith turned to summon her daughters and saw a bright forest scene instead of her own dark land.

"What the—" Her exclamation ended abruptly as Keyotie finally made his move. He launched himself from his hiding place behind the throne, landing square on her back. Lilith staggered, but managed to catch herself against one of the posts. When she turned around, he'd already bounced to the floor and was running away. Her eyes narrowed as she focused on the animal. Lilith pointed to the retreating Keyotie, but before she could use her power, he turned and came at her again, using the distance between them to pick up speed. This time, when they collided, she was thrown off her feet, flying backwards through the portal with Keyotie on top of her.

This was the Lady's cue to act and she ran over to the rune-covered doorway, yanking off the keystone and throwing it through the portal. She yelled an unladylike, "Take that, you bitch!"

The ancient magic in the key disrupted the fragile portal, causing it to explode in a shower of sparks. The web of fear flowing through the cavern evaporated.

Lilith was gone.

Keyotie was gone.

Framed between the upright columns, only the painted mural on the wall of three women bowing before a throne could be seen.

"No!" Rose pushed herself away from the Lady and ran over to where the portal had once shimmered in the air. She hit the post in frustration, then turned back to the Ladies.

"You let her escape! That was your plan, shoving her into some other world? What about the people she'll feed on there? And Keyotie! Is there nobody you won't sacrifice?" She turned to one of the posts, studying the runes. "Know this, Ladies," she added. "Lilith will pay for the death of my husband, this I swear on my true name. I will track the monster to wherever she is hiding, if I have to search all of creation."

The Lady tried to put a hand on Rose's arm and was shrugged off. "We could not avoid Tom's death," she told Rose, "but we would never waste his heroic sacrifice on tricking the monster into leaving." She traced one rune, rubbing out the additional lines she'd chalked over it. Keyotie had laughed with delight when told about this simple trap and his assigned role in completing it.

"Lilith has not escaped our vengeance and our beloved Keyotie is not lost or in trouble." She smiled. "In fact, he's probably enjoying himself, right about now."

The Weaving

***

Lilith and her attacker sailed through the portal together, but were knocked apart when she slammed into the ground on the other side. She had the breath driven out of her and lay stunned, looking up at a blue sky. This was certainly not her old world of twilight and terror. The Ladies had changed the destination settings of the portal.

Something bounced off her head and she sat up, seeing the keystone lying on the ground next to her. Lilith looked for the doorway and was not surprised to see it gone. It didn't matter. She would find this world's people and feed on them, as she had done countless other times in other lands. She would find or build another portal between the worlds, then seek out the Ladies again. She'd lost the first round, but figured this battle was a tie. The war would go on until she won, and that would be the final score.

Speaking of scores. Lilith scrambled to her feet and looked for the creature that had jumped her. This dog was first on her payback list. The animal was not far away, sitting and looking around. It was larger than she remembered, but now that she was braced, it couldn't stand a chance.

"You know," the dog remarked, "it's been so long since I left home, I'd forgotten how good this place smells." The creature took a deep breath and let it out with a sigh.

"Whatever you are," she said, "you should have run away when you had the chance. I'm going to skin you alive, then tear the beating heart from your chest and eat it!"

He cocked his head at her. "Whatever I am? We haven't been introduced, have we? Lately, I've gone by the name Keyotie. As for what I am, that calls for a story."

Another damn shapeshifter. Well, in either form, this one was vulnerable to her power. She spun a line of terror his way. She'd have this dog whining and licking her feet and then force it to shift and bite off its own tongue.

The animal sniffed and reached forward, trapping the magic web in his mouth. He made a sucking sound. She staggered as he jerked the stored fear from her body, leaving her weak as a mortal!

"Nasty taste," he said, curling his lip. "Please don't interrupt again. Now, here's how the story goes. At the beginning of time, Old Man Creator was playing with some mud. First he created the Ancients and breathed his spirit into them. He allowed the Ancients free run of the greater and lesser worlds. He had a little clay left, and rather than waste it he made the first people, breathing his spirit into them also. But since there was only a little clay left, the people only had a little of his spirit. To make up for this, the Creator gave these people the gift of change, so one day they could grow stronger and wiser than even the Ancients."

She stepped back, deciding to leave and wait until she was stronger before taking on this lunatic. The dog stood and walked after her.

"Now, the Ancients were powerful beings," he continued, "and thoughtless in their power. Some of the Ancients were jealous of the favored people and treated them badly. They began hunting the people for sport or to put in their stew pots. Old Man Creator was troubled by this and one day called on an Ancient named Coyote for help. He knew this particular being loved the people, and if asked would be willing to keep watch over these weaker children until they came to their full power."

The animal was growing bigger as it came nearer, its head up to her waist. She began to doubt she'd be able to escape, but at least she had her last resort. She'd let it kill this host body and then she'd find another woman to possess. This one was ruined, anyway. Lilith listened to the dog ramble on.

"Coyote made war on his brothers and sisters who were hurting the people, driving them away or hunting them in turn. He followed the people in their migration throughout the worlds, never forgetting his promise to Old Man Creator."

Lilith stumbled and fell backwards. The dog, now a beast as big as a horse, stood over her. He planted a paw on her chest. She shut her eyes and waited for the excruciating torture of her spirit being ripped free from its host.

The Weaving

His deep voice echoed throughout the forest. "What am I? I am Coyote the Trickster, who sat at the feet of the Creator and watched the first people being made. You dare lay claim to the Master's finest creation? I have dealt with your kind before, little spider. This entire world is my place of power to draw upon. Here, I can devour your spirit along with your flesh. This is your true death. I am Coyote, I am hungry, and this time you are the one on the menu."

Lilith's eyes snapped open and she screamed as she realized the truth of his words. She continued screaming and thrashing around in terror until the teeth clamped down on her throat, cutting off her breath and her life.

***

Keyotie finished burying what remained of Lilith, then sat licking his lips and digesting the rest. He looked around at his homeworld. The Happy Hunting Ground was a nice place to live and the people who spent eternity hunting and fishing the endless bounty were old friends. This place was beautiful, but dull as only a paradise can be. Nothing much happened here.

He burped and shook himself, giving the borrowed power back to the land and shifting to his human form. A shiny object in the grass caught his eye and he bent and picked up the keystone. He examined it, impressed at how far the people had come from their crude stone chipping. Keyotie hung it around his neck. The Ladies might want it as a souvenir.

He shifted to his four-footed form to begin the long journey back. There are paths that connect all the worlds, if one knows how to sniff them out. He ignored Raven, who had arrived and was calling from a tree, asking what all the commotion was about. Keyotie didn't have the time to play yet another trick on that gullible idiot. First he would visit Rose and pay his respects to the widow of a brave warrior fallen in battle.

Then Keyotie had a date with a Lady, and she didn't like to be kept waiting.

Epilogue

9 Months Later

Beatrice walked along the line of trees, checking the wards she'd placed there the day before. The life in the woods sighed with the same relief Beatrice felt, now that the blessed event was over. None of the animals had been able to sleep last night, not with Rose giving birth. It wasn't just the woman's impressive vocal range. Rose's link with her place of power meant every creature shared in the experience. It also meant anyone daring to intrude on the nest of their beloved mistress would meet an army of defenders. An elf would not make it past the first few trees. The Witch of the Woods was closed for business until further notice.

The young witch came to the two ancient ley stones and paused, noticing a wild grapevine had climbed halfway up one of the stones overnight. She went over to remove it. This particular patch of ground affected even the plant life. Once again, Beatrice felt around the area for any evidence of intrusive spellcasting, but all she could detect were faint echoes of powerful and complicated magic woven in the past, coming from the ground itself.

"Did you know," asked a voice from behind her, "the first Witch of the Woods built her place of power here because of those stones?"

Beatrice turned to see the short, black-haired Lady she'd come to know from the dungeon. The Lady rose from her seat on a bench and walked toward her. The shading trellis over the bench had hidden the woman from view before now. Beatrice wasn't the only one getting a bit of fresh air.

"According to the dragons," the Lady continued, "the Old Ones

The Weaving

brought the ley stones with them from the stars and used them to worship their own version of the Lifegiver. Even the elves treated this as a sacred grove." The Lady held up a rose blossom. "You've created a beautiful garden here. Smells lovely. You seem to know your way around flowers."

"I didn't mean to intrude, Lady. I was checking the wards before returning to help clean up." Beatrice looked around at the flower garden. The gilded lilies were in full bloom, but most of the pleasant scent came from the rosebushes. "These are just local varieties. Rose has encouraged me to continue my study of flowers, but I lost my collection of seeds and cuttings in Morania."

"This is a good start," the Lady said. "Some of the varieties here are new to me. You'd be surprised at the treasure that can be found in the most unpromising of places. Like in a dungeon."

"I...thank you, Lady...I planted this garden because Rose comes here a lot," Beatrice explained. "She gets in a mood and wants to be alone. She misses her husband so much. I hoped it would cheer her." Beatrice stuck her hand into the space between the stones. "It almost feels like I can reach out and touch the Mother of All when I'm standing here. Rose told me about the portal she built at this spot, how it started all the trouble. She meant it as a warning. But to actually meet the Goddess..."

"Everyone meets the Goddess, sooner or later. Your turn will come soon enough. Relax, Beatrice. The cleaning is about done and the wards aren't really needed. The Witch of the Woods has enemies who would try to take advantage of her vulnerable state, but we Ladies made sure they have other things to worry about right now. You've finished your private godmother ceremony?"

"Yes, your...that is, the...Sisterself...instructed me on...but you'd know that already, wouldn't you?" Her curiosity couldn't be held at bay. This might be the last time she talked to one of the mysterious Ladies without the rest of the trio standing close by, and having all three present made her tongue-tied.

"Lady, please call me Bea. All my friends do. Beatrice is so formal. And, please forgive me if I'm being presumptuous, but do you have names, individual names I mean? I've never heard you called anything but Lady."

"Names?" asked a voice from right behind her. "Every living thing has a name. Didn't you know that?" This was from another of the Ladies, the red-haired one, who had snuck up her somehow. Beatrice was sure they must be doing it on purpose and resolved to watch for the last of the three. Before she could answer this question, the first Lady chuckled.

"Bea here might be young, but she's still a witch and knows all about true names. Stop teasing her. Yes, Bea, we're known by many names. Let's see...I've always been partial to Selene, so you may call me that if you'd like. How about you, Sisterself? Do you have a favorite?"

"None in particular, but that name certainly takes me back. Why not Persephone for me, then? That keeps the theme going."

This time Beatrice saw the door to the cottage open and the remaining Lady walk out, the tall blonde. She was drying her hands on an apron as she came over to join them. "Nostalgia on a day like this? We should be celebrating the new, so I'll go with a new name." The Lady took her customary place between the other two women, addressing Beatrice. "What would you suggest, dear?"

A naming? This was the second such unexpected honor in one day, and Beatrice blurted out the first thing that came to mind. "Artemis! It's the name of a plant that grows in marshy soil. It only blooms when the moon is full and the aroma from boiling the petals can soothe the mother during childbirth. Your body odor smells like them when you sweat." That last sentence escaped as an afterthought and Beatrice turned red as the roses around her when she realized what she'd said.

But the Ladies only laughed together, before the blonde one spoke again. "Artemis it is! We of all people should know the past has a way of repeating itself. Now, Rose and the baby are sleeping off the exhausting business of squeezing a new life through the Mother of All's tiny portal to the world. Why don't you go inside and keep them company, perhaps stretch out on your own cot. A nap will do you

The Weaving

good."

Beatrice took the suggestion as a request for privacy, heading back to the hut but resolving to keep vigilant.

***

The Ladies watched her go, certain there would soon be three sets of closed eyelids. Once they were alone, the Lady Selene motioned to the little cottage in the clearing that Rose, her baby girl and the apprentice called home. "She certainly has talent in abundance, but she's only begun her training. Is Bea ready to be a godmother?"

The Lady Persephone shook her head. "Considering our role in the death of the father, her decision *not* to choose us wasn't a surprise. Besides, you'll never find a more dedicated guardian. Beatrice...Bea would sacrifice her life to protect mother or child."

"Rose blames herself for Tom's death," the Lady Artemis said. "She's forgiven us, but she'll never trust us again. Speaking of children, I want to check on Hardy. Keyotie has many attributes, but child sitting is not counted among them."

"A waste of time," the Lady Selene insisted. "Keyotie will still be telling those stories of his and Hardy will be hanging on every word. What ideas he's planting in the boy's mind, only the Creator knows, but trust Keyotie not to let a fresh audience get away." She walked over to join her Sisterselfs at the ley stones. "Let's get this over with."

The three Ladies joined hands, this time moving to complete the circle. When the two outside Ladies touched, their forms seemed to melt and flow into the center. Where three once stood, a single form appeared. This woman was wearing a deep purple robe, the shimmering cloth sprinkled with silver. It looked like the Lady had wrapped herself in a piece of the night sky. This combined being reached forward and the portal sprang back into existence. The Lady stepped forward and out of the world of earth and sky.

***

Gerald Ghostlow

The world she stepped into consisted of a small room containing a desk with several chairs, a wooden cabinet, a small table with a tea set and a startled cat. The Mother of All stood with her back to the visitor, looking closely at one of the paintings on the wall. She turned to confront the intruder. They stared at each other for a moment, then both smiled as they met and embraced. The Lady pulled back first and looked at the framed picture. It showed a small forest clearing with a familiar cottage. "I knew you'd still be watching this particular birth, so I didn't bother to announce my arrival. I hope you don't mind, Sister."

The Goddess pulled her close once again and kissed her before letting go. "I was hoping you'd come visit, Sister. You've outdone yourself this time. Somehow you brought all the threads together and repaired the web, in spite of the mess I made of everything. Can you ever forgive me?"

The Lady walked over and poured herself a cup of tea from the ever-present pot on the table. "I had to deal with Lilith eventually, I suppose. And the Keeper of Stories can't hide in there forever, you know."

The Goddess sat down in the chair at the desk and picked up her cup. Her features shifted as she became a younger, less careworn woman. "Greetings, Weaver of Lives. I liked that business with the names. Should I call you Hecate, for old time's sake?"

The Lady perched on the desk, the only other chair being occupied by the cat. "I've never placed much importance on names, you know that. I perform my function with no regard to what people call me or how desperately they plead for special favors. You should do the same."

The Keeper of Stories nodded. "A gentle rebuke, much less than I deserve. Still, you could have warned me you were going to have Rose send all that magic my way. She almost caught my office on fire. That was quite a gamble you took."

"All of life is a gamble, Sister. Those who should know better most often call upon me in my aspect as Lady Luck. What's your

The Weaving

opinion, Tom? What do you think of how this ended?"

The cat looked up from its washing. "Why ask me? I'm dead. My opinions don't matter anymore."

The Keeper of Stories shook her head. "Don't pay attention to him. He's in a snit because we won't let him be a guardian spirit for the baby."

The Lady bent over and picked up the cat, sitting down in the chair and placing Tom on her lap. He submitted with flattened ears and twitching tail to being stroked, but began purring when she scratched at an old scar behind one ear. "It's for the best, Tom," she said. "Having your ghost show up would reopen a wound just beginning to heal. Do you regret being human? You paid the biggest price in this."

Tom sniffed, then jumped on the desk for a better look at the scene of his old home. "The woman I love with all my heart loves me in return, and you ask if I have regrets? I regret only that it had to end so soon. The human in me also regrets he cannot be a part of raising our daughter. On the other hand, tomcats aren't so concerned about their offspring, usually having too many to keep track of. Being both cat and human is confusing at times."

The Goddess reached over and tweaked his tail. "Would it help if you knew the child has your Sight? And something else caused by her bath in the wild magic Rose summoned, a gift of your dual nature?"

"So that's it!" the Lady exclaimed. "There was something I couldn't pin down without my main scrying pool. The child is a shapeshifter? Rose is going to call the girl Katrina, but she'll come to be known as Kat. A fitting tribute to her father." The Lady put her cup down and stood. "It's time I returned. The final war between humans and elves is on the horizon, and half my players aren't in position yet—one of them has just been born. I envy you the solitude of your office, Sister. Even when I am three, there's too much work to do."

The Goddess also stood and they hugged again before parting. "And I envy you your station, Sister," she said in return. "You have the freedom to walk the land, being among and part of my children's lives. I can only send them out into the world, then watch and worry and gather them into my arms once their story is told."

***

Tom and the Mother of All sat in silence for a while after the Lady left. They watched her appear again in the picture, blowing a kiss in their direction before splitting into the three Ladies and heading toward the cottage. Tom jumped off the desk to continue his hunt for ghost mice among the labyrinth of shelves in the mansion of past lives. Occasionally, the Keeper of Stories would entertain Tom by reading to him from the books, and he would marvel at the strange worlds and even stranger behavior of the people.

This time Tom stopped and turned before leaving the office, shifting to his human form. "Will they be all right, Goddess?" he asked. "Do you know how the story will end? Rose and my daughter, Kat, and this talk of coming trouble—will they make it through?"

The Goddess sighed, sipping from her cup and looking at the cards laid out on the table before her. "Tom, their stories have still to be written. As for what is going to happen, there is only one answer I can ever give to that—their future is in the hands of Fate. I never know what my Sister has planned."

***

Rose lay on the bed, holding the baby to her breast. She could swear she heard the tiny little girl making a small purring sound.

"Welcome, little marvel, to a world of marvels," she whispered, drifting off to sleep.

About the Author

Gerald Costlow lives in Michigan, USA, surrounded by his wife and dogs and grandchildren. He has had numerous short stories published in magazines, anthologies, and webzines. This is his first published novel but definitely not the last.

Pill Hill Press

Now Available
From Most Online Retailers

$15.95
(Trade Paperback)
ISBN: 9781593306113

$15.99
(Trade Paperback)
ISBN: 9780984261000

$15.99
(Trade Paperback)
ISBN: 9780984261017

$15.99
(Trade Paperback)
ISBN: 9780984261024

$15.99
(Trade Paperback)
ISBN: 9780984261055
(Also Available in Hardcover)

Visit www.pillhillpress.com
For the best in speculative fiction!

Pill Hill Press

PROXIES OF FATE

The world teeters on the brink of hope and despair during the worldwide Great Depression of the 1930s.

Out of the darkness come the Krush, brutal warriors and destroyers of worlds. Drawn by the Earth's glow, they seek death and conquest. Their genocidal invasion is halted in orbit by the last of the Theria, godlike protectors of the universe. Forced into an unsteady armistice, the two factions agree to a battle by proxy to settle the fate of Earth.

Chris Donner, a jaded Great War veteran, is granted the divine powers of the Theria and strives to understand why he has been given such a gift. Li Chen, an idealistic Chinese peasant, is chosen by the Krush and becomes the fabled Dragon King. Both men irrevocably change history as they are drawn together in a final battle to decide the outcome of mankind.

NOW AVAILABLE FROM MOST ONLINE RETAILERS!

MATTHEW MOSES

THE PLACE TO GO FOR ZOMBIE AND APOCALYPTIC FICTION

LIVING DEAD PRESS
WHERE THE DEAD WALK
www.livingdeadpress.com

Wicked ZOMBIE Fiction

by Eric S. Brown
from COSCOM ENTERTAINMENT
www.coscomentertainment.com

In the heat of World War Two, a threat far worse than Hitler and his Third Reich has risen: the dead are walking and have an insatiable hunger for living flesh.

WORLD WAR OF THE DEAD

ISBN 978-1-926712-00-0

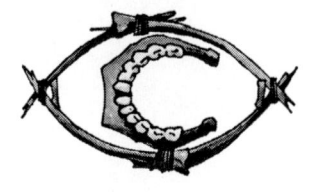

There's panic in the streets of London as invaders from Mars wreak havoc on the living, slaying the populace. Humanity struggles to survive, meeting fear and death at every turn.

But that's not the only struggle mankind must face. The dead are rising from their graves with a lust for human flesh. It's kill or be killed, if you want to survive, otherwise you might become one of the walking dead yourself.

THE WAR OF THE WORLDS PLUS BLOOD, GUTS AND ZOMBIES

ISBN 978-1-897217-91-7

Amazon.com | Amazon Kindle | Barnesandnoble.com | Ask Your Local Bookstore

Lightning Source UK Ltd.
Milton Keynes UK
09 April 2010

152497UK00002B/12/P